KING TOWNSHIP PUBLIC LIBRARY

TRISAN

Aug. 23.

TRI

32170130779211

38.99 The Crow Valley karaoke champ

S0-BBT-613

THE CROW VALLEY
KARAOKE CHAMPIONSHIPS

THE CROW VALLEY
KARAOKE CHAMPIONSHIPS

ALI BRYAN

Ⓗ

HENRY HOLT AND COMPANY

NEW YORK

Henry Holt and Company

Publishers since 1866

120 Broadway

New York, New York 10271

www.henryholt.com

Henry Holt® and ⒽＨ® are registered trademarks of
Macmillan Publishing Group, LLC.

Copyright © 2023 by Alexandra Bryan

All rights reserved.

Distributed in Canada by Raincoast Book Distribution Limited

Library of Congress Cataloging-in-Publication Data

Names: Bryan, Ali, 1978– author.
Title: The Crow Valley karaoke championships / Ali Bryan.
Description: First edition. | New York : Henry Holt and Company, 2023.
Identifiers: LCCN 2022052776 (print) | LCCN 2022052777 (ebook) |
    ISBN 9781250863430 (hardcover) | ISBN 9781250863447 (ebook) |
    ISBN 9781250291349 (Canada edition)
Subjects: LCGFT: Novels.
Classification: LCC PR9199.4.B7978 C76 2023 (print) | LCC
    PR9199.4.B7978 (ebook) | DDC 811/.6—dc23/eng/20230202
LC record available at https://lccn.loc.gov/2022052776
LC ebook record available at https://lccn.loc.gov/2022052777

Our books may be purchased in bulk for promotional, educational,
or business use. Please contact your local bookseller or the Macmillan
Corporate and Premium Sales Department at (800) 221-7945, extension
5442, or by e-mail at MacmillanSpecialMarkets@macmillan.com.

First Edition 2023

Designed by Meryl Sussman Levavi

Printed in the United States of America

1   3   5   7   9   10   8   6   4   2

This is a work of fiction. All of the characters, organizations, and events
portrayed in this novel either are products of the author's imagination or
are used fictitiously.

We acknowledge the support of the Canada Council for the Arts

Canada Council   Conseil des arts
for the Arts   du Canada

for Sandra McIntyre
for Bianca Johnny

THE CROW VALLEY
KARAOKE CHAMPIONSHIPS

Chapter 1

ROXANNE

Dale?

Dale?

Roxanne nudged open the sliding door with her elbow, the screen a bloated stomach, ash-specked and patched with fire tape. A fresh tear ran perpendicular to the door handle. One of the boys. She sighed.

Dale?

She stepped onto the A-frame's second-story deck overlooking the backyard, Dale's workshop, the clothesline, and the limp cord of chili pepper novelty lights he'd strung last summer. The lights drooped so low now that she had the option of ducking underneath or climbing over them. She always ducked.

She drew in a breath, the air a confusion of high altitude and midsummer heat. The beach towels, three of them, primary-colored and screen-printed with superheroes she couldn't name or differentiate from one another, had been baking in the sun for a week. Iron Man, Green Man, Charred Man. Dead Man. Or was it two weeks? She'd bring them in tomorrow when the boys came back from their grandparents'.

Dale?

Across the valley sloped an arboreal graveyard, the landscape mostly scorched but dotted with old logging camps and gravel pits and the powder blue Crow Valley Correctional Centre. If not for the high fence and seventies-era watchtower, it could pass for a school. The melted remains of a gas station sign towered like the spokes of a carnival ride.

Roxanne shuddered, glancing at her watch. The prison. Five o'clock. Dinnertime for Cell Block B. She stepped back inside the house, thrusting the screen door closed behind her, and passed through the master bedroom. A fastball trophy teetered on the dresser.

There you are. She gazed from the loft into the kitchen at the thermos on the island. *I've been trying to tell you something.* She hurried downstairs, fondling the warped box of orange Tic Tacs in her pocket, flicking the plastic tab with her thumbnail, and snapping it shut. Open, close, open. Close.

One more chance. That's what the mayor said to me. Can you believe that? She clutched Dale's thermos to her chest, the cup's camouflage design worn by fingertips. His, hers.

One chance, as if the last twenty-five years have counted for nothing. You know how many times I fixed the copier without having to call the rep? And you know how big a deal that is because he only comes to town once a month, if that. Roxanne paused to put in an earring.

Or what about the fact that I managed to save the files from the top drawer during the fire? Huh? Would've liked to see the town get through year end without those. She traced her left brow, the midpoint singed and scarred, giving her the appearance of a nineties rapper. *And speaking of twenty-five years, that asshole never even acknowledged my silver anniversary! No plaque, no "Thank you for your service, Roxanne." No card, no cake, no "Take the afternoon off"!*

Roxanne aligned herself with the brass mirror where Dale's quilted plaid jacket, key fob, and Corrections ID hung. *What do you think of these pants? They're getting a bit tight.* She blamed her excess weight on a pair of geriatric pregnancies. She'd had her boys late in life. They'd come out too big, already the size of hobbits, demanding Nerf guns and waffles and the Wi-Fi password. She smoothed a spot on her thigh. The pants were filing cabinet beige with serious pleats.

And of course, the mayor's going to be there tonight. You know his wife is going to sing the same stupid country song she sang last year, "Old Flame." Who the heck sings Alabama anymore? It was written in the bloody eighties. She's what, like twenty-three? Is she crooning about the boy who dumped her during recess in grade two? Honest to God. You'd think she'd be singing Taylor Swift or something.

Roxanne applied lipstick. *Do I look okay?* She stared at her reflection. She hadn't dyed her hair since the fire, and it hung below her shoulders, tinder-dry and tarnished. A Halloween wig. *I do, don't I?*

She stuffed her cheat sheet and the *Karaoke Judge's Handbook* into her purse and smiled. *Judges get free meals tonight*, she said, sticking the thermos under her arm. *I'm starting with the poutine.*

She grabbed her keys, but paused at the door. It was going to be a long night. She should feed Dale's goldfish. She dumped her stuff on the counter and pattered to the living room, where the fish tank was balanced on a rickety card table. The goldfish, once common and orange, was now abnormal and black. Ammonia, the vet had blamed for the fish's darkening fins, but Roxanne believed the color change was an act of love, not chemistry. A friend shaving his head or growing a mustache to support another man's malignant balls.

She gently tapped the glass. The fish was only a couple years old. Roxanne had given it to Dale in the spring before his death. That winter had been particularly harsh. There were polar vortices and budget cuts at the prison. A leak in the basement, low-grade tendonitis in his pitching arm, a stubborn bout of shingles. The fish was meant to give him some renewed sense of purpose. A project to snap him out of his post-winter blues. For the most part, it worked. Dale was meticulous in its caregiving. He kept the tank clean, indulged it with ornamental ruins, polished stones, and plants. A tiny decorative skull. Sometimes he would talk to the fish, sometimes he would serenade it, sometimes he would spend hours just watching it swim back and forth, the water thick as aspic, dim, silent.

Roxanne dumped a few flakes of food into the tank. She'd get the boys to help her clean it tomorrow. She gathered her belongings, kicked a football away from the door, and stepped outside. The July heat arrested the back of her neck. Her heel caught a rotting deck board.

Fuck's sake, Dale. I told you to fix that months ago. She set the thermos on the barbecue and used both hands to pry her heel free. Blood rushed to her head.

Okay. Calm. She exhaled, jamming her foot inside her scuffed shoe, edging cautiously down the back stairs toward her truck. *One more chance. He can't judge me outside of work hours, can he?* Roxanne clambered into her blue Silverado. The Tic Tac container dug into her thigh. She wrestled it from her pocket and tossed it onto the dash. From under the JEPSON FAMILY sign, she pulled out of the driveway onto Crow Mountain Road.

Roxanne had never judged a karaoke competition before, but she'd learned a lot sifting through Dale's old feedback forms. Pitch, tone, balance, staying on beat. The usual musical stuff, but song choice was important. Stage presence, performance. There was even a line for "costume." When Dale made it to Nationals last year, Roxanne had bought him a pair of blue coveralls and a headlamp to look like a miner. He'd worn his steel-toed uniform boots. She'd even loaned him some eye shadow—coal dust gray.

He'd been disappointed with his fifth-place finish, blaming his "poor enunciation" on his headlamp being too tight, even though his placing was the highest ever by a Crow Valley resident.

Roxanne's ears popped as she descended the mountain, eventually reaching the stop sign that marked her entry into Crow Valley proper, WHERE YOU BELONG. Gary rolled by in his Royal Canadian Mounted Police cruiser, leisurely like he was still in Newfoundland on his way to a whale-watching excursion, followed by the mayor in his Prius. Ugh. She snarled and inched forward as traffic continued at a pace she couldn't intercept. *I bet you he's going early to get his damn picture taken with the judge from Vancouver,* she said, shaking her head. Cars whizzed by. Roxanne laid on the horn. *Don't cry,* she told herself. *Don't cry, don't cry, don't cry.* She stared hard into the rearview mirror. *You got this,* she declared with the conviction of a Facebook meme.

But Roxanne didn't got this. She reached below her seat and pulled a paper bag from her stash, this one from A&W. She breathed in and out through clenched teeth. In. Out. She tasted ketchup, smoke, panic. Running at full speed, getting clotheslined by caution tape and expressions of sympathy, eyes and hands gesturing for her to turn back, look away. She had not.

An opening. The truck lurched forward. Roxanne stuffed the bag between her legs and turned toward the Crow Valley Town Hall, with its two-tiered roof and blistered siding.

Where there should've been a sign on the town notice board cautioning the residents of Crow Valley that a bear was in the area, there was nothing. Roxanne had forgotten to post the warning after the conservation officer faxed it late yesterday afternoon. She searched the back seat. Maybe one of the boys had left a drawing of a bear on the floor. All they seemed to do at school was eat snacks and color pictures of animals and maps of Canada and happy-faced pizzas sliced into fractions. Nothing. She found a blue pen and drew a bear on the back of her daycare bill. She wrote WARNING in block letters, got out of the car, and used a rusty staple to pin the sign to the board. The bear looked like Grimace from McDonald's.

She lingered then, her eyes flitting from notice to notice, from Dale to Dale. He was in the truck next to Brett in the recruitment poster for the local volunteer Fire and Rescue. He was mid-pitch on the mound in the flyer advertising the town's upcoming fastball tournament, the Crow Valley Classic. She recognized the tip of his work boot, scuffed and peeling, at the edge of a newspaper clipping celebrating Crow Valley Correctional's contest-winning Canada Day parade float. He was the notice board itself, having assembled the frame with his own tools and a pint of green paint.

Roxanne wiped a tear from her eye and got back in the truck. No seat belt. She crossed the road and pulled into her parking spot at the front of the hall, tires bumping the curb.

Showtime.

She slid out, taking her work sweater with her, though it was heavy as an afghan. The hall's front doors were plastered with more posters than the notice board. Summer camps and missing cats and housekeeping services. One of the Mains brothers was selling a dishwasher, and in the middle, the poster for the CROW VALLEY KARAOKE CHAMPIONSHIPS, IN MEMORIAM.

Dale.

She touched the image. Traced a line from his chestnut hair, down his throwing arm to the finger from which the headlamp dangled. He'd been right about the light. It was too tight. Roxanne had noticed weeks after the competition when she'd tried it on and it fit her much smaller head perfectly. She hadn't taken it off since.

She reached up, switched the lamp on, and charged through the door.

Chapter 2

VAL

A flyer advertising a daycare was posted on Crow Valley Correctional's staff room notice board. Val removed one of the sign's pushpins.
Forty, she muttered, transferring the pin to a hedgerow of tacks lining
the board's perimeter. *Sweet mother of Captain Morgan*, is that all it's
been? She crossed her arms, blew a kink of hair from her face.

Next to the flyer was Dale Jepson's funeral bulletin. Val snapped a
picture of the babysitting sign and placed a hand on Dale's photo. God,
it still seemed like yesterday even though it had been almost a year. A
year since his staff locker had been painted red and retired, a year since
the Crow Valley Heat had won a fastball game, nearly two years since
Benedetto was paroled and shot his parents with a sawed-off shotgun,
nineteen and a half since Dale and Brett joined Search and Rescue and
got lost during a training exercise. Brett. What was he doing? She texted
him.

Where r u?

*Getting ready. Should I wear the white shirt you like or my hunting
jacket?*

Who r u with?

He didn't reply. She slid her phone back inside her wool uniform
pants and sliced a bagel. Heat flared from the toaster element, warming
her cheeks, curling her hair, whispering falsehoods and what-ifs and
doubt. She reached for the bulletin board and counted the tacks from
one and then scrambled to remove her phone.

Now what r u doing?

Brett had sent photos. One of him in the white shirt, one in his hunting jacket. The other of him packaged into Dale's baseball jersey, the bottom buttons stretched brazenly like a corset. She enlarged the picture. He'd taken it beside the fridge. Daphne's horse painting curled from the freezer top. An upside-down *Frozen* magnet secured the girls' recent swim report cards and her fall AA meeting schedule. She stared at Elsa's witchy fingers and black eyes. *Let it go.* What a bozo. Someone hadn't put the broom away.

No way, she texted. *Too much. U look like Molly Chivers.*

What's that supposed to mean?

Tryin' too hard.

The toaster popped.

"Sonofabitch." She blew at her fingertips. "Why do bagels get so goddamned hot?" She searched the staff fridge, pushing aside a field-berry yogurt marked BLANCHARD for the cream cheese she'd brought in on Monday. Not there.

Val texted, *What r u doing now?*

She peeled the foil from a pat of butter someone had lifted from the prison cafeteria.

Changing my shirt, Brett replied.

Why did he think she liked the white shirt? She didn't remember telling him so. She'd never jerked off the buttons, never untucked it from his faithful jeans, ducked inside and made love to his chest. Val spread the butter with a plastic knife. No, Brett liked the shirt. It must make him feel good. Probably makes him feel like Dale.

"Valerie Farquhar." The prison chaplain sat at the table, folding his hands on his lap. Memories of a cleft palate were sewn into his smile. "You singing tonight?"

Val sat across from him, straddling the chair. "Can't find my cream cheese."

"I heard first place was ten grand." His eyes sparkled disco.

"And, a trip to Nationals," Val added, spewing crumbs across the veneer table.

"I thought you had to go to Vancouver to qualify. Or Edmonton. Isn't that what Dale did?"

"Yeah, but Crow Valley's a qualifier this year."

"No kidding."

Val sipped from a bottle of water. "Because Dale placed top five last year."

"Right on. Wish I could compete. Of all the gifts God gave me, singing isn't one of them." He pulled a wad of knitting from a canvas backpack. "How about Brett?"

"Oh, you know Brett. He's got this whole thing planned. For Dale."

"No doubt." The chaplain loosened his collar. "What's he singing?"

"Dunno. He's kept it a secret. Been practicing for weeks down at the old recording studio, serenading the one-way glass in his logging earmuffs." Val frowned. Had he been? Really? Yes, he had. She'd seen him through the window, choking the music stand, sucking in his gut, kicking at the sheet music when he messed up.

"Of course." The chaplain leaned in, face contemplative, gentle. The kind of look a parent gave before asking a child if anyone had touched their privates at summer camp. "And how are you doing, Val?"

"Forty days," she said, hands twitching. She set down her bagel.

"An important number in the Bible." He sat back, crossing his knitting needles. "You know the number forty is mentioned a hundred and forty-six times? Often symbolizes a period of great testing, a trial. Probation."

"Yes," Val managed. Trials she understood. Probation is exactly what she felt she was on. Permanent probation.

"Forty is the number of days Moses spent on Mount Sinai, the number of days and nights it rained while our good friend Noah was on his little sailing trip. But did you also know that Elijah went forty days without food or drink?"

Val didn't.

"Fought a lot of false idols, that one, but he also did some incredible things, like bring fire from the sky and perform miracles, including"—the chaplain paused, placed a hand on her shoulder—"resurrection." He gave her a little pat. "I think you're going to be okay."

Val hadn't thought of her sobriety in biblical terms. "Thanks."

The chaplain pushed away from the table and stood. "Will I see you at the hall?"

"Eventually." Val eyed the staff room clock. "I'm not off 'til eight."

"Eight? When's Brett up?"

"I think not 'til the second round."

"But you might miss him. You didn't think to trade shifts with someone?"

Val froze mid-bite, bagel lodged deep inside her cheek. The last time she'd traded shifts, Dale never made it home.

The chaplain covered his mouth. "Sorry," he mumbled, slinking toward the door.

Val swallowed. "Don't worry about it," she waved. "I got a sponsor."

He acknowledged with a salute, the door wheezing shut behind him. Break over, Val wrapped her bagel in a napkin and took the back exit, tracing the whitewashed cement walls down two flights of stairs toward Cell Block B. All but three of the inmates had gone to dinner. She dabbed butter from her chin with her sleeve and counted backward from forty.

Inmate 113 was Marcel, a transfer from a maximum security prison in Quebec, serving time for second-degree murder, weapons charges, and arson. Val had heard he was involved in some shenanigans with a female art therapist there.

"You're a tall motherfucker, aren't ya?" she said, passing his cell.

Marcel grabbed his crotch and thrust it between the bars.

"No, thanks. I got this toasty bagel." She proceeded to another cell. "You still sick?"

The inmate, boy-sized with track marks and farm teeth, nodded. He was sweating, wearing only pants, his shirt in a clump in the middle of his cell.

"You look like the time I mixed Bacardi Breezers with razor clams."

She shivered and wiped her fingers on her pants. "Only made that mistake once."

Bacardi. Now that was good for a summer throat lashing. Campfire, tank top, pint of rum. She'd hidden a bottle somewhere in the house. A flavored kind. Behind the ironing board? Or was it the yard? She needed to write this stuff down. She deliberately didn't write this stuff down.

The sick prisoner rolled onto his side and tucked his knees to his chest, exposing an octopus tattooed between his shoulder blades.

"Put a shirt on, would ya? That sea-bitch gives me the creeps."

The prisoner coughed into himself and Val continued on, shielding her eyes from his back, inspecting the empty cells, the paper-printed photos of family members and lovers left behind. Daughters with skipping ropes and missing teeth, girlfriends with lusty eyes and tidy cleavage. Shriveled grandparents, mutts, the occasional father. And mothers. So many mothers. She pulled out her phone.

I want a drink. I want not to want a drink.

Brett texted back. *Don't do it, Val. You gotta resist.* A flexed arm emoji. *Just don't. Maybe text your sponsor?*

Resist. Ha! Val squawked, pacing the hall. Had Brett *resisted* when that whore, Caroline, peeled the spaghetti straps off her beluga shoulders? "What are you looking at, Frenchie?"

Marcel yelled, "Take off your shirt." The handlebars of his mustache, blackened as though he'd gone down on a barbecue, poked through his cell, the expanse of his knuckles gripping the bars.

Take off your shirt. Is that what Brett had said before he'd slipped his fingers inside Caroline's ratty jeans? Shoved his thumb in her mouth? Tugged at her braid with his teeth? Before he took off his own shirt and yanked down his pants?

"You first," she heckled back, scrolling her contacts.

Marcel stuck his tongue out, waving it back and forth. It reminded Val of the banana slugs she caught as a child growing up in the British Columbia interior. She turned her back on the inmate and texted her sponsor.

I can't stop thinking about it.

I understand.

I want a drink.

I understand that, too.

Val had suffered frostbite as a child, a new school bus driver having dropped her off at the wrong stop on the coldest day of the year, her boots forgotten back in the grade three coatroom. She'd made the trek in pom-pom socks and discount sneakers—the kind you wore to summer barbecues and spring flings. At home, she'd marveled at the sight of her toes: thick, pale, rigid, and the bizarreness of not being able to feel them. So peculiar, so absolute. So horrible. And now that's all she sought. Numbness. Nothingness. Life was the coldest day of the year, and she wanted to feel none of it. She held the phone to her chest.

The air-conditioning groaned and Val finished her bagel. A prisoner at the end of the block caressed a photo of his wife. The wife visited him regularly. She told him stories from the outside about the chickens in their backyard coop, the new furnace, their daughter's latest part-time job or college application. Val wondered how their prison marriage seemed happier than her own. Separate houses?

Even before the affair. That was the thing about marriage; it was good until all of a sudden it wasn't. Like meat in a refrigerator. Prime, pink, and reliable one day, gray and questionable the next. You ate it anyway, ignoring that it might be off, ignoring the pain in your gut, in your heart.

Val scanned her proxy card to exit Cell Block B. She always thought the pale blue doors were better suited to a nursery.

Her sponsor texted, *When I really want a drink I count to ten in another language.*

Val looked back at Marcel. *Un, deux, trois.* As the door swung shut, she heard someone vomit.

Chapter 3

ROXANNE

The Crow Valley Town Hall was a work in progress. The main room contained a stage, no curtains, worn wood floors, and seats that had been recovered from a derelict theater. There was a gap between the stage and the theater seats so the space could be transformed into whatever Crow Valley was hosting: a wedding, a craft market, a trade show, a karaoke night.

Roxanne wove through tables and chairs and climbed the carpeted stairs to the back of the hall, her headlamp illuminating the town's history, a Bayeux tapestry of cigarette burns, glitter, and gravy. Between a faded blue fleur-de-lis and a gold wisp survived the barf stain Dale had left at Val and Brett's wedding when Dale won the limbo contest.

Roxanne smiled. A makeshift judges' platform draped with a plastic tablecloth had been erected over the back few rows of seats. Roxanne set her purse on one of the two judges' chairs and examined the stacks of materials spread across the table. Score sheets, songbooks, felt pens in a rainbow of colors, a triangle of bottled water. The hall's colossal wooden ceiling fan rattled overhead.

Below, the stage was empty, except for a single traffic cone beside a hole. Where were the mics? Molly Chivers was supposed to have arranged the AV. And where was Judge #2? She'd told him to be here at least thirty minutes before the show, to review the rules. She checked her purse for the thermos. It should've been on top, right there when she reached in, her fingertips catching the polished steel. She pulled out a roll of melted Mentos.

"My God. I've left him at home."

Dale hadn't missed karaoke in fifteen years. Even after that horrible winter. She glanced at her phone. If she hurried, she could make it back with a few minutes to spare. Roxanne snatched her keys and headed toward stage right. She'd go out the side door, circle round to the parking lot. They'd see her purse on the chair and assume she'd gone for a hotdog.

"Roxanne!" The mayor barreled through the door, his shoes polished, smile charged. "This is Silas Baker," he said, gesturing to the man beside him. "Judge number two."

"Nice to meet you." Roxanne shook the judge's hand.

Silas winced, shielding his face from the headlamp. The mayor's tiny taxidermic eyes bulged. Roxanne's hand darted to the lamp. She switched off the light.

"Sorry," she mumbled. "It's . . . a . . ." Her voice trailed.

The mayor rocked forward on his toes, loafers folding, teeth bared.

"A statement piece," Silas finished. "Totally get it. I once pierced my ear with a C-section staple."

Roxanne recoiled. The mayor chortled, reddening.

"Kidding," Silas laughed, pointing to his mangled earlobe. "It was just a regular staple. Pulled it from my grade ten trigonometry exam. I had a troubled youth."

The mayor clapped his hands. "Roxanne, I thought you could show Silas to the judges' platform, get him settled."

"Of course," Roxanne said.

"Great," said the mayor. "Then I shall go finish my speech." He tugged a crumpled yellow paper from his sports coat. "Silas, if you need anything, Roxanne's got you covered."

"After you," Roxanne said, motioning for Silas to go ahead. She eyed the door. If she left right now she could be halfway up the mountain before he even reached the judges' table. Sigh.

Silas took the stairs two at a time. His pants were short, cinched mid-shin in a style she wasn't familiar with. Urban, woke. A flotilla of embroidered pink jellyfish stretched across his linen shirt. Roxanne tilted her head back as though she were at the dentist. Silas had to be at least six five. He set his bag on the table.

"I'll make this quick," Roxanne said. "You got your pens, your score sheets, extra songbooks, and your water. Canteen opens in fifteen minutes. I don't recommend the nachos. Bathroom's down the hall. Muster point is on the edge of the parking lot by the notice board. And if you do go outside, be careful. There's a bear in the area."

"Grizzly, or black?" Silas asked.

"A big one," replied Roxanne.

Silas removed the lid from a felt pen. "So tell me about Crow Valley."

Roxanne looked at the clock. "What do you want to know?"

Silas shrugged. "Like, what do people do here for fun?"

"They make bad decisions and sing karaoke."

"My kind of place," Silas said, setting down a gas station iced coffee. "Heard you were a first timer. You've reviewed the handbook?"

Roxanne nodded, reaching for her purse.

"Any questions?" He ran his fingers through his hundred-dollar haircut.

She did have a question. "What if you just don't like the song?"

"Happens all the time." His nameplate, JUDGE #2 written in Magic Marker on a cardboard tent, had tipped over. He righted it and pulled out the contestant list for round one of the Crow Valley Karaoke Championships. "The trick is, is it the right song for *them*. A sexed up rendition of Anne Murray's 'Snowbird'? If the beak fits. A rap version of 'Sweet Caroline'? If you're inclined."

No sweet Carolines here, Roxanne thought. *Just slutty ones.* She flipped through an industrial-sized binder of songs, each title in capital letters and number-coded. She landed on the *I* songs. "I Can't Help Myself," "I Can't Tell You Why," "I'm on Fire." She snapped the binder shut and pushed away from the table, heart tripping.

"You okay?"

"Yeah," Roxanne stumbled. "I just forgot something at home."

"I probably have extras." He pointed to his man bag. "What do you need?"

"Dale."

Silas looked thoughtful. "As in In Memoriam Dale?"

They both glanced at the fan of karaoke posters on the edge of the table. There had to be at least twenty. Twenty Dales.

"I left my thermos on the barbecue."

Silas slid his iced coffee across the rough plywood. "Here, haven't even taken a sip."

Roxanne guided the straw to her mouth, inhaled a cloud of whipped cream. Onstage the mayor was back, directing Molly Chivers's placement of the mic stand, a herd of boys carrying on behind her. Roxanne sat up straight.

"A little to the left," he waved.

Molly made the adjustment, flinging the cord to the side with the tip of her stiletto and smoothing her hair.

"Almost showtime," Silas said, selecting an orange pen. "Let's go."

"Let's go," Roxanne echoed, cupping the headlamp. "Let's go."

She would never let go.

Chapter 4

MARCEL

Marcel plugged his ears, his hard-on fading as the inmate in the cell across from him retched into his sink. The noise reminded him of his mother after his father had beaten the shit out of her, Marcel's years of wiping her mouth, changing her bandages, fixing her clothes, righting whatever furniture had been knocked down or thrown or set on fire.

He wanted the guard with the big ass and frizzy hair to come back. He wanted to get a better look at her full and fuckable hips. She was different from the art teacher at the Sainte-Anne-des-Plaines Institution. That one was French, a tiny little thing who looked like she hadn't slept in years. Tits all washed up from age and weight loss. Petal-pink lips, hair dyed and dead, shoulders, nil. Her entire portfolio consisted of sketches of sugar shacks and kettles. It took Marcel only three classes to put his fist inside her. His mustache twitched thinking about it. He thrust his hand down his pants and grabbed his junk. The inmate across from him, now on his knees, puked into his T-shirt.

"Fuck off," Marcel hollered, withdrawing. He kicked at the sink, flopped on the bed, and imagined the ductwork above. He'd been mapping the prison since he'd arrived over a year ago, searching for cracks and opportunities. Holes, weed, lonely women. In the yard, he counted bricks, memorized doors, noted prison vehicles, deliveries, trains. He sniffed the air, surveyed the mountaintops, kept his body thin.

He peeled the picture of his daughter off the cinderblock wall. On the back, her age had been recorded as five months. The ink was red and smeared. He studied her tiny features. Her nose, a felted button, cheeks blowsy, eyes a limpid blue. He wondered what a five-month-old baby could do. He placed the photo on his damp chest. What could she do now that she was five?

Down the hall, the door buzzed and clicked open. A parade of inmates sauntered back to their cells, smelling vaguely of peas and tap water. Marcel stuck the picture back on the wall and watched for Val. Instead, the long-haired male guard with the CrossFit body and biting eyes passed by. Marcel feared him, felt the guard could see right through him. He was sure he could hear all Marcel's thoughts. After only his second week at Crow Valley Correctional, Marcel had started confessing things to him. *I stole my grandmother's piano and sold it on Kijiji! I drunk-pissed in a girl's closet and never told her. I feel better gluten-free.* To which the guard—Norman Blanchard was his name—would simply raise his chin.

Marcel stood, stretched his gaze. There she was, standing with her feet wide and her arms crossed. He imagined her in skimpy armor, a Viking maiden with blood on her cheek, her hair blowing off her face in a northerly wind.

"Hey, one-thirteen," Val yelled. "Whatcha looking at?"

Marcel jumped.

"You bored? Need some crayons? Go find yourself a coloring book."

He puckered his lips and retreated to his bed while Val stopped at the sick inmate's cell. She called for Norman Blanchard, cocked her head to the side, and spoke down into her radio, as though conversing with hell. Her profile was lovely.

An inmate at the opposite end of the hall sang "The Star-Spangled Banner." Marcel hummed along, waving his shirt away from his body. The prison air was warm and textured—how Marcel imagined the air inside a locked trunk. He shucked his socks, folded them in half, and sat upright on his bed, allowing his feet to cool on the tile floor as gloved medics entered Cell Block B.

Marcel closed his eyes and listened to the sounds of treatment. The physicality of the assessment. The murmur of planning. The grating of the stretcher against the floor. Breath under a ventilator. Marcel felt the weight of his youth, the Halloween he broke into a McGill University anatomy lab and stole specimens on a dare. The hot hot heat of his breath inside the rubber mask. The shame that the specimen might have been a fetus. He thought of his mother's ashen skin and sharp cheekbones and empty pine bed. The blurred red of ambulance tail-lights in December.

Marcel opened his eyes to watch the gurney pass. The fingerlike tips of octopus tentacles wrapping around the inmate's biceps and chest, holding on for dear life. Killing him. His wet lashes and heavy head.

"My mother," Marcel burst out.

Norman Blanchard strolled quietly toward Marcel's cell, pausing in front. "Marcel." Norman motioned to the shrinking gurney. "He'll be okay. Hospital will look after him."

The hospital hadn't looked after his mother. Hadn't saved his father.

Norman's gaze fell to the scars etched across Marcel's collarbone like a runic inscription. Was he counting them? Marcel wondered. There were nine. Six Molson, three Canadian Club. A dozen if you counted the spike impressions. His father loved to ice climb. Loved to be on top. Loved to look down.

"I got to get out." Marcel paced.

Norman stood tall. "You're exactly where you belong."

Marcel stepped backward, crawled into his bed, and pulled the sheet over his head, hands drawn into explosive fists so that he didn't inadvertently suck his thumb and weep.

Chapter 5

MOLLY

Song lyrics tripped through Molly's head. She kept screwing up the verses even though there were only two, and it was a country song, slow and simple: "You Don't Even Know Who I Am."

"Hey, Mol."

Molly looked up from the table, her left eyelash sticking. She'd used too much glue. She blinked at Caroline Leduc. "Hey," she replied. Molly had babysat Caroline's son from the time he could walk until he started kindergarten. He'd been a good kid, despite his cheating mom, clownish hair, and aversion to cats.

"Your boys here tonight?" Caroline asked.

Were they ever not? Roaming around in their fat sneakers, looking for iPhone chargers or twenty bucks or five more minutes, looking for ways to make mistakes. She'd made four of them and they all looked like their dad.

"All of them." Molly, smelling permanently of socks and Saturday morning, gestured under the table where half of her brood was playing Roblox or Minecraft. "Nate not here?"

"He's at his dad's this weekend." Caroline reset her smile. "Good luck tonight."

"Thanks." Molly watched her choose a table near the back, where the alcoholics quivered and the outcasts slumped. She wondered if Caroline was going to sing. How would Brett react now that her divorce was final and she was living in the Lodgepole Pine Apartments, a sports field away from the logging camp? Would he see her from the punch clock, hanging her laundry, twirling her braids, spreading her legs? More importantly, would Val?

The hall filled, many arriving straight from work, still in their fatigues, their steel-toes, their scrubs. Molly thought of last year's evacuation, the sky an otherworldly orange, the string of cars that came down the mountain glutted with sleeping bags and suitcases and hamsters in cages. One family drove by with a foosball table strapped to the roof. All of them headed to the hall. All of them wondered why Molly was parked on the shoulder alone, waving them by. All of them obliging, except for Dale. And why? The only time she'd expected anything from Dale was the movie date they'd planned on the last day of grade nine, but he'd stood her up without explanation. Was this why he stopped? Some kind of resurfaced guilt? A way to make things right between them? She shuddered. The bottle was still in her glove compartment. Nine and a half pills. All of them blue.

The DJ, in baggy Wranglers, performed sound checks, his voice Western, steady, cool. Onstage, the lights alternated from white to blue to red, an inauguration of color, each change complemented by a pleasing click. The mic stand was perfectly centered. Molly visualized herself standing behind it, belting the chorus, Roxanne nodding, Judge #2 enchanted. She had to remember to project. She had to use the whole stage, the way Dale used to. She had to win. She had to.

Molly brushed salt from the table and hiked up her strapless gold dress. Even though she'd bottle-fed the last two, her body was ruined. She was a war vet, all scar tissue and stretch marks and displaced parts. At four hundred dollars, plus tax, duty, and shipping, which she'd earned by weeks of babysitting extra kids, including Roxanne's oversized and low-functioning pair, the dress could at least fit.

"Let go," she said lifting the tablecloth and hunching down to speak. Malcolm, her youngest, four years old with a head the size of an excavator, squeezed her ankle. His hands were tacky. Half a granola bar and his tablet were parked beside him on the weathered hardwood floor.

"I'm going to the bathroom," she said. "Stay here." She paused, assessing her other son. "Xavier, pull up your pants."

Molly struggled free and slung her purse over her shoulder. She wove through tables of ten toward the back of the hall. The women's washroom hadn't been added until the early eighties and could only be accessed through the kitchen. A man wearing an apron that read ITAL-IANS DO IT BETTER shredded lettuce behind a prep table. He looked up as she passed. "One of your boys was on the roof earlier."

"I'll talk to him," she waved.

"He was vaping."

Of course he was. She slipped into the tiny bathroom. With the hall's new walk-in freezer on the other side of the wall, the bathroom was cold as an ice pack. She leaned over the sink and examined herself in the mirror. "For fuck's sake." Her left eyelash was now peeling and her expensive lipstick was faded as an entry stamp. Molly looked like the morning after.

She rummaged through her purse, upsetting McDonald's toys and matchbooks and pine cones she'd been asked to preserve, and found the lipstick. It was supposed to last twenty-four hours. Had she not applied it correctly? Was the clear end supposed to go on first? The fine print was too small. Someone tried to open the door.

"Nope," she called, shoving it closed with her hip. She swiped a layer of color over her lips, pressed the rogue lash onto her lid, and reached for the knob. Outside, her eight-year-old paced, mouth bleeding, a blot of black marker on his hoodie.

"Xavier, what did you do?" Molly lifted his chin.

"Malcolm didn't have enough Robux to buy the horse he wanted so he hit me."

"Because of a video game? Why can't you guys just get along?"

"He attacked me."

"Where is he?"

"Hiding in the laundry room."

"Couldn't you have watched him for five minutes?"

"I tried! He was having a rage fit so I took away his tablet and he punched me in the face." Xavier cradled his cheek.

Molly guided her son through the kitchen to the men's bathroom. "Give your face a good wash and then put pressure on your lip." She dug a pair of underpants out of her purse, folded them in thirds, and handed them to him.

"I'm not putting underwear on my face."

"They're clean. From when Malcolm needed spares."

"When he was three? When's the last time you cleaned out your purse?"

"Just take them."

"I'll use paper towel."

"Fine." Molly stuffed the underpants into a side pocket. "I'll deal with Malcolm. Meet me back at the table."

"Can I have ten bucks?"

"No. And which one of your brothers is vaping? Cole or Dylan?"

"Both. Though Cole's is better. His smells like Froot Loops."

Molly closed her eyes. "Just go get cleaned up."

She scuffed down the hall in the heels she somehow thought would exempt her from parenting and flung open the laundry room door. The linoleum floor was slanted, the windows unwashed and covered in grime from last year's fire.

"Malcolm?" She peered at the washer and dryer, which were set just wide enough apart for her son to wedge himself between. The space was full of lint and place mats. A dirty teething ring. When was the last time Roxanne had the cleaners in?

"Come on, Malcolm. I know you're in here." She opened the bi-fold doors to a supply closet. A mop timbered, grazing her shoulder. Once Gary had answered a call at Crow Valley Elementary. A class mom had drunk Lysol in the library. Molly stared curiously at the toilet bowl cleaner in front of her. It contained bleach. Maybe just a sip? Her phone rang.

"Molly, whadda y'at?"

"You know I'm at karaoke."

"Did you forget one of the kids?"

Molly looked inside a washtub and then out the window. Dead flies lined the trough between the panes. "No, I didn't forget one of the kids."

"You sure, b'y? Because I just found Malcolm a gunshot away eatin' a pizza crust in front of the bank with his Crocs on the wrong feet."

"He's with you now?"

"In the back of the cruiser. You think I'd leave him to prowl the streets like a sailor on a pub crawl? I'm out front. Come get him."

Molly hung up and darted down the hall toward the entrance, the dead eyes of a mounted whitetail deer judging her as she passed. One of the Mains kids ate candy bananas from a dispenser near the office.

The RCMP crest on Gary's car was visible through the double main doors. Molly barreled into the parking lot, shielding her eyes from the sun.

"Where'd you get that dress?" Gary looked his wife up and down. "I never seen it before."

"I bought it. For tonight."

Gary raised his eyebrows. "How much dat cost?"

A transport truck's retarder brakes kicked in on the highway twisting above them.

"It was on sale."

Gary opened the back door of the cruiser and Malcolm scooted out, licking an ice cream cone the size of his face. His Crocs were on his lap.

"You got him ice cream?"

Gary threw his arms up, incredulously. "You lost him?"

"I didn't lose him. He ran out a few minutes ago when I went to the bathroom, after, I might add, punching his brother over some dumb video game."

Gary turned to his son. "You hit your brother?"

Malcolm shrugged and bit into the cone with his baby teeth. "Is the cone made of wood?"

"Sweet Jesus, no. The cone's made of food. Now go back with your mom and you listen to her, right? You can't go around attacking your brother and runnin' out of the building." He put a firm hand on

Malcolm's shoulder. "This competition's real important to your mom. Now, go."

Gary nudged Malcolm forward. Molly took a step back.

"Geez, Molly, take his hand or something."

A bald eagle circled overhead and disappeared into a scrum of junipers.

"Can't you just take him?" Molly said.

"Can *I* just take him? G'wan with yourself, b'y." He gestured to his squad car, bird shit caked on the windshield. "I'm working."

"But you just said how important this competition was to me. Don't you still do ride-alongs? Can't you just pretend he's one of your ride-along passengers?"

"Sure! Why don't I just draw a mustache on him and let him sit in the front seat." Gary shook his head and went around to the driver's side. He pointed his finger at Malcolm. "You be good. Don't give your mudder a hard time." He got inside the car and put on his seat belt.

Molly hurried after him, motioning for him to roll down his window. "Please?"

"You're worrying me."

"You should be worried."

Gary frowned and then his eyes saddened and softened as though there'd been a tragedy.

"Take him for an hour," she pleaded. "Just until I've sung." Molly pulled out her phone and checked the time, counting in her head. "I should be up in about forty minutes or so."

Gary hard-sighed. "You all right, love?"

Molly took another step back.

Gary opened the door and came around the side. "Okay, buddy, get in de car."

Malcolm wiped his hands on the cruiser. "Where are we going?"

"We'll go check out the school. Make sure no one's on the roof."

"Can we shoot someone?"

Gary shut the door on his son and looked back at Molly. "Long may your jib draw. You look real pretty. Just make sure you sing from your diaphragm."

"I'm tired of being a mother."

Gary yanked his hat off and held it to his chest. "Tired of being a mudder?"

Molly nodded. Gary sank into the front seat, hands heavy on the steering wheel. Then he flipped on his siren and fishtailed out of the parking lot.

The upended dust settled into the sweat on Molly's exposed back. The chorus swirled in her head: *You don't even know.*

Chapter 6

═══

BRETT

You know why most marriage counseling fails?

Brett slapped water on his face.

Because couples come five years too late.

Gah! He rammed the hall's porcelain sink with the heel of his hand, causing a pipe to creak. His chest hair was visible through his white shirt. Was this a bad thing? He pressed the offending section. Or was this why it was one of Val's favorites? He turned to the side, examined his profile in the pocked mirror: a bit tight, stiff collar, a condor's nest of chest hair. The sleeves were a problem. Maybe he should roll them up? That's how Dale used to wear his.

Brett fiddled with the cuffs, his fingers calloused and trembling, smelling of sap.

Too late.

Why would the counselor have said that? He checked his teeth, readjusted his shirtsleeves, loosened the part tucked into his jeans. Was this even the shirt? Brett didn't recall owning anything else white and he distinctly remembered wearing this exact one to Dale's service award ceremony. Val had worn her Corrections uniform but had kept her hair down, and they'd snuck away early to play the slots at Big Al's. That was five years ago. Before it had been *too late*.

A parting glance in the mirror. *You can win this, Brett.* And as Dale used to say in the pre-game huddle, gum in his mouth, jersey clay-stained and untucked: *The only loser here is the one who done lose.*

Brett ducked out of the men's room and drifted back to the main hall. The sign language interpreter was positioned at stage right and the MC was already introducing the judges. At the announcement of her name, Roxanne stood, headlamp switched on and hijacking her forehead, her pants unusually formal. Judge #2 was eight feet tall. Brett spread a paper napkin over his lap where'd he dribbled piss on his jeans and took the program from the seat he'd saved for Val. "Opening Remarks."

The MC said, "I'd now like to invite the mayor of Crow Valley, Reg Dunn, to say a few words."

The mayor jogged up the stairs with the sort of fake athleticism politicians adopted to appear young and healthy when they were really a handshake and an enlarged prostate away from Crow Valley Extendicare. Brett offered a lazy clap.

"Welcome to the sixteenth annual Crow Valley Karaoke Championships."

Cheers erupted across the hall.

"As many of you know, tonight's competition is a little more special this year, as we remember longtime Crow Valley resident Dale Jepson. During the Cougar Creek fires last year, in a brave effort to help a stranded motorist, Dale lost his life."

Brett scanned the crowd for Molly Chivers but recognized only her boys.

"Dale was a dedicated member of our Search and Rescue, one of Crow Valley Correctional's finest guards, a loving father, husband, friend, and the best darn pitcher ever to come out of Crow Valley."

Brett made the yiffing sound he used to make when Dale was on the mound.

"But what made Dale Jepson really special was his love for karaoke. So tonight . . ." The mayor paused for dramatic effect. "Tonight, we sing for Dale. And one of you, like Dale before, one of you will qualify for the National Championships."

Another midway of applause.

"I also want to remind you not to water your grass in the heat of the day and that I have new lawn signs available for my reelection campaign. Please see Roxanne in the office afterward. They're fire retardant and made of recycled plastic."

Brett's stomach growled. He rushed to the canteen and ordered a hot beef sandwich as the first contestant, Kabir Abdul Wahid, was called to the stage.

"The heck?" Brett slid a ten-dollar bill across the counter. "Why's Kabir here?"

The counter attendant shrugged. "Where you sittin'?"

Brett gestured to a table near the front, stage left.

"The one with no one at it?"

"I'm waiting for people."

A nod. "I'll bring it over."

Brett returned to his seat. Kabir moved the mic from center stage off to the side. He'd brought his own mic, a glitzy wireless one with an elongated shaft. Kabir was from somewhere in the Middle East and had the global look and temperament of a World Cup footballer, earning him the right to cry in public, bank shirtless, and arouse good people with good values. The very best values.

Kabir cleared his throat. The hall silenced. "Hello."

Serious? Brett muttered. *Adele?*

"It is me."

A woman in a stretchy Reitman's dress yelled, "I see you, Kabir!"

Come on! Brett looked around. *Was anyone buying this shit?* Of course it didn't help that Kabir was a firefighter. The kind that saved baby deer from wildfires by putting oxygen masks on their little faces and making them pose with him for selfies. A story from the *Crow Valley Tribune* with one of the rescue photos hung on the bulletin board beside the hall's municipal office. Kabir's brown eyes and the deer's spindly legs broke the town's heart. Brett regularly caught himself gazing at the image. It made him simultaneously want to cuddle someone and slap himself in the face. He pulled out his phone.

Kabir's singing Adele.

Val replied. *Adele? Nobody can beat that. You're fucked.*

Can't u say something encouraging?

I'm busy.

I really want to win.

Kabir's pelvis was positioned at such an angle and with such presence that it was as if his pelvis was singing. Brett gaped.

Val typed. *Can't really help you. Inmate barfed all over his cell. Ambulance just took him.*

If I can just qualify I think I have a good shot. Top 3.

At Nationals???

You don't think?

I would just focus on tonight first.

You don't think I could make top 3?

Dale barely made top five.

Dale had NO stage presence. I HAVE STAGE PRESENCE.

Brett yelled, "I have stage presence!"

A man from the adjacent table looked up. Brett smiled as if he'd made a joke and stared indignantly at his screen.

He typed: *When are you coming?*

You know I'm not off until 8.

Brett sighed. Kabir had dropped to his knees and everyone but Brett and the wheelchair table was on their feet, cheering wildly. Fuck. Brett slammed his fist on the table, tipping a vase of faux carnations. Half a dozen scrunched Hershey's Kisses wrappers and a cigarette butt tumbled out.

He typed: *I have no one here to watch me.*

No response. Brett stared at his phone, at Kabir's right dimple, at the flap of beef bouncing from the approaching sandwich, Kabir's shoulder, back at his phone.

Not what I heard.

He slow-turned toward the corner table where Caroline sat, cross-legged, denim shorts faded and tightly rolled, her milky thighs, bigger than Val's, flowing over the fabric chair, fingers he'd nearly gagged himself on stirring a drink, the mole on her left cheek. He could still smell her. Still feel her weight. It had been like making love to a landmass. Something hilly and breathtaking and organic. Like fucking New

Zealand but waking up in Detroit. The regret had nearly done him in. He was the aftermath of the explosion that took Dale. Broken, melted, ruined.

He stuck his fork into his sandwich. *The only loser here is the one who done lose.*

Chapter 7

ROXANNE

"Can he see me?" Roxanne bent behind a stack of songbooks and jammed a forkful of poutine into her mouth.

Silas gazed toward the mayor's table. "Nope, he's on his phone."

"Good," she mumbled, gravy on her chin. A wet fry and a cheese curd dropped on Kabir's score sheet. "He can't see me eating on the job."

"You know, he might see you less if you took off the headlamp."

"Never." Roxanne recoiled, fingertips stroking the gadget's neoprene straps. "Then *I* wouldn't be able to see."

"See what?" Silas asked.

"I just need to keep it on, okay? In case . . . so I don't miss him if he . . . comes back."

Silas raised his hands, then brought them down gently. He withdrew a vape from his man bag. The device made a clicking noise. He blew mint clouds at the ceiling fan where a strand of metallic ribbon caught on one of the blades whipped around violently. Roxanne remembered that ribbon. It had been used to decorate the hall for Molly and Gary's wedding.

"So, what did you think of . . . how do you say his name?"

"Oh, I just call him Kebab." Roxanne smoothed out her score sheet and whispered. "Grew up in a refugee camp. Doesn't even know how old he is."

"I love him," Silas pined.

"But did you hear him? The lyrics are *it's me*. He said *it is me*. Hello, it is me. Doesn't even know the words."

"He doesn't need to. That's the je ne sais quoi we're looking for. Karaoke is about taking a song and making it your own. Go easy on him."

"Easy? You don't make it your own by changing the lyrics," Roxanne argued. "Next you'll tell me they can do an interpretive dance in lieu of singing."

"No, but I do love a good interpretative dance. Besides, he's gorgeous." Silas circled a series of tens on Kabir's judging form.

"A ten for costume?" Roxanne gaped. "He wore his firefighter uniform!"

"And a very tight undershirt."

"Because he just got off work." Roxanne tugged at her hair.

Silas shook his head. "It was deliberate. The song is about lovers displaced by time and space. And what do we call lost lovers? Flames. The uniform is a metaphor. His love still burns hot, but with love there is pain, so in a way, it offers protection and defense, but the fact he left the jacket unhinged, heart exposed, means he's open to reigniting things. It's brilliant, really." Silas scrawled "brilliant" across the bottom of the score sheet and underlined it with jelly-black strokes.

Roxanne considered this interpretation. Since the wildfires last year, Kabir rarely changed out of his uniform. The tragedy had invoked national media attention, and Kabir wanted the town to remember he was a hero. *Hero firefighter recycles a plastic grocery bag. Hero firefighter stops to let child cross crosswalk. Hero firefighter gives up his shirt to man who spilled mustard on his.* She gave him a five for costume and lifted another stack of wet fries to her face.

"Mayor's staring at you," Silas nodded. "Looks like the MC is waiting to introduce the next contestant."

Roxanne concealed herself behind a napkin and gestured to the stage. Silas gave the MC a nod.

"All right folks, it seems our judges are ready, so we're moving on to our next competitor." The MC had the look of a pinup. Her dress was cinched and polka-dotted, her lips bold. The toes of her white stilettos kissed. She read from her phone. "Please welcome, Alan."

Roxanne rolled her eyes, nearly choking on a cheese curd. "Ugh."

"What's wrong with Alan?" Silas asked, etching the name on a score sheet.

"He borrowed my whipper-snipper a month ago and hasn't given it back. You should see my yard."

"Ask him for it."

"I've tried. He lives in the trailer two lots up from me, but he's never home."

"Speaking of trailers," Silas interrupted, "I had a hard time locking mine. The door doesn't fully latch."

"Didn't Brett show you how to lock it? You pull the blue wire and then feed the—"

"Orange coil through the hole, yes."

"It'll be fine, then."

The DJ worked fastidiously to cue Alan's music.

"You didn't say anything to the mayor, did you? About your accommodations? They're okay otherwise? He insisted that I find you something classy because you were coming from Vancouver, but kinda hard when we lost Crow Valley's only motel in the fire last year." She leaned into him. "It was right near the gas station."

"The trailer's fine."

"Good, because I had them install a flat screen TV and I put in new bedding. What about the towels—they okay?"

"The towels look like they were used to line a dog's crate, but it's all good—I brought my own."

"Damn it. I meant to check them. Normally, that would have been Dale's job. The towels and repairs and stuff."

"It's fine, honestly, but if you could find me a corkscrew . . ."

"What are you drinking wine for? You're in Crow Valley. We drink hard stuff. Lemonade, rum, every flavor of vodka you can imagine. Beer."

"For later. I brought a few bottles with me." Silas pulled out a flask. "For now, it's Scotch." He took a long haul and exhaled, licked his lips. Alan's music finally kicked in, volume set to a theme park. Roxanne winced. The telltale intro to "Ring of Fire" hat-danced through the auditorium like a mariachi band. Alan tugged his Los Cabos souvenir shirt over his belly and performed what one might call a jig. The audience, against Roxanne's rules, joined in the chorus.

"They can't be singing like that!" Roxanne scolded.

Silas remained entranced, bobbing his head a chipper side to side.

Roxanne gave him an elbow. "Silas," she whispered. "They're singing." Roxanne looked down at the mayor, who was leading the congregation and swaying like a palm tree, clapping his tiny, meaty hands.

"How can you *not* sing? It's Johnny Cash." Silas took another swig from his flask. "Roxanne." He had to shout now, over the clapping. "You gotta relax. Karaoke is supposed to be fun. Everyone out there is putting everything they got into being someone else. Here." He handed her the Scotch.

Roxanne stroked the sleek steel flask. It didn't fit her hand the way Dale's thermos did. Dale, who was still on the barbecue, missing karaoke for the first time ever. How could she have let this happen? She unscrewed the cap, brought the metal lip to her mouth, and tipped her head back. The Scotch tasted three-dimensional, like she'd swallowed an amplifier. She shook her head.

Silas winked and mouthed the chorus while the mayor, in his navy suit and happy shoulders, turned jovial circles, fingers up, feet down as if he was dancing on her job. As if he was dancing on a grave, and Roxanne started singing, her throat burning, Crow Valley burning, the gas station burning, Dale burning, forever on fire, forever in flames.

Chapter 8

VAL

Val hauled her acrylic sweater up over her nose, shifting away from the inmate's vacated cell. Gurney marks ran through a flood of vomit. "What the hell did they serve 'em for lunch today?"

Norman Blanchard shrugged. "Tuna casserole, judging by the density." He radioed Control. "We need a wet clean-up of biohazards in Five B." The radio squawked as though it had tripped over a curb. "Have you heard anything from over at the hall?" Norman asked.

"Kabir sang Adele. Killed it. Wore his PPE too."

"Of course he did," Norman replied. "Hard to pull off, no?"

"He got a standing ovation."

"It's a very nice uniform."

Val watched an inmate stack books by his sink. Norman continued to patrol Cell Block B, a few paces ahead of Val, chin out, hands linked behind him in a princely stroll. "Seems like everyone's at karaoke but us."

"Everyone," Val agreed, voice tightening. "Everyone."

"Even . . ."

"Yeah, her too." *Uno, dos, tres.*

An inmate grunted through a speedy set of push-ups.

"Ten more, you pussy-bitch," another yelled.

Norman stopped in front of Marcel, who had his forehead pressed against the bars, arms heavy. Norman raised a hand, like a witness sworn into a trial. He spoke quietly. Val tried to lip-read but couldn't make out their conversation. She turned and paced in the opposite direction, unearthing her phone from her tight back pocket, and texted her sponsor: *Caroline. She's there. At karaoke. And I'm here. In prison.* Her sponsor already knew this of course, but she texted him anyway.

Val called her thirteen-year-old. "Hey, Liv. How's it going?"

"Fine."

"Daphne being good?"

"Kind of. She's watching some mermaid show on Netflix."

"Dad leave?"

"He left a long time ago."

"Like a long *long* time ago?"

"I don't know. Like a while ago. An hour maybe?"

The inmate with "Hello Kitty" tattooed on his forehead sat on the end of his bed talking animatedly to his hands. Val paused to watch.

"Mom?"

"Huh?" She lifted the phone to her ear.

"He wasn't with anyone," Liv said.

"Right," Val swallowed. "Wait, what? I didn't ask that." She held her stomach.

"Can we bike down and get a Slurpee or something?"

"No. You don't need Slurpees. And I told you guys to stay in tonight and clean your rooms. I found a moldy cheese string on Daphne's pillow."

Down the hall, Norman's radio blasted. He halted to listen. "Problem in Commissary." He gestured. "They're out of ketchup chips, and they've substituted the Aquafresh with that real minty Crest everyone hates."

"No kidding. It burns the shit out of your tongue." Val held her throat.

Norman waved her over.

"What?" Val leaned in.

"Keep an eye on one-thirteen," Norman breathed. "He's a bit of a mess."

Val nodded.

Norman turned, speaking into his radio as he strode away.

Val casually strutted toward cell 6A. Marcel was slumped on his bed, knees tucked tight into his chest. A Polaroid of his mother was plastered on the wall across from him. A slight woman, hair swept off her face, bruised. At her hip, a toddler Marcel, long-legged and sad-eyed, as if he'd known at the ripe age of three that the photo would end up in his future self's prison cell. A beer bottle rested on a picnic table in the picture's foreground. Val squinted to read the label as an overhead fluorescent light flickered.

"Hey, one-thirteen," she called. "Heard you got your panties all in a knot."

An inmate whooped, "'Cause he's a little bitch."

Val replied, "A little bitch who set his house on fire." She spun back to face Marcel. "That right, Frenchie?"

Marcel wiped his eyes.

Val lowered her voice. "You're fine," she said, body thronged against the bars. She raised her chin like Norman, hoping she might have the same hypnotic effect, but Marcel leapt out of bed and approached the bars, his erection leading the way.

"You're going to sit on my face."

His spittle landed on her cheek. His breath, heavy as a mastiff's and tinctured with alcohol, toppled her. "Sit down, one-thirteen," she managed from a closed throat. "No one's sitting on anyone's face today."

Marcel stepped back, but somehow stayed. It made Val want to run for her life. It made her want to drink for her life. Shots and coolers and canned wine. It made her want to . . . touch herself? She crossed her legs, horrified, aroused. *Forty days*, she thought. *Make it to forty-one.*

Her phone buzzed inside her pocket: a text. She carried on through the narrow hallway, chin up, shoulders back, gut wrenched, face pink. Her sponsor: *He's not going to do anything.*

Val paused at the exit of Cell Block B and looked back at Marcel.

Chapter 9

BRETT

Brett coiled the wire stem of a faux pink carnation around his finger like a tourniquet. The same flower he'd worn pinned to his lapel at Dale and Roxanne's wedding. Dale's best man. The man who was best, off to the side, older, and in smaller shoes. Brett watched his finger turn blue.

The MC had labored up to the judges' table. Brett ordered a beer and ran through his performance in his head. He planned to start in the dark, likely stage right, and then move into the light, fourteen steps to get there for the chorus. Then, as Val had suggested, he'd look up, eyes to heaven. He'd wanted to do something more dramatic. Dale was always finding innovative ways to make a stage entrance—rollerblades, an exploding crate, rappelling from the rafters—but Val had said these were too extravagant for a tribute song.

He checked the time. There was no way Val would make it, even if she came straight from work, which was unlikely. Her work pants were too tight in the crotch. She'd definitely go home first to change her clothes.

A woman with gold earrings placed a hand on each of two empty chairs set at Brett's table.

"Anyone using these?" she asked, voice a can opener.

Brett shook his head. She winked and dragged them away. He stared at the vacated space. The table looked bigger now, an empty theater.

He called Olivia. "Hey Livvie, it's Dad."

"I know who it is."

"It'd be nice if you and Daph came down to watch me sing."

"Mom said we had to stay home and clean our rooms."

"Mom's at work."

"No offense, Dad, but I'm not really into karaoke."

"There's other kids here." Brett relieved his sweaty palms on his lap. Olivia paused. "Like who?"

Brett scanned the hall. "The Chivers kids."

"I hate them."

"Okay, what about Lennie Dixon? He's here. Didn't you have a crush on him?"

"Not since grade four."

Two tables away, Kabir appeared to be autographing programs. A line of women in floral stretch dresses and orthopedic sandals formed. Brett's mouth gaped. He squeezed his eyes shut. Focus. "Daphne likes music. I'm sure she'd want to come," he said exhaling. "Where is she?"

"I'll show you."

Brett pulled the phone away from his ear as Olivia switched the call to FaceTime. *Connecting.* Within seconds, he was squinting at his youngest daughter sitting fully clothed in the bathtub. There was no water in it.

He held the screen closer to his face. "What's she eating?"

Olivia zoomed in on Daphne cradling a bag of frozen green beans, the other hand splayed in front of the phone's camera like an irritated celebrity. She scowled.

"What's in there with her?"

Olivia spun away from the bathroom. "Oh, she emptied all the knives and forks into the tub."

Brett scoffed. "Why would she do that?"

Olivia turned the camera on herself and shrugged. Something green was caught in her braces.

"Olivia, aren't you supposed to be playing with her or something?"

"I only play with her when you guys pay me to babysit."

"You can't just let her go around putting clean dishes into the bathtub."

"You can't expect me to go around babysitting without getting paid."

Brett whispered into the screen. "Liv, I could really use your help. I'm the only contestant here without anyone to watch me. I kind of need you and your sister right now."

Liv frowned. "But I'm in the middle of watching a video."

"I'll pay you."

"How much?"

"Twenty bucks."

"Forty."

"Liv! Fine. Just hurry up."

"And you can't embarrass me by singing anything hideous."

"Everything I do is embarrassing."

The MC descended the back stairs sideways, knees bulging out of her fishnets, a fresh stack of cue cards clenched in her hand.

"Should we bike down?" Olivia asked.

"Yes, and take your key. And don't forget to lock the door. Text me when you're on your way."

"Can I get food there?"

"Sure, fine. Whatever. Just hurry." Brett finger-counted the names in the program. "I'm up in six."

"K K, I have to curl my hair." She hung up.

Brett slid the phone under his napkin and twisted the tab on his beer can. Lyrics cycled through his head, and he wondered whether he would ever see Dale again. There were times when he thought he had. Standing in the outfield, ankles crossed, left shoulder dipped, waiting for a line drive. Another time floating above the gravel pit. Was Dale in heaven, shrouded in a robe, the best robe, embroidered with his number, nine, stroking lambs at Jesus' feet, fixing things and coaching children, convincing women they were beautiful and sinners they were redeemable? Was there karaoke in heaven?

He leaned back in his chair, causing the metal frame to gently bounce, and awaited the next contestant. The MC crossed the stage and halted, pigeon-toed and mascot-large. "Before we welcome our next singer to the stage, the mayor has asked that you open your hearts and your wallets to help out the Dewitt family." She flipped to the next cue card. "As many of you know, Adam Dewitt regularly has to travel to Kelowna for cancer treatment. Adam"—she swallowed—"is only six years old."

Brett pulled a five from his pocket while members of the Ladies Auxiliary passed collection plates through the hall. Brett deposited his donation into Kabir's helmet. His eye twitched. Once the offerings had been gathered and brought to the DJ booth, the mayor gave a cursory wave and mouthed "Thank you" to the audience, his hands and expression locked in prayer.

The MC clapped, then cleared her throat. "Up next, we have the top qualifier from the regional north karaoke championships, coming all the way from Beggar's Creek and singing Wiz Khalifa's 'See You Again,' please welcome to the stage, Barney Somer."

"What?" Brett jumped from his chair, smashing his knee into the table and upending the saltshaker with a clatter. "I'm singing that." He pointed to himself. One of his shirt buttons had come undone.

The MC smiled apologetically, her lips full and flag-red. "There's no rule in the handbook stating that two or more finalists can't sing the same song." She tilted her head and touched her hands to her knees, a teacher addressing a kindergartener. "So, Barney will sing first, and then we'll hear your version." She scrunched her nose. "What fun."

Brett stomped his foot and then half-kicked the air. "But it's my song!"

The MC replied, "Does anyone really own anything?" Then, with a sweep of her tattooed arm, she shouted, "Let's give Barney a warm Crow Valley welcome."

A crescendo of nausea crashed through the gap in Brett's shirt, squeezing his chest, while Barney strutted across the stage.

"Not that guy!" Brett covered his face. Barney Somer pitched for the Beggar's Creek Buffaloes and had twice hit Brett with a fastball, once in his shoulder and a second time in the neck. He instinctively grabbed his throat as Barney opened his, belting the song as if he owned it. As if he owned grief. As if he'd watched his best friend burn in an inferno and then had to give the eulogy.

Brett glanced up at Roxanne. She sat tall. Brave. He snatched the songbook from the center of the table, bypassed the men's bathroom, and charged out to the parking lot. He'd have to petition for a song change. "God, now what am I going to sing?" He gazed up at the sky, kicked an empty pop can, and shouldered the vending machine. Olivia texted *we're on r way* as a passing seagull shat on his head.

Chapter 10

MOLLY

Molly slouched against a charred support beam outside the Crow Valley Town Hall, the wood kneading her exposed back. She lit a cigarette, tipped her head, and exhaled into the sun. In the daylight, her dress resembled a foil blanket. The kind Kabir had wrapped her in after the explosion. He'd never mentioned the pills, her full tank of gas. She traced the hem of the dress with her finger.

She wished she hadn't said anything to Gary. Motherhood was right up there with cod and good times as things Newfoundlanders held sacred. Professing to be tired of motherhood was akin to putting a padlock on your door and painting your house gray. It didn't help that Gary's own mother was something of a legend in Torbay, where she'd raised eight boys with only a hot plate and a wooden spoon. Nor did it help that she'd died last year, a week shy of her seventy-fifth, buried in a party hat and her slippers, a wooden spoon tucked under her arm. By the end of the visitation, the spoon had been moved a dozen times: laced through her fingers, crossed on her chest, balanced on her forehead, in her front pocket, her favorite sock. The brothers took great amusement in this, laughing until their eyes wept and their pants split and their faces turned the color of a Maritime sunset. And then they cried. They blubbered and they sniffled, and only when she was lowered into the ground did the Chivers men go silent.

Molly took another haul off her cigarette, staying hidden behind one of the town's mobile grills, and watched Brett stomp on a pallet and kick a fast-food bag. When the bag's contents spilled, he gathered

the mess, violently shoving it into a garbage can, not bothering to separate the recycling. She was certain she heard him tell a ketchup packet
to go fuck itself when he reached for his head.

"Stop!" Molly shouted. "That's bird shit."

Brett jumped, withdrawing his hand.

"Sorry," she said. "I had a bad feeling about that bird." She nodded
toward a seagull, tall and smug. "Saw him eating a sandwich earlier."
Molly extinguished the remainder of her smoke, grinding it into the
ground with the tip of her shoe. "I think it was ham and cheese. Come,"
she gestured. "There's a hose around back."

Brett followed Molly to the side of the building, past the storage
shed. "You're up soon, no?"

"Very soon," she agreed. "Here, bend down."

Brett complied, stooping as Molly cranked the wheel, the tap hic-
cupping into action. She stuck her finger inside the nozzle to goose the
water pressure and sprayed Brett's hair.

"Is it safe now to touch?" Brett asked, straightening, wiping his face.

Molly turned off the hose. "Should be."

"Thanks," Brett shook his hair, assessed the dampness of his shirt.

Molly set the hose on the reel and led Brett back toward the main
entrance. "Gary says it's good luck if a bird shits on your head," she
offered.

"Well, I need it. That friggin' Barney Somer sang my song."

"Already?"

Brett held up a trio of fingers. "Third one in."

"That's no worse than Kabir singing Adele."

"Right? I think they give him extra points for being a refugee."

Molly shrugged. "He did look hot in his uniform."

They rounded the corner to the front of the building. Half a dozen
bighorn sheep stood in the parking lot.

"I really want to win this," Brett pleaded.

"I do too," Molly replied, checking her reflection on the door. Dale
stared back from the karaoke poster. It wasn't the most flattering picture of him. He'd put on weight in his last year of life and the photo

amplified his pulpy midsection. It reminded Molly a bit of child Dale. She remembered the day his family's moving truck rolled into Crow Valley. She'd been hanging out with her uncle at Big Al's and he'd climbed down from the truck's cab, weary and round as a hamburger bun. But Molly could see why Roxanne had chosen this particular picture for the poster: his winning smile. It was quintessential Dale. Warm, worthy, heroic.

Brett gestured. "I was going to sing for Dale."

"You still can."

Brett pulled the crimped songbook from his rear pocket. "I don't even know where to start."

"Close your eyes and pick something. Maybe you'll get lucky."

Brett swallowed.

"I meant that maybe you'll pick the right song." Molly remembered the day Val found out about Brett's affair. Val hadn't picked up the girls from Molly's daycare and Molly had to drive them home. She arrived to find the lawn covered in Brett's possessions with Val passed out in the middle of it, body in the shape of an X, still in her Corrections uniform, Brett slumped on the porch using a safety vest to stop his forehead from bleeding. "Why are my parents having a garage sale?" Daphne had asked.

"You know, you could sing something for Val. Instead of Dale."

Brett looked up at her, surprised, curious. "Like what?"

"Like an *I'm sorry* kind of song."

"I already told her I was sorry. I've told her a hundred times." He threw his hand in the air. "It's never enough. I can't go back."

Molly knew what he meant by this. He couldn't un-have an affair. She couldn't un-have children. Couldn't un-mother. Couldn't pack up her stuff and move back into the tiny apartment above the bank where she lived after high school. The place where she smoked out the window and wore pretty bras. The home without cribs.

"Have you shown her?" she asked. "That you're sorry?"

"Why do you think I'm wearing this shirt?" he said, plucking the damp fabric. "Of course I've shown her. This is her favorite shirt. I wore it on our third date and she told me I looked good. That's why I get it dry-cleaned. It's the only thing I dry-clean."

"She might appreciate the gesture."

"She's probably not even gonna make it."

Molly shrugged. "Just a thought."

"Sorry," Brett sighed. "You don't want to be late." He opened the door and motioned for her to go.

"Thanks," Molly said, teetering through. "Whatever you decide, good luck."

"You too," he said following behind. "And thanks for . . ." He pointed to the top of his head, making a circle with his finger. "The hose job."

"Mom!" Xavier slid down the hall in his sock feet, hair standing on end. "You're next! They just called your name!" A poster fluttered to the floor as he passed.

"I'm coming," she reassured him, adjusting her bust.

"Hurry," he coaxed.

She stooped to pick up the flyer that had leapt from the bulletin board. It was the newspaper story of Kabir saving the fawn from the wildfire. The deer looked tragic, almost stillborn. Kabir resembled a cross between Snow White and Jesus. She pinned the clipping back to the board.

Xavier reached out his hand. "Come on, Mom."

She left a note on the counter, next to the grocery list. Was that the line?

"My God, I don't remember the lyrics."

"It's okay," he said thoughtfully. "No one cares."

She took his hand. She hadn't written a note. She'd thought about it only after she'd pulled out of the driveway, the pills like anchors on her lap, past the pile of scooters and skateboards and Gary's 4-wheeler. What could she have possibly written other than *Sorry?*

Chapter 11

ROXANNE

Roxanne was distracted, curious that Molly Chivers wasn't fidgeting nervously in the wings, trilling her tongue, and pretending she didn't make a living reminding people to wash their hands and empty their lunch kits. She knew tonight was important. She'd heard Molly'd dropped nearly a grand on her dress, which looked to Roxanne like a *Star Wars* costume. R2-D2, C-3PO, General Grievous.

Silas busily scratched comments on a score sheet. Hers was blank. How long had she not paid attention? This was the kind of behavior the mayor cited in his performance review. *Easily distracted. Doesn't complete work. Heats leftover salmon in staff microwave. Wears headlamp. Short fused.* She grabbed a pen and scrawled "excellent song choice" in large letters. But was it? She listened. *It's getting dark, too dark to see.*

Fuck. She scrambled for a Sharpie and blacked out her comments. A redaction.

Silas leaned in, puzzled. "You don't like this song?"

They both gazed at contestant number whatever she was, swaying in her safari outfit, hair angled and dyed the color of protest. Roxanne didn't know if she was a real lesbian or just worked at the Crow Valley wastewater treatment plant.

"I hate this song."

"How can you hate it? It's a classic."

"Do you believe in heaven?"

Silas loosened his collar and reached for his vape. He didn't answer right away. Roxanne waited expectantly. It was very important that people believed heaven was real, that it did in fact have a door, and that Jesus had opened it when Dale had knocked. That he might open it for her too.

Silas smiled. "Yes, I think so."

A baby at a middle table fussed. The father, still wearing a tool belt, rose from his seat, scooped the baby from the high chair, and carried him out.

"Do you know anyone who went there?"

Silas paused mid-inhale. "To heaven?"

"Yes." Roxanne withdrew a notebook from her purse. "Okay, go ahead," she urged, pen poised below a column marked *HEAVEN* in block letters.

"I guess, my uncle Philip went there. And my grandma—the Scottish one, not the French one—the crossing guard . . ."

"Hold on," Roxanne waved, scribbling.

"And the agouti we found beside the beach bar last year."

"What the hell is an agouti?"

"It's a Mexican rodent."

"And you're sure it went to heaven?" Roxanne's pencil hovered over the *HELL* column, with its dozen names etched in dull grade school pencil. Onstage, the contestant felt for an imaginary door, and Roxanne wondered if when Dale had arrived he'd shown up burnt, black as the duck she'd overcooked on their tenth anniversary, or bright-eyed and clean-shaven, and if the paramedic who had tried to save him ever did something about his face eczema.

"Of course. All agoutis go to heaven."

"That in the Bible?" Roxanne looked suspicious, though she'd already printed the letter *A* under the *HEAVEN* column.

"I just know," Silas said, circling a series of threes on the score sheet. "Why do you do this?"

"To see what they have in common. I can probably tell you where everyone in this room's going."

"Okay," Silas crossed his arms. "What about Kabir?"

"Heaven, but the Muslim one."

"All right, guy down there with the big hair and chaps."

"Hell."

"How come?"

"Screws up his taxes every year, doesn't prune his juniper, and talks through movies."

"Her." He pointed to woman in bleach-washed shorts and ropy braids, scrolling her phone at a corner table.

"Also hell. Hussy. Slept with a married man, Brett." Roxanne searched for Brett's table. "Dale's best friend. Plus, she voted down a motion to fix the playground on Crow Mountain Road because it, quote, 'wasn't accessible to most children in Crow Valley.'"

Silas rubbed his temples. "And Brett?"

"Heaven."

Silas opened his mouth to speak, but words failed to form.

"Brett goes everywhere Dale does, so it's only logical that he'll end up there too. They were like brothers."

"You know, Roxanne," Silas folded his hands on the table. "I don't think you understand how it works."

Roxanne shrugged, satisfied to leave Silas in suspense.

"And the mayor?"

They both looked down on the small man coddling his much younger wife, her hair like a Pixar film, big and full of promise. He kept an elbow on the table, a primate smile on his face. Even from the back rows of the hall he smelled like an election.

"Well?" Silas asked.

Roxanne tapped her pen. "Hell," she replied, mock-circling his name, which was third under the header.

"Because?"

"He's trying to get me fired. Working for the town is the only job I've ever known. I was here before him." She felt a tingle in her nose. "I can barely look after the boys on my own. I can't tie their skates or make pancakes the way Dale did and I don't know the difference between a split-finger fastball and a slider—they all look the same to me, chunk tuna, flaked tuna—and yet they always ask 'What was that, Mom?' and

I don't know the superheroes, except for Spiderman, and as far as I know he's no longer relevant. There are hundreds of superheroes."

"I'm sure you're a fine mom," Silas offered.

"But I'm not a dad."

"No, and you never will be. You can't be. And that's okay." Silas took a drag off his vape. "Teach your boys to ask questions. Encourage them to be seekers. They want better pancakes, get them to look it up on YouTube. They don't know how to tell a slider from a fastball, tell them to ask Brett."

"Half the time, Brett doesn't even know which base to throw the ball to."

"I can sympathize. First base, third base, home?"

The contestant whispered the remaining lines of "Knockin' on Heaven's Door." The hall was quiet except for the industrial dishwasher rattling in the kitchen as though it was a space shuttle preparing for orbit, preparing for heaven.

"I don't know if you're right about the mayor going to hell, but it sounds like you need to keep your job. For you, for the boys."

Roxanne sat tall, tidied the table papers into organized stacks, replaced the lid on a pen. Her heaven and hell lists remained visible in her notebook. Silas stared, eyes warm. Roxanne slid a splayed hand across the page, concealing the details. The contestant returned the mic to the stand, igniting a concert of applause. The MC let out a whoop and rushed the stage, her dress a candy store. The lights dimmed. Roxanne's headlamp pulsated.

Silas marked his score sheet and slid the completed evaluation to his right. "What about you?" he whispered. "Where are you going?"

And that was the thing. Roxanne didn't know. She worked hard and she tried harder. She fed the birds and kept up with the home reading and the driving and the endless requests for snacks, the glasses of water in the middle of the night. She answered when the boys mistakenly asked where their father was, controlled her rage when they touched his thermos. Sometimes she waived the penalties on overdue municipal accounts. Sometimes she said hello to the staff in the morning. Once she participated in the office potluck, even though she had a bunion on her foot.

But there was also darkness inside her. As if all the remnants of the fire—the melted playground equipment, the burnt cars, charred trees, chair springs, and gas nozzles, the singed bed frames—as if all of it had been shoveled into her chest, the ash settling into the chinks and gaps, cloaking her heart, her lungs, her ability to forgive. Someone had to be blamed for Dale's death, multiple people, actually. She had a list for that, too. It was pierced on the tip of her tongue, branded on her brain, burnt into her heart, a rotting agouti in the Mexican heat.

Silas pointed to the *HEAVEN* column and whispered, "Add my mom, please. Her name was Shelley."

Chapter 12

MARCEL

Marcel fished his socks from the floor, unfurled them on the bed, and closed his eyes. He detected the distinct rumble of the tanker truck emptying the Crow Valley Baseball Diamond porta-potties near the north yard. Service had switched from bimonthly in the spring to weekly in June. He'd already noted the stomach turbulence from the inmate across from him in 7D. Whatever his condition, it regularly peaked after a meal and was always more prominent in the evening. That meant it was almost six thirty, time for scheduled athletics.

"Hey Stalin," an inmate heckled, "you runnin' tonight?" Nash was a rapist from Thunder Bay. He was excellent at basketball and tasks requiring fine motor skills. On the outside, he'd been a pastry chef, self-taught and award-winning, an expert in fondant, sugared flowers, and marzipan fruits. Marcel liked that he called him Stalin, having twice read the Soviet politician's autobiography since arriving in prison.

He shook his head. "Field events tonight. We're jumping."

Nash scratched his balls and horked in a garbage can, something Marcel's dad had done with irksome frequency. Horking, swallowing, throat clearing, grunting, the abrupt release of breath when he lobbed a fist or kicked the dog, the expanded, more guttural release whenever he finished, no sound from his mother, the snoring that followed so deafening that Marcel couldn't hear the drip of an expired icicle, the violence of a lit match.

He paced his cell, visualizing what he'd mapped of Crow Valley Correctional's floor plan, adding recently acquired details—a narrow storage closet on the second floor by the prison chapel, a length of obsolete ductwork near the cafeteria, loose Gyprock in the last stall of the men's room across from the prison welding shop.

Marcel wedged his face through the bars. "Nash," he called. "Roberta Bondar awake over there?"

Nash finished a set of push-ups, sat back on his heels, and surveyed the cell diagonally across from him. "He readin'."

"Tell him we got a date tonight."

"You're a horny bitch, Stalin," he replied, spreading his hands back into a push-up position. He lowered himself to the floor, tongue hanging like a dog's.

Marcel needed Roberta Bondar—nicknamed for his physical likeness to Canada's first female astronaut—to fill in the blanks of the prison's kitchen, particularly the receiving area and dry storage. One of three possible escape scenarios he'd devised since arriving in Crow Valley was to go out with the compost. Unlike the garbage and recycling, the compost was stored in segregation, where it couldn't attract bears. Marcel had already noted that a woman picked it up on alternate Thursdays.

The second option was to bust out through the ceiling of the gym's storage room. Last year, the prison inherited a fat crash mat from the condemned junior high school where Norman Blanchard used to coach track and field. Marcel's plan was to remove pieces of the mat's foam stuffing so that he could eventually zip himself inside and get dragged into the equipment room. From there he'd figure out the ductwork.

Scenario three was, of course, seduction, but there were few candidates. Most of the women were punchy and post-menopausal, with soft arms and hard hearts. A few were lesbians, the nurse a newlywed. The Crow Valley Correctional women were more likely to humiliate him than succumb to his advances. He'd hoped for a lonely program officer in her twenties, one who hosted paint nights and curled her eyelashes and was always trying to lose weight. Instead, he got Val: tough, calm, aware. She demeaned him in a playful way, humored him with jokes that were dated, inappropriate, crass, but underneath her institutional exterior, other than a ripe and freckled rack, was something murky and suffocating, a tailings pond of sorrow. He didn't know why she'd become an alcoholic or why it was such a struggle for her to maintain her sobriety, but Marcel could detect the exact moment her mind switched to that of a drunk. It was a pathetic look, one his mother had perfected when her cheek was pressed against the floor under his father's knee.

The lock clicked, and the door to his cell eased opened with a mechanical *whoosh*. Marcel followed a line of inmates through the corridors of Cell Block B into the yard. He blocked the sun with his elbow. The air smelled like dead grass. A new bench had been installed beside the basketball court, the legs green and bolted in place.

Norman Blanchard stood in the middle of the yard with a clipboard, flanked by the setup for high jump. A terry cloth headband stretched across his forehead. He summoned inmates with a wave and sent them on a warm-up run.

For a second, Marcel remembered the guard with the charming face and impossible grip strength. The one who'd put him to sleep with his forearm, broken his rib, pissed on him in the yard. The one who'd told Marcel he was a piece of shit, that he'd never get his GED or be a dad or have a lawn to mow or a house to hang Christmas lights on, a car or a woman to bend over, wash his shirts, or make him lunch. Motherfucker sang like a boys' choir. *What happened to him?*

"Three laps," Norman motioned.

Marcel kept pace with Hello Kitty, notably Crow Valley's fastest prisoner. He was out of breath by the time he assumed a spot up front, hoping Norman might praise him.

"Feel the length in the side of your body as you reach your fingertips to the sky." Norman said, exhaling.

Marcel felt his rib cage expand as he mimicked the guard's movements. He enjoyed exercising in the fresh air, even though it was nighttime and humid as fuck.

"Good, Marcel." Norman set his clipboard on the grass. "A real high jump approach only requires about ten good strides." Norman was a lefty and demonstrated opposite where Marcel paced. "I want to see everyone's run."

The line in front of Marcel vaulted forward, each inmate readying himself for the approach with a different set of mannerisms. Roberta Bondar did some capoeira shit, a series of stutter steps and then three long strides. The inmate behind him jumped up and down and hammer-punched his quads. The only other lefty ran in a sweeping arc.

"Let's go, Marcel," Norman commanded. He stood on the crash mat with his arms crossed, ponytail over his shoulder, eyes gazing above the bar. "Long, clean strides."

Marcel rocked on his lead leg, and then shifted back on his hind one. His arms jutted out to his side like tree branches. He couldn't control them, or his fingers, which contorted and bent inward like they'd been lopped off by frostbite. He propelled himself forward but was on the wrong foot by the time he reached the jump spot.

"Fuck," he shouted, turning away from the apparatus, purposely smashing himself in the head with the heel of his hand.

"Marcel," Norman called calmly. "One cannot jump from a place of darkness. Take that bird over there." He gestured toward a sparrow. "See the light in its movements."

An inmate yelled, "Bitch can't jump because he's a little Frenchie bitch."

"I'm not sure I understand that logic." Norman raised a hand to silence the inmate while Marcel punched himself in the head. "Let's do it again, Marcel. Start from where you'd take off, and then count ten paces out."

Marcel approached the bar where Norman was stationed and walked the ten paces back on a curved line. "From here?" he asked, pointing at an intersection of lines that had once meant something on a soccer field.

"That'll do." Norman nodded. "Now relax. Feel the tension leave your body through your fingertips."

Marcel shook his hands and exhaled, causing his mustache to flutter. He glanced at the sparrow. He imagined it whispered good tidings as it bowed its thumbprint head. As Marcel shifted his weight into his lead leg, an RCMP cruiser pulled into the parking lot on the other side of the fence.

"Focus," Norman directed from a stepladder adjacent to the mat. It made him look like a giant. An ancient alien. A god. A father.

Marcel pulled back, then catapulted himself forward. When he felt his fingers kink, he made fists and pressed his arms into his rib cage to keep them from flailing. He counted four strides but became distracted by a small boy exiting the back of the police cruiser. The boy was shirtless, his shoes large and lime green, his head a cake pop.

Three more steps, and Marcel closed in on the high jump. He heard someone say "That's it," and he was unsure whether it was Norman Blanchard or Roberta Bondar, or anyone at all.

"Hey!" the Mountie shouted. "Get back here, b'y."

What the fuck kind of accent was that? Marcel tried to stay focused, but he glanced to his right. The Mountie scrambled over the hood of his car. The boy squealed and darted toward the fence.

"Watch out!" Norman called.

But Marcel, with the momentum of a rhinoceros and arms fixed to his sides, plowed into the high jump bar with his face. A few inmates jeered. Norman clambered down from the stepladder and placed a hand on Marcel's heaving spine.

"A little too much speed, that's all," he coached. "Look at me."

The Mountie yelled, "Get down from there, b'y!"

Marcel, slumped on the mat, high bar at his ankles, raised his chin. Norman held up a finger and waved it slowly from side to side in front of Marcel's face.

"Follow my finger," he directed.

Marcel obeyed.

"I think you're going to be okay," Norman declared after several passes. "But you're going to have a heck of a bruise across here." Then he placed his hand on Marcel's shoulder, a Jesus touch, firm and loving. Marcel started to cry.

"I said, get down from there this instant or I'm going to phone your mudder."

Norman turned toward the fence. The boy was climbing at an alarming pace, vertically and then laterally around the side of the prison yard, away from the main door, away from the police cruiser. Norman mumbled something, seized the stepladder, and raced toward the scene, metal clanging, stopwatch thumping his chest.

Marcel scrambled off the mat and joined the surge of inmates gathered along the edge of the yard staring dizzyingly up at the fence top, right into the boy, into the sun. Hello Kitty had ripped off his shirt and was whipping it in NASCAR circles over his head. An inmate yelled, "Jump, motherfucker!" Another urged him to "hang on" and begged for him not to look down. A third was doing Tai Chi.

The boy continued, sidestepping the metal links, his elongated head and kid hair grazing the barbed wire coils, the Mountie below blabbering instructions with his neck cranked upward, his arms raised in holy prayer.

"Grab the mat!" Norman shouted.

A mob of prisoners yanked the red crash mat from its station, knocking down the uprights. Marcel tried to help but there were too many helpers. Before the crew reached the fence, the boy lost his footing, a single green Croc tumbling to the pavement. The crowd reacted with a collective gasp and a solo "Motherfucker almost fell."

Norman raised his voice. "Climb down, boy."

But the boy continued to circle, the sun continued to throb, and the high bar was suddenly in Marcel's hands, stretched across his calluses, balancing on his scars. At some point the bar had been painted orange.

The throng of inmates moved with the boy in frenzied unison, with Norman at the helm. Another guard stood below with a bedsheet. A lone prisoner lay in the basketball court, legs crossed and arms spread pleasingly as though it was the last day of summer. Marcel tightened his grip on the bar. The boy dangled by his arms, white and fleshy, the remaining Croc now wedged into the fence. The jeering, the pleading, the prayers, the threats intensified.

Marcel retreated to the fringes of the yard where the dandelions grew and the prairie dogs burrowed, where the parking lot pavement

on the other side of the yard wasn't maintained. In less than three minutes, he used the high jump bar to pry an opening at the bottom of the
fence and slither underneath. The bar clanked to the ground. Filings of
orange paint dusted his mustache, imprinted his forehead. Freedom
rushed through his hair, tugged at his joints, shook his equilibrium.
The RCMP cruiser, idling in the lot with the door open, beckoned like
a beach slut, only ten strides away. Ten long, clean strides.

Chapter 13

VAL

Val ducked into the boiler room. During Brett's ball tournament last weekend she'd found a pinkie finger of Russian Prince vodka behind the porta-potties. She was fairly certain it fell out of one of the Chivers kids' backpacks, the oldest one, Cole.

She squatted down and ran her fingers under the lip of the steel shelving along the left wall where she was sure she'd hidden it. Nothing but an oily film and a single Tic Tac. Prolly Dale's. She heaved herself upright, leaning heavily on the wall, accidentally switching the light off. All she needed was a sip. Anything to quell the curling rock of anxiety parked in her chest. Anything to silence the thoughts, erase the shame. Anything to numb. Fuck a sip. She'd swallow the whole goddamned bottle. *Just make it to forty-one.*

The tiny room hummed and spat, her phone chiming inside her pocket. Now what? FaceTime. Why? Her cheeks were still flushed from Marcel's face-sitting comment. In her ten years at Crow Valley Correctional, she'd heard all the things, both graphic and benign, that the prisoners wanted to do to her. *Let me come on your tits! Suck my dick! Read me a story! Touch yourself while I cry!* So why, then, had Marcel's invitation to sit on his face been so appealing? She fanned herself with a dustpan. Brett was a cautious and predictable lover. Always on top, nostrils flared, patting her head with a boyish innocence. It was like making love to a stuffed animal. He would never talk to her like that. Val swallowed. Was that how he had talked to Caroline? When she'd come to drop off the catering that day, had he put the skidder in Park and motioned for her to climb aboard, through the wood chips, up the metal rungs, and onto his chin like a white trash Dora the Explorer? *Where are we going? Brett Farquhar's face!* And there it was on the screen, Brett's desperate face. She flicked on the light.

"Where are you?" she asked.

"The hall. I still don't know what to sing."

Val could vaguely make out Roxanne's office in the background. She squinted. "Is your hair wet?"

"A friggin' bird shit on my head. Where are you?"

"I'm in the break room."

"There's a water tank in your break room?"

"Go like this." Val ran her fingers through her hair, tousling it at the top.

Brett copied.

"That's better." She caught herself smiling. Anguish looked good on him.

"Song?"

"I can't help you," she said, the HVAC kicking in, hissing and wheezing the way Val did when she took the stairs. Somewhere a whistle blew. She paused.

"What was that?" Brett asked.

"Dunno. Look, I should go." The screen froze. Val said, "I love you."

It came out as a whisper. She hung up, slipping back into the prison hall, vodkaless. Sweat beaded on her chest, and again she thought about pinning Marcel down on the big red crash mat with the high jump bar, his long muscular legs, the scent of his sweat, French and delinquent, the curve of his mustache grazing her thighs. He was all of twenty-four years old. A baby. *The fuck is wrong with me?* she muttered, shaking her head. The radio squawked from her hip. She jumped.

"We got a minor problem in Cell Block D," a guard said. "Need you to cover for a minute."

"Copy," Val replied into her mouthpiece. "I'm on my way."

Val hated D Block. It was in the prison's older south wing, which hadn't been updated since the early seventies. The cells were smaller than those in Cell Block B and it smelled permanently of mildew and mental illness.

She buzzed herself through two sets of metal security doors, then navigated the slim hallway to D Block, running her hand along the rough concrete wall. Inside the block, three guards knelt on top of a prisoner. Val couldn't tell which inmate it was. He was facedown, forehead rammed into the floor, still managing to writhe under the guards' weight. One of his pant legs was bunched. Val's heart rate quickened.

"There's nothing to see here," she shouted at the inmates pressing their faces against the bars. At the opposite end of the hall, a young guard shook. New kid. Ranch boy with a pudding face.

"Y'all right?"

The guard trembled. "He spit in my face."

Val looked back at the prisoner, tattoos crop circled across his forehead, mouth bleeding. Guards wrestled him to his feet. All four of them were sweating. One of the guards' shirts had popped a button. Another guard was gasping for air but posturing like he could go another round.

"Mackowitz," Val nodded. "He's got nothing."

"But it got on my lip."

Val winced. "He's clean. You'll be fine."

"I'm pressing charges," Pudding Face stuttered.

"For spittin'? You can. Although he'll already get an institutional charge."

"There was a lot if it."

"You want me to call the cops?"

"They already have." He gesticulated at the other guards.

"All right then." Val checked her watch. "Gary should be here any minute. You meet him yet?"

The guard shook his head.

"The Mountie. He's from Newfoundland. Talks like . . . Well, you'll just have to listen. Sounds a bit like an Irishman but without a mouth or an alphabet. What you'd expect from a place with its own time zone. Why don't you go on up to the office and wait for him there."

The young guard nodded and charged down the hall.

Pussy, Val whispered, shaking her head. There were much worse things to get hit with. *The hell's he going to do when someone throws jizz on him?*

Mackowitz's lip was swollen. His pant leg remained twisted as the guards led him down the hall to Solitary. He reminded Val a bit of Benedetto, not in action but in looks. Same bald head, similar face tats and wiry limbs. Unlike Mackowitz, Benedetto had been a model prisoner. Sang in the prison choir, taught other inmates to read. Val knew it was Dale's glowing behavior reports that aided in Benedetto's early parole, and his release on the first day of spring. She remembered the look on Dale's face when he learned Benedetto had waltzed out of Crow Valley Correctional and gone straight to his parents' house, where he shot them both in the head. An untouched cake was found on the counter with the inscription in yellow icing: WELCOME HOME BENNY!

Val shook her head. Dale was never the same after that. At least not at work, anyway. His mistake consumed him. It was the deception that did him in, and that Val understood. But fuck, if she'd had to spend one more shift with Dale listening to him talk about his goldfish, she'd have drowned herself in a tank.

"All right, show's over." She paced the hall, crossing and uncrossing her arms. A prisoner sat on his bed, expressionless, a taxidermy version of himself, like he'd fallen asleep on a long bus ride with his eyes open. Risperidone, Val recognized. An antipsychotic that turned inmates into manageable space cadets. His mouth hung open like a bull's-eye. When she paid attention, she could see his cheek twitch.

Her radio blasted. "We have a problem."

Less than an hour until her shift was over. It was always this way. "Copy, everyone has a problem. What is it?"

"A boy's escaped." Norman Blanchard's voice crackled.

"What boy? A prisoner?" Val tried to recall Crow Valley Correctional's younger inmates. Other than Marcel, there weren't many, and the few under twenty-five could pass for forty. They all looked like they'd spent their formative years sleeping in bus terminals or serving in Afghanistan.

"There's a child on the loose. In the yard."

"Catch him," Val puffed, climbing the two flights of stairs to the main office. "Mountie should be here any minute."

"The Mountie is here," Norman replied.

Val paused to look out a second-floor window when the alarm blared, triggering a full prison lockdown. "For fuck's sake."

Brett texted her a selfie. *Does this look better?*

His hair was brushed to one side and had a wiry bounce that reminded her of pubic hair.

Sure, she replied. *Lockdown, gotta go.* She pressed her face against the window next to a finger-drawn happy face and watched the RCMP cruiser reverse through the prison gate, turn, and fishtail down the arcing road toward town.

Chapter 14

MOLLY

Molly was freaking out at the bottom of the stage right stairs, out of breath, waiting for her name to be called again. The MC, in a blurred spotlight, made an announcement about the rec center's upcoming pool closure. The mayor stood to offer clarification on the anticipated length of the project and then asked the audience if they were having a good time. Molly tuned out their response, attempting to smooth the skinny fat that hung around her waist. Six hundred calories a day and it was still there, like an inflatable ring. Her phone buzzed.

"Moll," Gary panted. "Malcolm's run off. I need your help."

"I'm literally next," Molly whispered, shielding the phone to conceal the anticipated volume of her husband's response.

"Lard dien dumpin', woman, you're deef as a cod. The boy's run off."

"Please welcome our next contestant onstage, Molly Chivers, singing song number 78, Patty Loveless's 'You Don't Even Know Who I Am.'" The MC flung a red ringlet over her shoulder.

"Hear that? They called my name. Just tell Malcolm to come back or we'll take away his X-Box."

"Better to talk to the snow than talk to him," Gary wheezed. "He's climbed de fence, all the way to the top. Get down from there, b'y!" he shouted.

The MC cleared her throat. "Paging Ms. Molly Chivers."

"What fence? Are you at the school?"

"I'm at the prison."

"You took him to the prison?"

"Wus ya born on a raff? You forced me to take him on a ride-along and I got a call. Malcolm, get down from the fence dis instant. I got your mudder on the phone and she's some vexed wit ya. She's taking away your X-Box."

Molly hiked up her dress and whispered sternly into the phone, "I have to go."

"Shag it," Gary replied. "I'll just get the skeet wit da Hello Kitty tattoo on his face to coax him down. Maybe he can take Malcolm back to his cell after and play a nice game of bludgeon." There was a pause. "Where's me car?"

Molly hung up and jammed the phone inside her dress beneath her armpit. The MC, smiling like a dental hygienist, passed her the microphone outside the spotlight. "Good luck," she mouthed, her breath a cinnamon heart. "Your bra's showing."

Molly yanked up her dress for the umpteenth time, stepped into the spotlight with a sultry kick of her hips, and replaced the mic on the stand. The DJ, offstage left, watched, his expression kind, encouraging. Molly gave him a nod, closed her eyes, and waited for the music to start.

She sang the first verse to the audience, trying not to focus on the gentleman at the wheelchair table openly chugging from a bottle of neon-pink wine, or on Xavier, who was sniffing his hand. Why was he sniffing his hand? Where were the people who could relate to the song? Where could she find an amen, a hallelujah, a *Preach it, sister.* Where were the caregivers? The mothers? At which table did the invisible sit?

Under her armpit, the cell phone vibrated, complicating the arm movements she'd choreographed for the chorus. *Fuck off, Gary,* she thought, improvising. The spotlight changed to a hazy blue. A man near the DJ table dropped his hotdog on the floor. She saw the waistband of his underwear as he bent to retrieve it. She strutted to the opposite side of the stage and stopped. A ceiling fan lifted her hair. She stood in the same spot she'd sat during her wedding reception, when Gary'd removed her garter with his teeth and spat out a pearl. She remembered the way he'd looked up at her, eager and devoted, their firstborn already a bloom of cells, already making her cry.

Verse two: Molly turned her attention toward Roxanne and the judge with the flawless skin from Vancouver. She bet he had a bamboo duvet. She bet he never mowed the lawn or kissed the cod or cooked breakfast in a sou'wester. He probably didn't have a lawn. He probably lived in a museum.

Roxanne swayed in her seat. A good sign. Judge #2, however, sat tall, unmoving and serious. *Damn it*, Molly thought. *Maybe he hates country music.* Maybe she had completely miscalculated. Yes, he's from Vancouver. Of course he hates country music, especially the kind she was singing: old and clichéd, a dilapidated barn, a farmer in a kid's book with overalls and a pitchfork and hay in his teeth. Oh my God.

Then she forgot the words.

The chorus played, but she wasn't singing. She made the sort of noise people made when they forgot the lyrics to a song, an extended-release hum, off-key, the words a single unintelligible drawl, a low-battery Fisher-Price. She looked at the DJ. He nodded encouragingly. Judge #2 covered his eyes. Roxanne set her score sheet on fire, burning a hole through the center with her headlamp.

"Sing, Mom," Xavier chanted. He sat on his plate twirling a tiny drink umbrella. A muffle erupted from the back and spread like a gas leak through the hall.

Molly blanked. She shouted random lyrics: *laundry! pillow! gro-cer-ry list.* In front of the stage, the MC squeezed a stack of cue cards until they crumpled, her jaw clenched. The man who'd chugged the neon-pink wine accepted an exaggerated piece of lemon meringue pie. The spotlight swapped to a basement red. The DJ looked as though he'd come in his pants and Brett jumped up on his chair, eyes fixed to his phone. "Holy shit, there's been a prison break!"

Molly stumbled backward, dropping the mic, her moment over. She was over, like a canceled celebrity. The truth was that she was over long ago. Motherhood had given her four boys and they were lovely and smart and horrible and in exchange it had taken her. Motherhood was a con man. Motherhood was a thief.

Whispers ballooned to a roar.

"How many?" a woman asked, emptying a packet of sugar into her tea. "Just one prisoner? A single break? Or like a whole cell block?"

"Did they catch him?" A mechanic fed his baby with a spoon.

An old man waved. "Gary'll get 'em."

The mayor scrambled to the stage, "As mayor of Crow Valley, I want everyone to please remain calm. You have my personal promise that we will find these prisoners and have them returned to Crow Valley Correctional immediately and that starting tomorrow we are closing the left lane on Main Street for three months please see Roxanne if you have any issues may justice prevail."

Molly stood in the mayor's shadow, lyrics trickling back to her. *So what do you care if I go.*

Chapter 15

MARCEL

It was Marcel's eighth time in a police cruiser, his first in the driver's seat. He clutched the steering wheel and cranked it left and right, side-swiping the chain-link fence as he passed through the prison's exterior gate. He flashed back to the coin-operated police car his mom let him ride in the back of the convenience store where she bought white bread and cigarettes. The car was small, too narrow for his clunky snow boots amid the empty cups and chewed straws and makeshift gas pedal. He remembered the smell of his unwashed hair, damp with sweat and Quebec winter, the remnants of the Vicks VapoRub his mother ritually applied to his chest. He recalled the pleasing mechanical clatter of the ATM that dispensed cash beside him, the obscene gnashing of the same ATM when he later dragged it out of the store with a chain and a stolen F-150.

Marcel spun, the back tires flirting with the ditch as he put the cruiser in turbo and tore down the road toward town. The computer screen blinked beside him. In the back seat a crumpled T-shirt, in the front a rosary dangling from the rearview mirror. The cruiser smelled like a house that had only known a single owner, comfortable and sour. He crossed himself and for a speed bump of time, he thought of Norman Blanchard. The disappointment Norman might feel on learning of the escape, and perhaps, Marcel fantasized, perhaps even a prick of sadness that his favorite prisoner was gone. He reveled in the possibility of being missed.

He rolled down the window, gravel spewing from the tires, and inhaled the snow seven thousand feet up. He rounded a sweep in the road and came to a dead end. A sign pointed right for DOWNTOWN. Another, left, to the CROW VALLEY ACRES INDUSTRIAL PARK. A third sign advertised fresh local eggs. No one would expect him to head toward town. They'd be searching the campgrounds and the abandoned weekend parking lots of the sawmills, schoolyards, and logging sites.

Marcel spun the steering wheel and drove with his head out the window, gulping air like a road dog. He'd gone less than a few kilometers when he saw something ahead. A clump at a junction with a road that stretched down the mountainside perpendicular to the one Marcel was driving on. He slowed.

A girl, maybe twelve or fifteen, peeled herself out of the clump and waved.

"Fuck." Marcel slammed his head into the window frame when a second girl, smaller than the first, crawled out from under the heap, which he now recognized as a pair of bicycles. He pulled over and simultaneously reached into the back seat for the T-shirt.

"What the fuck?" The T-shirt looked and smelled like a daycare. There were grass stains and brown marks and holes along the neckline, like it had been chewed. It was still damp. He stuffed it into a seat pocket as the older girl approached. A ribbon of blood trickled down her cheek, and she cradled her elbow. Marcel looked down at his prison-issue jogging pants.

I'm off duty, he said to himself. *I'm an off-duty RCMP officer coming back from the gym.* He opened the car door. "Everything okay?"

The girl glared at him. "Um, no. I'm bleeding." She pointed to her cheek, showed off her elbow. Her T-shirt said PIZZA IS MY BAE.

"That your sister?" Marcel asked.

The girl nodded. "Daphne, get over here."

The younger girl kicked one of the bikes and then rage-limped across the street. "It was your fault," she shrieked, striking her older sister across the back. "You cut in front of me."

"Hey, whoa," Marcel said, reaching for the girl's arm. "You can't go around hitting people."

"Yes, I can," she replied, hands in fists. "I do it all the time."

Marcel believed her. The rabbits on her shirt were dressed in fatigues and there was chain grease on her neck. She was missing some teeth, maybe four. He bent down, looked her in the eye. "Do you want to end up like me?"

"What, like a cop?" She crossed her arms, her entire left kneecap sticking out of a tear in her pants.

Marcel blabbered something unintelligible. *You're a cop*, he said inside his head, turned his back on the girls, and punched himself in the face exactly where the high bar had landed.

"She wants to be a bartender," the older sister said, digging at her braces. Marcel noticed that her eyebrows were a different color than her hair. His noticing seemed to make her uncomfortable and she touched her face. Her shoulders fell.

Marcel examined Daphne. "How old are you?"

"Seven."

Two years older than his daughter. "What kind of things could you do when you were five?"

"Huh?"

"Like could you read? Do a cartwheel? Cut up your own meat?"

"She's a vegetarian," Olivia interrupted.

"If your dad was in prison, could you have written him a letter?"

The older girl stared at Marcel, her eyes narrowing. "Where's Gary?"

"Gary?" Marcel stuttered.

"Uh, like the only male Mountie in Crow Valley?" She stepped back and took Daphne's hand. Daphne wriggled free.

"He's sick. I'm filling in."

"Where's your uniform?"

"I left it at the gym. On accident."

"*By* accident," Olivia corrected.

"Why do you talk like that?" Daphne asked.

"Like what?" Marcel shifted, embarrassed.

"With a dumb accent."

"I'm from Quebec."

"Is that why you have that stupid mustache too?"

Marcel winced. He knew his mustache, though styled, was patchy and ugly, but it was the only thing that made him look different from his father. Why hadn't he heard sirens?

"Are you really a cop?" The older one picked dirt from her skinned elbow.

"Yes."

"Then why are you wearing prison-issue jogging pants?"

"How do you know these are prison jogging pants?" Marcel gaped.

"Because my mom has a pair."

"Your mom's in prison?"

"She's a guard."

Marcel stopped himself from asking who. "Look, I am a cop."

You'll never be more than a criminal.

He listened for traffic. Still nothing. He grabbed a plastic bottle from the back seat of the cruiser, poured some water on a napkin and handed it to the older girl. "What's your name?" he asked.

"Olivia."

"We call her Liv, as in the opposite of dead." Daphne picked up a bottle cap, pressed her finger into its crimped metal edge, then flicked it into a pothole.

"You girls okay then?"

Olivia wiped her face. "I think so," she said, handing him the soiled napkin.

He turned toward Daphne. There was a clot of blood on her hand. "Can I?" he asked.

Daphne stuck out her arm. Marcel took her wrist and gently wiped the blood. It was the smallest wrist, vulnerable and slight. Tragic. It took away his breath. He let go and gathered himself.

"Where were you off to?"

"Karaoke."

"Our dad's paying us to come, because he sucks."

"That's not a nice thing to say about your dad. Does he read to you? Build you forts? Cook you pancakes?"

"Sometimes," Daphne said. She walked heel-toe down the white line as if she'd been instructed to perform a sobriety test.

"When I was your age, my dad stuck a burning cigarette between my shoulder blades until I pissed myself."

Olivia flinched. "I don't think that's the kind of story you tell kids."

Marcel thought about this.

Daphne sidled up beside him. "Do you have a scar?" she asked. "Can I see it?"

"You girls untangle your bikes and get going to the . . . Where are you going?"

Olivia rolled her eyes. "The hall."

He thought she might have added a "duh." "Right, the hall. And be nice to your dad or I'll give you both a ticket."

"For what?" Daphne threw her hands up, crossed the road to the bikes, and yanked mercilessly on a set of purple handlebars.

"For riding without helmets," Marcel called.

Daphne adjusted her seat, climbed on her bike, and pedaled violently down the road. Olivia followed, steering with one arm. Marcel got back in the car and suffocated the rosary with his face. He'd done good. He'd only punched himself once. He'd helped the girl with her elbow like a nice dad. Made threats like a cop, spoken like a real man.

Marcel turned up the mountain road the girls had ridden down. Away from them. Away from the Crow Valley Town Hall. Away.

Chapter 16

BRETT

Brett was still standing on his chair when the MC joined the mayor onstage and yanked him into a huddle. Molly remained rooted behind them, a statuette, the mic at her feet. Brett noted the time. The girls should be here any minute.

"I heard it was the guy who ate his wife's eyes after he caught her having sex with his boss," whispered someone at the adjacent table.

"It wasn't his boss," another replied. "It was their financial adviser."

A woman hunched over a walker stopped. "You think he went north?" she asked. "I didn't lock my door."

Brett shrugged.

The woman carried on, cutting the line where people waited to top up their sour cream, their drinks, their feelings. Everyone else texted with the zeal and madness brought on by a town emergency. A more subdued response than to last year's wildfires, but a response nonetheless. Those who'd refused the mandatory evacuation last year remained seated, picking their teeth, cleaning their plates, contemplating how they got so fat or why they got married, or what took them so long to discover online grocery shopping, or their own mediocrity.

The MC recovered the mic from the floor and clipped it back onto the stand. "Everyone please remain calm," she advised. "We're going to take a ten-minute intermission to verify whether there has in fact been a prison break, and in the event that that information is correct, we'll consult with police for instructions."

The mayor added "Pray for Crow Valley" before clasping his hands and swallowing dramatically, an act he'd perfected last year for the national news outlets and the reporter from Idaho with the very important questions. He hurried away. The MC followed, making a beeline for the DJ booth, leaving Molly alone, upstage and downtrodden. Brett wanted to rescue her, offer his friendship, escort her to safety, wash the shame from her eyes, as she'd washed the shit from his hair, but just as he stepped off his chair, Kabir the archangel ascended the stage and guided Molly down the stairs to the partitioned area.

"Ah, come on!" Brett yelled. "Isn't there a cat stuck up in a tree somewhere?"

In the shadows behind the curtain, Kabir removed his coat and draped it over Molly's shoulders.

"It's a hundred friggin' degrees in here," Brett hollered. "Ever hear of climate change?"

No one paid attention. Brett tried to call Val, but her phone went directly to voice mail. He reread her last message: *prison break*.

A man wearing a bolo tie claimed there were two, possibly three escapees. A woman with cornrows insisted it was five. She was a probation officer and could probably name them. A boy in pajama pants was asleep on the floor, a soother balancing on the rise and fall of his small chest. The contestant who'd been on deck adjusted her wig and reapplied lipstick. The sequins on her dress winked when she moved.

Brett followed up with a text: *R u safe?*

He'd accepted Val's working in a men's prison. He'd even grown comfortable with it, as he had other areas of his life: his hourly wage and soft middle, how much he was willing to parent, how much he was willing to help around the house. He didn't do lunches. He didn't do home reading, class blogs, agendas, concerts, toilets, birthday cards, birthday parties, or school projects of any kind. He'd never cleaned a microwave, or called the school to report an absent or a late.

Dale had done these things.

There were times Brett wanted to do them, or thought maybe he should do them, usually when he was sprawled on the couch after work, one foot on the floor, his symbol of readiness, but it was too hard. Logging was exhausting. Averageness was exhausting. Pine needles were regularly lodged in his socks, his shoulders ached, and there was always a game on TV, perpetually in overtime, in extra innings, on a fourth down. He'd never match Val's energy, but he admired it from the comfort of the couch, the way she signed the permission slips and bleached the sinks. The couch, olive-colored, overstuffed, microsuede, so comfortable he lost his marriage in its seams.

Tell the girls to make sure the door is LOCKED.

Brett dropped the phone. The girls. Val still thought they were home. He stared at a wall clock nailed above the double doors and tried to figure out the time, but it was like reading a sundial at midnight. It didn't matter anyway. Enough time had passed; Olivia and Daphne should've been here by now. He grabbed his cell and staggered away from the table. He had to find them.

Halfway down the hall, Brett paused to steady himself on a bench covered in donated books. His legs wavered, hand sliding across a presidential memoir, a swirl of nausea surfacing in his throat. A picture book die-cut like a fire truck slammed to the floor, alarming Roxanne and Silas, who were communing outside the municipal office.

"Brett?" Roxanne called. "Are you okay?"

Brett stumbled toward her, a wash of supernatural heat assaulting him from the inside, and then fainted, landing facedown in the office doorway.

"Jesus, Brett!" Roxanne croaked, squatting beside him, her knee jammed against his rib cage. He felt her presence, hollow and heavy both, the heat of the headlamp.

Someone asked, "Is there an AED on site?"

Was that Silas? Brett wondered.

"He doesn't need an AED," Roxanne asserted. "He only fainted."

"It might wake him up?"

Brett's eyes fluttered. Were they going to shock him? Restart his heart? Maybe that's what he needed. A reset. Five thousand volts to send him back five years when his marriage and best friend were still intact.

"Get him some water."

"Maybe he's choking. Who knows the Heimlich maneuver?"

Another voice, "They don't use that any more. Just back blows."

"What did he choke on?" asked a man.

"Did he order the taters?"

Then a gallant voice, formal and dazzling: "Do not touch him."

The blur of feet by Brett's head retreated. Someone bumped into the Xerox machine, causing it to emit a mournful beep. A work boot came into a view and then a face. Kabir.

"You just fainted," Kabir said, muscling Brett onto his back.

Brett attempted to nod, sweat pricking his hairline.

A woman asked, "Is he going to live?"

"Liv!" Brett bolted upright. The girls.

"Easy." Kabir placed a firm hand on Brett's thigh. "You need a minute," he said, reaching behind him to where Silas unscrewed the cap from a bottle of water.

A milky way of stars flickered behind Brett's eyes as Kabir brought the bottle rim to his lips, tipping it at just the right angle, while simultaneously holding Brett's weight with a single hand spread across his back like a stretcher. Brett drank with desperation. He drank like Val. When he attempted to sit up fully, Kabir heaved him off the floor into a fireman's carry—the same way Brett used to carry Daphne home from soccer.

"Fresh air," Kabir sermonized, striding toward the main doors. "I'll take care of him."

Brett wanted to thrash. Wanted to buck free and find his feet and go after his girls, as his eyes finally focused, zooming in on the karaoke poster taped to the glass. What would Dale think of this? That he had to be bottle-fed, coddled, and carried away on another man's back—the wrongest place to be, apart from a burning gas station.

Blood rushed to Brett's head as Kabir kicked open the door. The sun matched the reflective glare of Kabir's uniform pants.

"Are you ready?" Kabir asked, a diminutive grunt suggesting the first signs of physical strain.

"Almost." Brett closed his eyes, savoring the final moments of being draped across the capable back of a real-life superhero, secure, safe, and completely uncomfortable, and then Kabir lost his grip and dropped him on his head.

"Sorry," Kabir apologized. "That never happens."

Chapter 17

VAL

How in the heck had they done it? There had been no indication of a riot. No explosions, extreme weather, or extraordinary sounds. The prison wasn't on fire. Val clattered down the two flights of stairs toward the yard, her legs quivering, pants hot, adrenaline zipping through her like a taser charge. She'd tried to call the girls to make sure they were safely locked in the house, but Liv hadn't answered.

The air whooshed as she flung open the door. The inmates from B Block were facedown on the pavement, on the grass, awkward and submissive. Routine. Lights strobed. The alarm continued its deafening wail. With the rest of the prison population locked down in their cells, the remaining guards had moved in on the yard.

"Let's go, astronaut." Val nudged Roberta Bondar's lower leg with her boot. "Ain't nobody going on a space walk tonight."

Roberta Bondar peeled himself off the ground, face and hands filmy with dust. His body odor was cabbage and violence.

"Keep your hands above your head where I can see them," Val said, transferring him to a row of prisoners lined up at the door, where guards in riot gear escorted them back inside.

Val scanned the line counting *1A, 3B, 3C, Hello Kitty, 4D, 2A, Nash, Bondar,* and then wandered toward the crash mat in the yard. The cover had been removed, the remaining foam block scavenged. An inmate was stuffing pieces into the waistband of his underwear. Who knew how the foam might be useful?

"Leave it," she hollered, motioning toward his bulging pants. The inmate obliged, ditching the salvaged foam. Val escorted him to the line, where a guard shouted incoherently at the prisoners. She stepped over a little green Croc. "The fuck is that doing here?"

In the adjacent parking lot, Gary climbed into the back of an ambulance.

A medic with a blond ponytail secured the doors behind him. Val surveyed the yard, confused. She'd seen Gary take off not ten minutes ago from the west wing's second floor window. It looked like it had been a serious call, more than a face spitting, the way he'd scrammed out of the gate, tires flinging rocks. Val paused. *Holy shit!* She just assumed the dickhead who'd escaped was on foot. Not that he'd taken the cruiser. She picked up the Croc and continued patrolling the yard, hustling inmates into line before moving alongside the fence.

A jungle canopy of barbed wire loops hung overhead and the summer sun was midday hot even though night was closing in. On the edge of the yard, she stopped. At her feet was the high jump bar, orange and peeling, wedged beneath the fence, a swath of fabric entangled in the chain link.

Who in the heck could fit through there? Val squatted, her head turned, face in the hole. She lifted the end of the high jump pole, jostled it sideways, and then dropped it to the ground with a thud. *Marcel.* The delinquent fuck had done it. Slithered his way to freedom like a goddamned circus act. Where the hell had he gone?

Val stood, shook off a head rush and stared at the prison's main gate. South toward the border? West to Vancouver? He couldn't have gone east. She'd read in the *Crow Valley Tribune* that the Cougar Creek Bridge was closed for repairs, slated to start Monday. She imagined him miming his way down Highway 2, juggling his options, slowing every five minutes to cry or punch himself in the head, stopping only to jerk off at something beautiful: a piece of obsidian, an abandoned carburetor, a bull thistle.

Val gazed into the neighboring baseball field, fixating on the empty pitcher's mound. She wondered what Dale would think of all this. Marcel escaping. Dale would've taken it personally. After Benedetto, he didn't believe in freedom or second chances or rehabilitation. He even stopped believing in time served. And he certainly didn't believe in French people, men that were taller than him, men that were younger than him. Marcel escaping Crow Valley would've felt for Dale like Marcel was escaping him. Climbing out of the cage of his ribs with a manhood souvenir.

"I see where he got out," Val garbled into her radio.

"Under the fence," a guard replied, radio blasting. "By the west gate. Took off in an RCMP cruiser."

Val swatted a mosquito. "I know that now. I seen him leave. Thought it was Gary."

"Negative. Main detachment's been notified. They're sending support."

Main detachment. Val shook her head at the mountains like they'd somehow enabled the escape. That was nearly a fifty-minute drive. Longer, if the officers were out on patrol or chowing down at the new Denny's.

"Everyone else accounted for?" she asked, shielding her eyes from the sun.

"Just waiting on confirmation from B Block."

Val looked out into the yard. The last of the inmates had been wrangled back inside. She kicked at a piece of foam and redialed Olivia.

"Hello?" Olivia shouted. "Mom?"

"I can barely hear you." Val stuck her finger in her ear. "Sounds like you're standing on the *Titanic*. Are you outside? Why are you outside?"

"It was just a truck going by."

"You *are* outside. Olivia, go back in the house right now and lock the door." Silence. "Did you hear me?"

"Can't hear you."

Val shouted, "I said, go back inside and lock the door. There's been a prison escape."

"I'll just text you."

Val hung up, stared at the screen, waiting, the green Croc still tucked under her arm. Who'd she know in town that wore them? Really no one since the splash pad burned down. She flipped the shoe over: MALCOLM. Of course, Val mumbled. Kid probably couldn't even tie his shoes. She'd warned Molly her eggs were getting old.

Her phone pinged.

We're inside.

Finally, Val replied. *Lock the doors and don't leave. I might be late.*

She crumpled at the edge of the basketball court, in a mix of relief and exhaustion. Val didn't just want a drink; she deserved one. She'd earned it. She brought her knees to her chest, plucking a buttercup from the yard, twirling the stem between her fingers in a meditative rhythm. *Buttercup.* Brett used to call her that. Didn't he? The memory cut her even if it had only been once, even if she'd made it up. She was starting to forget the early years of her marriage because it felt like she'd been married for a hundred.

The alarm had ceased and the yard had gone quiet, but it was a weighty silence, a timber on her shoulder, and it reminded her of their bedroom at night in those minutes after they'd both said good night but before they fell asleep when their thoughts moved in. *Did I forget to take out the garbage? Did I start the dishwasher? Did I leave laundry in the washer? What the fuck is happening? How did I get here? Is this it?*

She was off soon. One drink. The draw was extreme. The kind of forest fire rating that disrupted industry, shut down campfires, and incinerated memories. She should text her sponsor, confess her plan, acknowledge her failings, but she knew it wasn't a good time. Norman was busy. She eased herself up to head back inside, the buttercup flattened beneath her boot.

Chapter 18

ROXANNE

Roxanne and Silas stood at the end of the hall, fixated on the front entry. Brett and Kabir were blurred by the mosaic of posters taped to the door.

"What are they doing out there?" Silas squinted.

It looked as though Brett was back on the ground, legs in a knot. A recovery position? Roxanne shrugged. "Maybe he's giving him mouth-to-mouth."

"One could only hope." Silas crouched to get a better view.

The mayor quickstepped his way toward them, a spot of gravy on his lapel, his wife struggling to keep up. She was much taller than he, with dewy skin and a strip mall manicure. She sidled up beside him and took his hand.

The mayor said, "I just got off the phone with the RCMP detachment. They got a couple units on the way and they've already contacted Border Patrol."

"Did they say to do anything special? Cancel the show? Lock the doors?" Silas asked.

The mayor shook his head. "No one would be stupid enough to come to the hall. Have you seen the parking lot? Whole damn town's here." His chuckle caused his face to redden. "We don't have time to postpone."

"I get it," Silas agreed. "Nationals are next week."

"You judging those too?" Roxanne asked.

"Negative," Silas replied. "Booked a two-night trip in the wilderness to learn primitive survival skills. You know, shelter building, fire construction, game tracking, emergency response. That kind of stuff."

Roxanne had a hard time imagining Silas in the woods with a machete tracking anything more than the face cream he'd ordered off Amazon last week. Primitive survival was a manly skill. A Dale skill.

Silas must've sensed her disbelief because he put a firm hand on her shoulder. "Sometimes I identify as straight," he said, teasing.

The mayor laughed uncomfortably and pointed to his name tag, specifically his pronouns, which he'd begrudgingly agreed to have added. "He/him," he blurted.

"Yes," Silas said, "Aren't you an ally."

"Your kind are always welcome in Crow Valley. You know we hosted our first pride event this year."

Sweet Jesus. Roxanne covered her face. The "event" was simply a pride flag–raising ceremony at the library, at which time the mayor had asked if there was also a flag for straight people and if so, what did it look like.

"Splendid. I'll let my kind know."

Roxanne cut in. "Do they know where he went? The prisoner?"

The mayor adjusted his tie. "RCMP figures he went east."

"Why east?" Roxanne asked, aware that her pants had ridden up, exposing her poor choice in socks. She attempted to nudge them down.

"Some Frenchie. Wants to get back to La Belle Province."

Roxanne considered the dossier of prisoners Dale had talked about over the years. There were hundreds, the details scant and incomplete and random. She didn't know if any of them were French. *We got a guy who talks to dead people. We got a guy who's allergic to citrus. A guy who played Tom Hanks's son in that big movie. A transfer from Grand Cache with dwarfism. One who speaks six languages. A guy who has Hello Kitty tattooed on his forehead. A guy who murdered his brother. His mother. His coworker. His wife. His girlfriend. His girlfriend. His girlfriend.*

Silas swiped a mint from the fishbowl at reception. "You know what he's in for?"

"Murder, for one. And arson. The loser set his house on fire. Burned it right to the ground. Heard there was nothing left but a claw-foot tub and a can of coffee." The mayor paused, sparing a passing band of kids glued to an iPad further details. He lowered his voice. "His old man was inside. That's how he killed him. Nothing left of him but a . . ."

Roxanne gasped, legs buckling.

Silas grabbed her elbow to keep her upright. "Nothing left but a poorly directed and highly insensitive comment."

The mayor stuttered. "I'm sorry, Roxanne. I . . . I didn't mean to . . . I was just . . . repeating the story." His eyes were soft. His wife covered her face with a red pashmina. The mayor rolled his hands in a nervous orbit, opened his mouth, but didn't speak. Silas cleared his throat and put a hand on Roxanne's back.

"I didn't mean . . ." the mayor repeated.

"I know," Roxanne replied, woozy, tears burning. She pictured dead Dale, charred and angular, his shape only vaguely human.

The mayor's wife reached for Roxanne's arm. "I hope it's not too late to say this, but I'm sorry about Dale." She paused. "Remember a few years ago we had that huge September snowstorm and that massive tree fell across Main Street right by the bank? Well, I tried to go around it to get home from work but I got stuck in a snowbank. Dale pushed me out."

"Thank you." Roxanne forced a smile, both charmed and incensed by her sweetness, by her youth. Of course Dale had pushed her out. That was his thing. Shoveling driveways, fixing chainsaws, rescuing idiot motorists. Why would anyone attempt to drive around a felled tree? Roxanne had seen the pictures. The tree had pretty much cut Main Street in half. For her to go around it would have literally meant driving on top of the snowbank. Not grazing it with her mirror, not skimming it with her tires, but surfing it like a monster truck. And then Molly during the fire. Knowing they'd already evacuated the long-term-care patients at Crow Valley General. Knowing they'd already cut power to Elk River, closed Highway 44, Range Road 17. Knowing the fire had already reached Crow Valley like some kind of plague, and she runs out of gas?

"Do we have a plan?" Silas asked.

"Yes." The mayor exhaled, relieved the conversation had shifted. "We'll take another ten minutes and then resume where we left off."

He squeezed his wife's hand. "You should go warm up your voice," he said.

She nodded and tucked into a meeting room, heels tumbling out of her platform wedges. The mayor took a step closer to Roxanne. She raised her chin to prevent the headlamp from spilling into his eyes.

"There's no way he's making it to Quebec," he asserted.

"Why?" Roxanne wondered.

"The Cougar Creek Bridge is closed!" He beamed. "You ordered the signs for Friday. There's no way he'll navigate the detour. It's like a bloody corn maze."

"Right, of course. The signs. Perfect."

"Listen, I know you're not really *on duty*, but I have small favor to ask. Alec is turning two next week." The mayor pulled a piece of paper from inside his coat pocket. "We're having a little party for him over at the pavilion. Figured I could hand out the invitations tonight since everyone's here. You mind making me a few copies? Maybe ten, fifteen?"

"Sure."

The mayor winked. "I knew I could count on you." He took a few steps backward, nearly knocking over the book bench, and addressed Silas. "She's great, right? Isn't she great?"

Silas waved affirmatively.

"See you back"—the mayor checked his watch—"in seven minutes."

Roxanne gave a thumbs-up as the mayor slipped inside the main auditorium.

Silas turned to her. "You didn't order the signs, did you?"

Roxanne covered her mouth, eyes half the size of her face. "I remember seeing the work order but . . . no. I spent all week studying the judges' handbook."

Silas rapped his fingers on the reception desk. "Is it a big deal?"

"The signs were supposed to be up and he believes they are."

"But no one's going to plummet off the bridge or crash through a hole?"

"No. They're just replacing some capstones."

"Then you're fine."

"What if the prisoner gets through? What if he makes it back to Quebec and he sets someone else on fire? It'll be my fault."

"Blame it on vandals. That shit happens all the time in Vancouver. Anyone says anything, tell them the signs must've been stolen."

Roxanne exhaled, flattening the invitation on the reception desk before lifting the cover of the copier and setting the page on the glass plate. The machine chugged like an old generator. She punched in the number of copies.

"You good?" Silas patted her back.

She sniffed. "I'll be fine."

He shook his flask. "I'm going for a refill. See you back at the table."

Roxanne braced herself against the machine when it paused, an error message of broken text indicating it was out of paper. *I don't have time for this.* She bent to retrieve the spare case wedged between the copier and the mayor's favorite plant, which was chest-high, leathery, and parched. *Oh my God. I didn't water his plant.* She snatched Brett's half-empty water bottle from the hall and dumped the remains in the soil and then removed the lid from the paper case. Empty, except for a fly and a leaf, both long dead, and a No. 2 pencil. *How could they be out of paper?*

Roxanne went to her desk and fumbled through the drawer for the storage room keys, displacing wrappers and work orders, a picture of her boys. She hadn't even bothered to check in with them. They would be getting ready for bed now. She studied the photo, taken a few summers ago in the front yard, the boys in the sandbox with a pileup of dump trucks. She noticed Dale in the background, a sliver of him, bent down on the porch. A ghost.

No keys. *For fuck's sake.*

She returned to the copier and yanked open the reserve tray. A stack of cardstock, slim and dusty, was tucked inside. She transferred the bundle to the main feeder and hammered the green button, relieved the machine responded.

In the hall, a group of kids played floor hockey with mini-sticks. A paperback filled in for a puck. The squeak of sneakers on tile amplified the game. Beyond, Roxanne caught the bluesy echo of the MC's voice making an onstage announcement. Someone yelled, "The show must go on." A few whistled, others drummed the tabletops, producing a roar that in another setting, a prison, for example, might have been the precursor to a riot.

For a second she considered how it was possible the prison break had even occurred and whether Dale would have stopped it had he been alive. No one had escaped Crow Valley Correctional, or even attempted to, during his nineteen-year tenure. Dale wouldn't have allowed it. Second chances were only earned through time served. None of this early release for good behavior like you see on TV. Parole was a dirty word. And you sure as hell didn't get to escape.

With minutes to spare, Roxanne collected the birthday invitations from the tray, the paper tepid with a pleasing sheen. On the reverse side was the back page of Dale's funeral bulletin, the picture of him sitting on the quad in his quilted plaid jacket with his billboard smile, the dog in the foreground eating something dead. It took away her breath. She collapsed into an upholstered chair.

Roxanne had refused grief counseling. She'd read about the stages: denial, anger, bargaining, depression, acceptance. *Acceptance.* She would never *accept* Dale's death. A slice of cake, a hand, a raise, help. These were things one accepted. To accept Dale's death would be to abandon hope that he was coming back, and to have no hope meant she, too, would perish. She might drown in the bathtub, drive her car off the Cougar Creek Bridge. She might spontaneously combust and the boys would be orphans. She would never *accept.*

She flipped over each of the invitations. Same photo. She removed the remaining pile of cardstock. *How?* She thought. *Why?* She held the papers to her face, inhaling the industrial smell of mass printing, of portfolios and program guides and AGMs. Dale had smelled like starch and diesel and orange Tic Tacs. *God.* She slammed the paper tray and carried the invitations through the office to the preschool classroom with the blue recycling bins. It was a sad room with the lights off, the paintbrushes hardened, the coat hooks and whiteboards empty. So quiet. The center carpet was black. By the sink was a sneaker, Velcro matted with hair and thread.

Roxanne ran her hand across the red laminate countertop. Her boys had both come here. Dale had picked them up on his days off, sometimes on the quad. She thought about her boys now, tucked together in their dad's childhood bed, bellies warm with Zoodles or whatever canned meal they'd had for dinner, teeth unbrushed and hearts broken, Dale's parents hovering by the door trying so hard to be brave. She dumped the paper in the recycling bin, burying a painting of a family, and headed for the main auditorium.

Chapter 19

MOLLY

Molly slumped behind the stage left partition, her gold dress furrowed and foolish. She'd kicked off her stilettos and the sight of her feet, red-rimmed and punished, was unbearable. She tucked them under the stool she was hunched on, her disastrous performance looping through her head in real time, in slow motion: verse one, little bit of rasp, high note, drawl, chin tilt, wide eyes, tiny bit of twang, sad face, chorus, catastrophe. Kabir's insulated firefighter jacket with its panels and spring hooks, a weighted blanket, suffocated and comforted her both. Her phone buzzed on her lap.

"Moll, whatta yat? I'm in da back of de ambulance. Now don't panic, but Malcolm gone and fell off da fence and we're muckin' him off to the hospital. We're pulling up to it now."

Molly sprang from her seat. "Is he okay?"

"Nuttin' too serious. Medic says his leg's right broken, but kids fix up quick."

"Malcolm," she whispered, bracing herself on the stool, adrenaline flushing through her. "How'd he manage to climb high enough to break a leg? He can barely cross the monkey bars."

"Right? Don't know what got into 'im. I think it was the ice cream. He was clinging to the chain link like one of them gibbons we seen in Florida. Now we's safe, but dere's been an escape."

"I heard. They made an announcement." Molly freed herself from Kabir's jacket and looked for her purse. She'd set it beside a dirt pile that had been swept and then forgotten. "Should I meet you at the hospital?"

"Negative. Stay there for now. Deadbolt the doors. Help is coming from the main detachment, but it'll be a while. Officers was in de middle of eggs benny when the call came in. Malcolm, say hi to your mudder."

Malcolm's voice was faint. "Hi, Mommy."

He sounded much younger than four. A machine chirped and Molly's heart stopped. "Malcolm, honey. Why on earth would you have done that? Huh? What were you thinking? Of all the fences to climb you picked Crow Valley Correctional's?"

"It looked neat."

"It looked neat?" Gary interrupted. "Lots of tings look neat, but it don't mean we climb dem. Like dat neat-lookin' IV bag over there. You see me tryin' to scale it?"

Molly listened, pressing her ear against the phone.

"It told me to climb it."

"Lord lumpin' b'y. You keep talkin' like dat they gonna put you in de psych ward. You hear that Mol? The fence called to him."

Molly sighed.

"What's the psych ward?" Malcolm asked.

"It's de place they put kids who listen to fences." He paused to say something to the paramedic. "Sorry 'bout dat. They were checkin' his temperature. He's just hot from the sun. Just sec, we're parked now, I'm gettin' out of the back."

Molly cautiously wedged her feet back into her shoes and waited.

"You dere, Mol? They're wheelin' him in. How'd it go? Did you kill it? Do I need to book a week off for you to go to Nationals?"

"I forgot the words."

"Forgot de words? You've been practicing so much even I know them. *She parked her car in de driveway, she forgot de key in the front door, and you don't even knows who I am. She left de car.*" At the word "car," Gary's voice cracked.

"You still there?" Molly asked.

Gary cleared his throat. "Mol, had ya really run out of gas?" His voice quivered. "Last year, during the fires?"

A shriek of feedback blasted through the hall followed quickly by the holy opening of Aerosmith's "Angel." Molly dropped the phone and squeezed her eyes to fend off the volume, righteous and penetrating. Seconds passed before the DJ wrangled the knobs to a cooperative level. She retrieved her phone.

"Dat our song?" Gary asked, out of breath. "They're paging me to triage. Listen, lock up the doors and you ask Roxanne for a re-sing. They done it for Dale before. T'ree years ago when de power went out. He was singing that Coldplay song. Serious, Mol. You gotta ask, and if Roxanne gives you trouble, you remind her it was that sad song about fixing people. She can't say no."

"Look after our baby."

"Roger dat. I'll reach ya when we seen the doctor."

A woman with a receding hairline and clogs slow-marched through the crowd, protecting a wobbly piece of pie from sliding off her plate.

Molly headed toward the front doors, her feet swelling and stilettos clicking. Gary was right about asking for a re-sing. There were some concessions in the rule book about interruptions, and Brett declaring a prison break during verse two seemed as reasonable a disruption as any other.

She stopped to pick up a few books that had fallen from the sale table outside the office, an antiquated version of *What to Expect When You're Expecting*, the South Beach Diet cookbook, and a grade ten physics textbook, probably Cole's. She stacked them in a pile and paused to again admire the clipping from the *Crow Valley Tribune* of Kabir saving the baby deer from the forest fire. She could still smell him on her neck, industrial and sweet, a cargo ship of citrus and stowaways. She imagined him in a tight pair of underwear, leading her through the desert on a camel, stopping only to bend her over the ruins of a forbidden monument while the Spanish national team played soccer beside them.

"Mom!" Xavier ran toward her, a friend in tow, a girl with stringy hair and the enthusiasm of a child actor. "You forgot the words!"

"I did, didn't I?"

Xavier wrapped his arms around her, knocking her backward. "Sorry you choked. I know you wanted to win. Remember how bad I wanted to win that coloring contest and I didn't even come in the top five?"

Molly remembered that he'd "colored" the Santa Claus with pencil. "Yep," she replied.

"Are we going home?"

"No, I'm setting the deadbolt." Molly gestured down the hallway at the front doors. "Dad suggested we lock it."

"Because of the escaped prisoner?" The girl chewed a swath of her pink hair.

"Yes, but it's just a precaution."

"Is he going to come here?" Xavier asked.

"This is the last place he would come." Molly put her arm around Xavier's slim and freckled shoulders. He had a cowlick at the base of his neck that resembled a hurricane on a satellite map. She dug a handful of change from her purse. "Here, go get yourselves a treat from the canteen."

"Can I get a Ring Pop?"

"I don't care, as long as you brush your teeth before bed."

Xavier turned and wandered off, the girl following and gently shoving him from behind. Both tripped on the puckered carpet near the door where the fire extinguisher hung.

Molly continued down the hall, placed her hands on the front door, and looked out into the parking lot. It was full as far as she could see. Mostly trucks, a few cars, and the wheelchair bus with its fat tires and blue writing. She thought about the escaped prisoner, out there somewhere, running for his life, probably in the woods, tripping on tree roots and charging through brush. If he was smart, he'd jump on one of the freight trains, hitch a ride to the city, disappear for a while, emerging to work as a line cook or a barber or a FedEx driver, grow food on his apartment balcony, and read to his elderly neighbors.

For a moment Molly thought about joining him. Bursting through the front doors, shattering the glass, and running away from Crow Valley, from Gary and the boys, her crowded bed and jungle playroom, the size charts and food wrappers and roughed-up electronics. The sports team of hoodies that populated the house. But there was nowhere to run. No chance of running away to find herself or to start over. She could not get lost because she was here, a found woman. Her reflection in the glass said so, a shadow, dull and undefined.

Molly bolted the door, keeping the prisoner out, keeping her in.

Chapter 20

MARCEL

Marcel climbed the winding mountain road in the police cruiser past double-wides and log cabins. He'd seen little of Crow Valley beyond the prison yard and the hospital where he'd been couriered during a spring snowstorm zip-tied with a broken arm, hair soaked in Jepson's piss, the night almost morning.

A sign for MOLLY'S DAYCARE where WE NURTURE HAPPINESS was plugged into the ground. A teddy bear waved from the sign and Marcel wondered whether his daughter went to daycare, and whether it was a French-speaking one with a big yard and colorful walls and thinly sliced apples. *Was her happiness being nurtured?*

He wondered if the girls he'd encountered at the bottom of the hill had made it to karaoke to see their dad sing and whether they'd told him of their chance meeting. He thought not. The older one had looked scared, aware that something was off, uncomfortable and conscious. Her kind was the best for keeping secrets.

He leaned out the window. The trees were all needles and height. A chipmunk dashed across the road and Marcel thought of the rabbit he'd owned as a boy. It was a dwarf, and black as a Sunday shoe. It had slept on a pillow at the foot of his bed. The chipmunk stopped on the shoulder, stood on its hind legs and washed its face. Marcel thought about opening the door and inviting it inside, desperate to whisper sweet everythings into its tiny petal ears. Instead, he waved.

Midway up the hill, he passed a weathered A-frame. The front lawn was knee-high and gnarly. Junk and wildflowers poked though the grass: handlebar tombstones, truck tire monuments, fireweed. A hand-made sign nailed to a tree read THE JEPSON FAMILY. Marcel recognized the beveled edges and burnt letters of the prison woodshop. Only low-risk inmates were allowed to work there. Marcel was not.

He slowed to a stop and studied the house. *Jepson.* That thick-haired, broad-shouldered, commercial-faced motherfucker. Marcel held his rib cage, remembering the size of Dale's boot, the flaming orange scent of his breath, the terrible songs he hummed on patrol. The pleasure that tugged at his mouth and lit up his eyes when he felt his power.

Marcel slammed the car into reverse and turned into the drive, fol-lowing it around to the back of the house. He jockeyed the gearshift into Park and half-fell out of the cruiser, adrenaline-drunk and red-hot. He charged up the back steps, snatching a metal thermos from the barbe-cue, and wound up to throw. He felt the unnatural bend of his elbow, a wand of drool escaping from the corner of his lip as he drove forward, aiming for the back door, its filthy window. Before he could release the thermos, a deck board gave way beneath him, a trap, his left leg sinking up to his ball sack, snagging his pants, his dignity.

What the fuck? Marcel spat, dropped the thermos, and worked to heave himself out. He lost his shoe. Kneeling, he peered into the hole. *The hell?* Beside his prison issue sneaker, a toy. It was plush and pale. Marcel fished it out. An animal of indiscernible breed, a baby one, soft tail, face stitched to sleep, the ears crusted, loved to ruin in the smallest of mouths.

He replaced the toy and looked around. Behind the barbecue stood a tiny set of plastic golf clubs. Marcel smiled at their preciousness and then punched the deck, retrieving his shoe and stuffing it back on. *Who the fuck raises kids here?* He eyed the hole and clambered down the back steps, the cruiser still running, and made a beeline for the tree. With both hands, he yanked the JEPSON sign until it snapped clean off its post. *What kind of father keeps a rotten deck?* He followed his foot-path back through the bent grass, dragging the board, its beveled edge now splintered and nicking everything in its wake, nails bent but intact.

Then he halted.

Sirens.

For fuck's sake. They were coming for him. Marcel worked fastidiously, positioning the sign into place where the rotted deck board had snapped, sweat dripping from his forehead, the thermos a perfect hammer. The hardware groaned. Finished, he tucked the thermos under his arm and collapsed into the cruiser.

He pulled out of the yard. He had to ditch the car, but where? Park it in an abandoned lot? Put it in neutral and push it down the hill, letting it crash into a tree? He idled at the end of the driveway. The only way to go was up. He accelerated, giving himself whiplash, and searched for a chained-off side road, a private property. His ears popped during the ascent. A hairpin turn, then another, and finally the road turned to gravel, the police car jerking over the uneven surface with a breakfast cereal crunch.

Marcel had a sudden paralyzing thought. What if the car had GPS? What if he was being tracked? He punched the cruiser's computer, shook the monitor, nearly driving off the road. He thought maybe he should set it on fire. He could watch it burn. It had been a while since he'd seen a good fire. Since he'd set one. He wanted it like Val wanted a drink. He slapped himself in the face, causing the finest and faintest stars to appear, lit buoys twinkling over the Gulf of St. Lawrence, his father swiping him so hard in the middle of the night Marcel thought he'd been hit by a bear. He missed a turn. The trees came at him, a broken black wall. He wrenched the steering wheel, causing the back end of the cruiser to fishtail, forearm veins throbbing, rocks spewing from the tires like confetti. For a moment the car hung in the air, weightless, silent, as though he was driving through space, until it flipped once and then again before stopping at the base of a century-old tree.

Disoriented, Marcel was aware of his breath. Of his brain inside his skull. For the first time, he understood that it was a separate entity from the rest of his head. A different color, a different weight, a different texture. He viewed the landscape sideways, through the cracked windshield. It was like looking at the top of the earth through a spiderweb.

He saw a nest, gray and elaborate, in the tree opposite. A bloody cheek print clouded the window. On his lap was a pile of glass. He examined a shard and tossed it behind him. Maybe this was a good thing, he thought. The computer screen was black. Maybe the GPS had died. He was off the road, hopefully twenty or thirty feet down, so he wouldn't be visible from above. He whooped, and then he worried. They would send helicopters. Mountain towns owned all kinds. *Motherfucking mountain rescue heli-skiing sons of whores.*

Marcel tried the driver's side door, but the frame was crippled. It made a junkyard sound when he tried to kick it open. He climbed across the front seat to the passenger door, which opened with surprising ease. Chest tight, breath labored, Marcel dragged himself out of the car, the thermos rolling out after him, and onto the rock shelf.

He could push it. He could push the car off the ledge it was balancing on and pray it landed upside down on its lights. An inmate in Quebec had once told him the key to burying victims was to make sure they were facedown. The inmate had accompanied the advice with a gesture, his hand a paw, like Marcel's father's, pushing down.

Marcel threw himself at the car. It slid a foot, scraping the rock. He lunged again, wedging his shoulder under the front bumper. The headlight was broken, the bulb like the eye of a whale staring him down. And then the car started to creak. It fell straight, rear bumper leading, hit the side of the cliff, and tipped sideways.

Marcel knelt, exhausted, relieved. It was nothing like how he'd planned to get rid of the car, but then escaping from the prison with a high jump bar wasn't either. Using blood from a gash on his face, he twirled the ends of his mustache into submission, stuck the thermos in his pants, stood, and sought a line, a freedom line, back up to the road. Up and away.

Chapter 21

BRETT

Kabir helped Brett to a park bench a few meters from the hall's main doors. A brass plate bearing Dale's name had been drilled into the backrest. Brett hadn't fainted since watching a cow give birth on a cattle ranch when he was ten. His legs were wet sand, and heat pulsated from his pores.

He wiped his forehead with a napkin. "Thanks," he muttered.

"Just doing my job." Kabir stretched his arms overhead, squinting at the sunlight. His hair had the sheen of an electric guitar.

A wren flitted through a crowded sumac bush nestled against the hall siding.

"When I was a boy in the mountains of Iraq, a songbird would be a feast."

Brett straightened. "That little thing?"

"That would feed my whole family." Kabir sat down on the bench, hunched, resting his chin in his hand.

"But who would want to eat a bird?" Brett looked at him, wide-eyed.

"Most of them were already dead." Kabir continued. "I was born in a cave." He bent down, flicking a leaf from the hard tip of his uniform boot. "My mother had no anesthetic. There were no doctors."

Brett thought about stories of his own birth. He was born in a gas station restroom outside Butte, Montana. "My wife, Val, wanted an epidural, but we got to the hospital too late with both girls. Heck, Daphne was almost born in the truck. I just kept shoutin' 'Hold it in,

Val. Hold it in.'" Brett chuckled and then exploded off the bench. "Oh my God. The girls."

Kabir's eyebrows contorted.

"My daughters. They were supposed to be here a while ago. I told them to come watch me sing." Brett paced, nearly falling off the sidewalk into the grille of Roxanne's Silverado. "My wife's going to kill me." He grabbed Kabir by the shoulders. "You have to help me find them."

Kabir extracted himself from Brett's panicked grasp. "Let me grab my keys. I'll drive." Kabir paused and then pointed to Brett's chest. "And you look."

Brett nodded, running his hands nervously through his hair.

Kabir went to the door and yanked on the handle. "It's locked."

"Fuck."

Kabir tried again, tugging violently. "My keys are in my jacket," he said. "And I gave my jacket to the Mountie's wife after she forgot the words. Molly. Can you text her?"

"I can't." Brett held out his phone.

"Why not?"

"Just can't. Other than my wife and my girls, no women in my contacts."

"Probably a good thing." Kabir nodded. "Then you drive."

"I took a cab here." Brett patted his pockets. "Had a few beers when I was getting ready. They help me sing."

Kabir bent to peer through the glass. He banged on the door. "I don't see anyone."

"Well, you're from Syria, aren't you? Or Iraq. Or Kurdistan . . . is Kurdistan a real place? Like Poughkeepsie?"

"What is Poughkeepsie?"

"Can't you hot-wire one of these?" Brett gestured toward the parking lot.

"You think because I'm from Iraq, I am also a criminal?"

Brett's face was a heat lamp. "I didn't say that."

"I suppose you also think I'm a terrorist."

"No!" Brett argued. "I think you're a very good, handsome firefighter." *What the fuck.* Brett cupped a hand over his mouth. *Had he said handsome? A very good handsome firefighter?* "You do handsome work. Your work is handsome." He talked with his hands. "You rescue people and mice from fires and emergencies, so that's a really handsome job that you do handsomely."

"I rescue mice, Brett?"

"Cats!"

Kabir took a step, pinning Brett against the hood of Roxanne's truck. "Do you think I'm handsome, Brett?"

Brett cowered. "I . . . I . . ."

"I'm kidding," Kabir smiled, punching Brett right in the sandwich and fries.

Brett didn't have time to flex. Fuck.

"Let's go," Kabir waved. "Of course I know how to hot-wire a truck."

Brett exhaled, the relief almost euphoric. He checked the door to Roxanne's Silverado. Unlocked. They climbed inside.

Chapter 22

VAL

Val was a hot mess when she returned to B Block. The underwire in her bra poked her armpit and sweat bubbled in her cleavage. She still wanted a drink. She thought of Brett preparing for karaoke alone in the hall bathroom, warming up his voice and his face muscles. Mouth open, mouth closed, lips curled, smile stretched, random jumping jack, tongue out, tongue in, tongue. Dale had once explained the importance of a relaxed tongue in creating beautiful tone. That was before Brett had used his to masticate their marriage. She exhaled a weary breath, then threw her shoulders back and chest up.

Norman Blanchard's hair frizzed in the humidity. He paced the block.

"It's not your fault," Val said, reaching him, resting a hand on his shoulder. "It's Gary's. I mean, who takes a kid on a friggin' ride-along? Christ."

Norman shook his head. "I'm concerned about Marcel."

They both turned to the prisoner's empty cell, his foolishly short wool blanket, the orphan bed, the *National Geographic* with the capybara on the cover. Textbooks for high school math, Stalin's memoir, and his favorite book, a tattered copy of *Hero: Becoming the Strong Father Your Children Need.*

"Concerned about him?" Val scoffed. "What in the hell for? He's probably out there stealing cars and watching sad movies."

"His file said he had a history of suicidal thoughts."

"It also said he stabbed someone with an ice pick."

"He had an extremely violent childhood."

Hello Kitty jumped up and down in his cell as if psyching himself up for a fight. Val could tell he was grieving for a missed opportunity. He was too thick to fit under the fence. Too many chin-ups. She crossed her arms and gazed at Norman. "Marcel's not going to go through the trouble of escapin' to throw himself off a cliff."

"He needs a little more treatment," Norman said. "He's not ready yet."

"Well, if they find him on a ledge somewhere, maybe you can talk him down with that."

Somewhere in the row of cells, an inmate beat-boxed, a baritone rhythm, moist and thick.

"I don't think he's coming back."

"Why not?" Val made a sweeping gesture. "We got all of H Division searching."

"He's very bright."

"He thinks he was Stalin in a past life and he punches himself in the face."

Norman and Val paused to listen as the far door reverberated, announcing a shift change. Val checked the three-dollar wall clock. Trevor, the guard replacing her, strode down the hall and nodded, his cheeks outdoor pink, uniform rumpled, beard the color of Heinz spaghetti. Norman excused himself as Roberta Bondar hollered from his cell.

"Heard it got a little wild in here," Trevor said, raising a fist. "*Liberté, égalité, fraternité.* Cocksucker Frenchie. Hasn't been here long enough to earn the right to escape."

"Hasn't had enough treatment either." Val nodded toward Norman Blanchard standing at the end of the hall, conversing with a prisoner like they were old squash partners.

The block still smelled of antiseptic from the sicko they'd wheeled off to Crow Valley General. Val wished for a drop on her tongue. The electric sting of alcohol. The taste of escape, searing and pleasing both. She should really try her sponsor again.

Trevor shook his head. "This is the treatment," he argued. "You serve the time." He stopped in front of Roberta Bondar's cell. "What's up, astro boy? How come you didn't go with him? Rocket ship broken? You know, I was only twelve years old when you got here? Used to bike down the back road with the boys and sneak onto the prison grounds near the reservoir. Drank all my dad's beer." He stopped, whispered over his shoulder at Val. "Lost my virginity out there, too. Good ol' Molly. That was before she had a litter of kids." He put his freckled hands on his hips and faced the prisoner. "How come Frenchie left you behind?"

Roberta Bondar sank into Child's Pose. Trevor shrugged and looked at Val. "Brett singing tonight?"

"He is," she replied. "Think he's up real soon."

"You tell him I said good luck." Trevor saluted and then bowed to Roberta Bondar. "Namaste, space cowboy," he said, moving to inspect the next cell.

Val waved good-bye to Norman and buzzed herself through the labyrinth of doors to the staff room. Safely inside, she collapsed at the table. She lifted her hands alternately, as if she were a marionette, and observed their trembling. She stopped herself from crying. She texted Liv again: *YOU SURE THE DOOR IS LOCKED???* Olivia replied with a simple *Ya*.

Val dropped her phone, her hands slapping the table, and went to the fridge. She'd drink kombucha at this point, but there was none. The last chunk of carrot cake from Norman's birthday was a corner piece with heaps of icing. It reminded her of the time Brett used too much spackling paste on the basement wall and how hard they'd laughed at it. She wolfed the cake back in three bites, then emptied the contents of her locker into a trash bag like a foster child.

"Hey, Val."

"Norman, you're not off for another hour."

"Taking my break," he replied, opening a Coke. The label said #BESTDAYEVER.

"Look, I'm sorry I wasn't there with you. When Marcel escaped. I should've been."

Norman waved. "No one could have predicted that." He took a long sip and twisted his hair into a man-bun. "It's just, I was reaching him. You know? It sounds ridiculous because he's only been here a year, but he was different. Some education, training, counseling . . ." Norman's voice trailed off. He sipped his Coke. "Rehabilitation was a real possibility for him. I had high hopes."

Val shrugged. "You can't save 'em all." She patted Norman on the back and held up her garbage bag. "Finally cleaned out my locker." She smiled.

"No bottles in there, I hope."

Val smiled. "No bottles."

"Thatta girl." Norman winked. "Have you checked out the new lockers? Got mine yesterday. They're great. Finally enough space to fit my violin. Don't have to leave it home between practices or drag it on my bike."

"That's great, Norm. That'll save you a lot of time." She glanced back at the old row of lockers, narrow and bent, all gunmetal green, with the exception of Dale's, which was red and empty save for a box of Tic Tacs and a bundle of zip ties. His favorite things. She nodded. "What are they going to do with those ones?"

"Taking them to the dump. They're gonna spray-paint one of the new ones in Dale's memory instead. Paint's over there on the counter. *Fire Red.* One of the inmates will do it."

"Right on." Val swung her trash bag over her shoulder. "All right, partner, I'm out."

"You be safe out there."

"I'll be fine."

"If you run into our boy Marcel, you tell him Norman wants to see him."

If I see Marcel, Val thought, *I'm going to sit on his face.* "See you at karaoke."

Norman raised his Coke, and Val made the arduous trek through security to the parking lot. There was a little liquor store on the edge of town. Maybe she'd drive by and see who was working. It might be someone new.

Chapter 23

ROXANNE

Silas peeled the liner from a cupcake. "You get the invitations printed?"

Roxanne dumped her purse on the table, upsetting a sheaf of Sharpies. "No," she replied, adjusting her headlamp. "Ran out of paper. And all I could find was leftover cardstock from Dale's funeral bulletin."

"When my mom died, we didn't have a bulletin."

"Why not?"

"She would have thought it was too formal."

"But what about the hymns? How'd people know what to sing?"

"Everyone knew what to sing."

Roxanne waited for him to elaborate, but no explanation followed. She wouldn't have made it through Dale's funeral if it hadn't been for the bulletin, the service outlined in painstaking detail like a wedding menu, the hymns and eulogies, reflections and poems of remembrance. Roxanne had counted down the line items in desperation, waiting to explode out of there so she could go home and bury herself under a pyre of donated lasagnas and Dale's things.

"Where in the hell are we?" She flipped through the karaoke program.

"Contestant six," Silas said, pulling the judges' table toward him an inch. "I may have some blank paper in my bag."

"It's all right," Roxanne sighed. "I have some at home. I'll grab it during intermission."

"Randy Figg," Silas mumbled, inscribing the contestant's name on the top of a score sheet. "You know him?"

"Nope. Out of province. We automatically give them zeros on vocal performance."

"Why?"

"Because they fail to qualify in their own regionals and then come here to take one of our spots. It's not fair. The only other time Crow Valley was a national qualifier, some idiot from Winnipeg swooped in and Dale came second." She pointed to the zero on Silas's score sheet under vocal performance and tapped her finger.

"Absolutely not." Silas shielded his page, as if it were a math test. "You give him a zero and I'll have to report you to the International Board of Karaoke Judges."

"You wouldn't." Roxanne's mouth gaped.

Silas folded his hands. "Try me."

Roxanne selected a pen from the spread on the table and flicked off the cap. She held the tip over the zero on Randy's score sheet and made a circular gesture.

"Give me your notebook," Silas said.

Roxanne placed a protective hand on her purse. "Why would you need my notebook?"

Onstage, the MC cleared her throat into the mic. She'd made a costume change that included lace gloves and a girly bow tie. Her Crayola hair remained big and overwhelming. "From Calgary, please welcome our next contestant, Randy Figg."

The resulting applause was cautious.

"See?" Roxanne gestured toward the audience. "They agree with me."

"Give me your notebook." Silas waved.

"Why?"

"I need to add someone to the *HELL* column."

Roxanne withdrew the notebook from her purse. An ink bleed marred the front cover. She flipped to the page marked *HELL* and smoothed out the seam to flatten the book. "Figg with two gees," she instructed, sliding it over to Silas.

In a yellow shirt and crumpled jeans, Randy lumbered across the stage to the mic stand. His salt-and-pepper hair rivaled the MC's in size and madness. He took a wide stance and placed a firm hand on the mic. "I'd like to dedicate this song to my son."

"Of course he would." Roxanne rolled her eyes and leaned in toward Silas. "Next he's going to download some sob story about his son moving away for college."

Randy wiped his eye. A tear? "He died before I had a chance to meet him."

"Big mistake." Roxanne shook her head. "Bet he won't even make it to the chorus."

"I judged a competition in Toronto once. Guy gets up to sing a song for his late wife. She died in some sort of accident. Anyway, he gets up to sing and the sprinklers go off! But just on the stage. The other judges and I, we stand, ready to evacuate, but the DJ stays. He's in on it. Starts playing the song."

Roxanne leaned forward. "What was the song?"

"Blame It on the Rain."

"Maybe she'd hydroplaned." Roxanne whispered.

"So, what do we do? We sit back down and the guy has the performance of his life. He's kicking through the water, splashing it in his face."

"Did he win?" Roxanne was anxious now. She'd never heard of such an extravagant stunt. Why hadn't she thought of something grander for Dale's one shot at Nationals? A coal car, or a canary in a cage. A pit pony! She imagined the points Dale would've earned had he ridden in on a blind horse the size of a rail car.

"Disqualified."

"Why?" she slumped back in her chair, disappointed.

"Because he lip-synched the whole thing!"

"Get out."

"It was a gimmick."

They both went quiet as Randy fiddled with the mic. Roxanne knew it was to buy himself time, to get his emotions in check. She used the time to get hers in check too, breathing in through her nose and exhaling a silent breath.

The music started, a familiar melancholic trickle. Roxanne recognized it immediately but couldn't remember the name. "What song is this?"

"Listen." Silas held up his hand. "It's 'The Sound of Silence.' The original one."

"There's more than one?"

"Disturbed did a cover in 2015."

Roxanne had never heard of Disturbed or any other version that wasn't Simon & Garfunkel. She closed her eyes. Randy's voice cracked under the weight of the lyrics and she felt a wash of grief soak her insides. "That is not the sound of silence," she whispered, eyes shut so tight she thought the force might clot her blood, blow out her nervous system. "I can tell you exactly what silence sounds like. Dale's workshop."

The table jerked and Roxanne opened her eyes, disturbed. Silas regarded her contemplatively.

"Imagine standing in a room full of machines."

Silas exhaled. "I'm picturing a pasta maker and a Roomba."

"Nope." Roxanne gestured to the left, her palm open and facedown, fingers spread, as if she were feeling her way through the dark. "It's a workshop, ceiling's low. There's a planer and a sander over there near the sleds and Christmas lights." She raised her other hand and pointed right. "And in the corner is the whipper-snipper, the air compressor, and the ride-on mower or the snow blower, depending on the season." She looked at Silas. "Do you see it?"

"All but the air compressor. I don't know what that looks like."

"Close your eyes. Now imagine all those machines operating at once, everything grinding and grating and gnashing."

Silas nodded.

Roxanne choked, "Those are the sounds of Dale."

Silas dropped his pen.

"Now imagine all the machines stopped. Run your finger across the seat of the Kubota and feel the dust on your fingertip. It's a bit greasy. Look at the glass on the workbench. Is it empty? Has the water finally evaporated? Are the flies on the floor all dead?"

"Yes," Silas said. "They're hard and shriveled and broken."

"That's the sound of silence."

Silas opened his eyes and hung his head. "My mom started every day singing 'I'm Alive' by Celine Dion. No matter where I was in the house, even when I moved to the basement, the second I opened my eyes, that's what I heard. So for me, it's mornings. Mornings are the sound of silence."

Roxanne whispered. "I used to sing to my boys." She'd stopped after Dale's death. Songs belonged to him.

She picked up her pen, Silas adjusted his score sheet, and they quietly fixed their gaze on the stage, on Randy replacing the mic, triumphant and devastated. They remained quiet through the applause, through the MC's clunky walk and small talk, through the introduction of the next contestant, a woman with a prosthetic leg dressed as a bar wench. They marked their score sheets in private, Roxanne flipping hers facedown in a pile, Silas folding his in half.

"You still have that flask?" Roxanne asked.

Silas bent below the table and twisted off the cap. Roxanne took a fiery swig, exfoliating her senses. "I'm alive," she said, between sips.

Silas nodded, receiving the flask. "The service was at sunrise."

Roxanne took a new score sheet and scrawled a name across the top. Her notebook lay open on the table between them. Her name had been added to the *HELL* column in bold block letters and then crossed out with a thin red line.

Chapter 24

MARCEL

Marcel scanned the rock face, debating the safest line back to the road. His climbing experience was limited to second-floor break and enters, scaffolding, and the Montreal airport security fence, though he'd honed a certain degree of athleticism fleeing the police and his father. He clutched a root protruding from the mountainside and heaved himself up, finding a narrow ledge for his foot. He never looked down.

Halfway through the ascent, his limbs spread between the branches of two flimsy trees, Marcel heard the whoosh of a car passing above. *Fuck.* Didn't everyone in a small town do the same thing? Shouldn't they all be at karaoke cheering on their uncle's brother's half sister? What the fuck kind of donkey was pleasure-driving on a day like this? He swung his body over to the more stable-looking of the two trees and clung to it like a hurricane survivor. Ten feet to go.

He wondered if his daughter climbed trees. A specific curiosity given that he didn't even know her hair color, her middle name, where she'd be going to kindergarten in the fall. He imagined her clinging to the fireman's pole on the school's playground. Legs wrapped tight, ankles in a knot. He pictured her, this made-up girl extrapolated from a baby photo, smiling. He pictured her fearless. He pictured her safe.

Marcel unwrapped himself from the tree and pressed his body against the mountain. Even with the sun blowing up his back, the ancient cold of the rock made him shiver. He waited for the chill to pass before clambering up a nearly vertical stretch to the top, where a bleached chip bag bathed in the light. Exhausted, Marcel remained on all fours, the open road stretching on either side of him, until he regained his breath. It was now quiet as a graveyard.

Had the passing car gone up or down? He stood. The mess of tire tracks he'd left when he'd gone off the road resembled a hand-drawn map. He moved the gravel with his foot and then frantically with his hands. Dust billowed, blanketing his face, as he erased the evidence. He stepped back to assess his work and survey his surroundings, turning a slow circle.

Uphill there appeared to be another road, a vague clearing on the left. A driveway? He jogged, ignoring the heat in his knee, the joint swollen like a football, his hunger, nauseating. The exercise and elevation hijacked his breath, making his heart feel inadequate. Shriveled, Grinch-like. But his hunches paid off. There was a driveway, about twenty feet of one, and a trailer at the end of it, the beige and orange of the 1980s, of camping on the Saguenay with his mother.

Strings of patio lights drooped from trailer to tree, zigzagging across the property as though the place had hosted a hipster wedding. Marcel approached with confidence. The lights were off. He tried the door handle but it spun, unhinged. A piece of blue wire and an orange coil dangled from the mechanism. Marcel painstakingly maneuvered both, tugging and twisting until the door popped open.

To his surprise, the inside of the trailer had been modernized. A flat-screen TV was mounted on the wall above the dining bench. The dishes on the counter were sleek, oval, artisanal, the flatware, thick. A shiny rose gold suitcase lay on the bed. Marcel ran his finger down one of the grooves in the ribbed exterior. It looked more like a machine than a piece of luggage and he imagined inside it was a tiny operating city complete with escalators and conveyor belts and industrious-looking people dressed all in white.

The trailer smelled like the little bowl of guacamole browning on the counter and Thierry Mugler's *Angel Men*. Was a Frenchman staying here? What the fuck was a Frenchman doing in Crow Valley? He unzipped the case and shook out an impeccably folded pair of pants. Twenty-eight-inch waist. His hand dropped instinctively to his concave stomach, and his shoulders collapsed into a moment of silence. In his first week at Crow Valley Correctional, Norman had said something about signs from the universe. *They're all around us*, he'd prophesied. *You just have to pay attention.* And here Marcel was holding one, a soft-cotton sign from the universe in exactly his size. He felt a tingle in his chest, something childlike and unfamiliar. Something like hope.

He stepped out of his prison-issue jogging pants, looked down on his bulbous knee, his blood-spotted shins, the thermos sliding to the floor. He took off his underwear too, rooted through the suitcase and removed a handful of boxer-briefs in the colors of holiday drinks, choosing a cranberry pair and sliding them over his cock. Though the pants fit at the waist, they were cropped and clown-short, an odd style. He changed shirts, doused himself in *Angel Men* like a proper Frenchman, and washed his face. There was a tiny sewing kit in the suitcase. Marcel removed the scissors and cut the handlebars off his mustache. He ate the guacamole with his hands.

There was a leftover quesadilla in the fridge. He ate that too, and half a lime. There were several bottles of wine. Marcel appreciated the one with the screw cap and embossed label—a totem of baby goats standing on top of one another. They made him smile. He put the wine on the counter.

A backpack balanced on a shelf over the bed. Marcel filled it with T-shirts and socks. He added the thermos, sewing kit, the wine, a crumble of paper-wrapped cheese, a container of peanuts, and a toiletry bag. He collected his old clothes, then took a steak knife from the drawer and slipped it into the backpack, the handle sticking out from the zippered front pouch. He felt high, almost skipped out of the trailer, the door shutting behind him with a cap gun snap. Now it was time to go down. Now it was time to find a way out of Crow Valley and go somewhere where he might find a home, where he might find love. Where he might find a second chance.

Chapter 25

BRETT

Kabir drove Roxanne's truck like it was a rental, hopping the curb out of the hall, speeding. Brett wanted to tell him to slow down, but he'd emasculated himself enough for one day. God, why had Kabir insisted on carrying him in public? What next? Chronic fatigue? Menopause?

He steadied himself, placing a hand on the dash. "You drive the fire truck like this?"

"Of course," Kabir replied, coming to a hard stop in the middle of an intersection. He stared at the community notice board. "What is that sign warning of?"

Brett studied the drawing, the blue scratches of pen. "Looks like the Pillsbury Doughboy is in the area."

"Is he dangerous?" Kabir replied.

"If you poke him."

"Which way?"

"Left." Brett pointed. "You know Crow Mountain Road?"

"I know all the roads in the valley." Kabir cranked the steering wheel.

"You can't know all of them."

"Every single one."

"The logging roads?"

"Even those."

"All right," Brett challenged, crossing his arms. "Where's the Halo Trail?"

"Go south on the 537, cross the Cougar Creek Bridge, then at the Y, head east until you get to the gravel road, then make a right and follow it to the end." He looked at Brett. "Takes about fifteen minutes. Halo Trail splits off to the left from the main logging road."

"Wrong!" Brett blurted. "Halo Trail splits to the *right*."

"It used to. But because of the fire, it now splits to the left, only meeting with the original trail at about three hundred, maybe three hundred fifty meters of elevation." Kabir helped himself to a handful of orange-flavored Tic Tacs from the box on the dash.

"Damn it," Brett spat, looking out the window.

"When I'm not saving people, I spend a lot of time on those trails."

"Not me." Brett reached out his hand and Kabir shook a pile of Tic Tacs onto his palm. "I've been logging for almost twenty years. Since I was a teenager. Geez, not much older than Liv is now. Last place I want to be on my days off is anywhere near trees."

"You live on the mountain, no?"

"Yes, but it doesn't mean I do tree stuff."

Kabir smiled and Brett was struck by the whiteness of his teeth. Did refugee camps have dentists?

"The girls should be somewhere around here." Brett waved, crouching for a better view. "They were biking."

Kabir slowed. The road was empty in both directions. Brett leaned forward in his seat.

"Have you tried calling them?" Kabir veered toward the ditch, eyes downcast.

"They're not going to be in the ditch," Brett snapped, pulling out his phone. His hands trembled as he scrolled through his contacts and then he forgot who he was calling. He forgot that his phone was a phone. He stared at like it might be something else entirely. An elephant's pacemaker. Kabir placed his hand on Brett's to steady it.

"You're calling your daughter," he reminded him.

"Right." Brett gestured to the shoulder. "Can you pull over?"

Kabir obliged and Brett told Siri to call Olivia, drumming his fingers on the dash as he waited. She answered after the third ring.

"Where are you?"

"We're at Big Al's."

"I told you to come straight to the hall."

"We needed air. Daphne's back wheel has a leak."

"Thank you, Jesus."

"Huh?"

"You're at Al's right now?"

"I just said that."

"I'm coming to get you."

"Why? We're like two minutes from the hall."

Brett gestured for Kabir to turn around by twirling his finger and nodding to the rear. Kabir put the truck in gear and executed a shoddy U-turn. The Princess Leia bobblehead on Roxanne's dash quivered. Brett remembered it had been a Secret Santa gift from a prison Christmas party Dale and Roxanne had hosted. The girls were still in diapers then, his marriage still a holiday of colored lights and warmth. It was the same Christmas he'd bought Val tickets to a comedy fest in Vancouver and she sobbed tears of joy.

"Have you talked to your mom?"

"Yeah. She thinks we're home. She was acting all worried because she said there was a prison escape." The gas station's indicator hose dinged in the background.

"There has been," Brett replied. "That's why I'm coming to get you."

"K, but we're literally, like, two minutes from the hall."

"I know that, Liv. Just stay where you are. No one knows who this guy is or what he was in for."

"Everyone here says he's a murderer."

"See? That's what I'm talking about. Just stay put and I'll be there in five minutes."

"Can I get a Slurpee?"

Brett sighed. "Fine, but drink it inside. And make sure Daphne doesn't get any flavors with caffeine."

Kabir pointed at a pair of mule deer grazing by the side of the road.

Brett nodded. "Where is Daph? How come I can't hear her?"

"She's in the bathroom washing her gum. It fell out of her mouth and she wants to keep chewing it."

"Fuck."

"That's what I said, but whatever. She's your daughter. And you need to fix my handlebars. The left side is bent. She ran into me at the bottom of the hill."

"Are you okay?"

"Yeah. We both got a few scrapes. A police officer checked us and said we were good."

Brett exhaled. "Okay, I'll be there soon. Remember, wait for me inside."

"K, I'm hanging up."

Brett dropped the phone onto his lap and slumped heavily into the headrest.

"They're safe?" Kabir asked.

"Yes, thank God." He wiped his face with his hands like the entire nightmare had been just that. "That Liv. She's a good kid. Always looking out for her little sister." Brett swallowed. "You got any brothers or sisters?"

"Three older brothers." Kabir's gaze was steady through the windshield.

"They live back in . . ." Brett still didn't know exactly where Kabir was from. "Arabia?" Fuck. He didn't know for sure, but he didn't think that term was correct. Maybe he'd even made it up. Was it a Disney movie? Was that where Aladdin was from?

"They're all dead, as far as I know. Captured in the mountains, forced to become soldiers. Karrar, he was only twelve at the time. My mother pleaded, but they took him at gunpoint." Kabir shook his head. "I have a sister, too."

"And she's still alive?" Brett's palms were sweaty. He tucked his hands under his legs. Why had he asked?

"She's a dental hygienist."

Brett tried to think of an Iraqi city. He was pretty sure there was one called Mosul. Or was that in Syria? Was Raqqa in Syria? What about Aleppo? That was always in the news. "Back in Mosul?"

"Atlanta."

"I never knew there was an Atlanta over there."

"Atlanta, Georgia," Kabir corrected. "She's married to an engineer. He's a professor at Georgia State."

"Right," Brett replied. "Huh. What's that up ahead?"

Kabir squinted. "Don't know." He eased off the accelerator. "Check-stop?"

Chapter 26

MOLLY

Molly borrowed a bag of frozen corn from the hall kitchen and held it to Xavier's eye. He'd been pelted with a tennis ball in a game the kids had invented that centered on hitting your opponent in the head. With the other hand she called Gary, but he didn't answer, only texted that they'd been moved to an examination room and were waiting to see the doctor. The woman who'd bought the vacant three-lane bowling alley near Big Al's took the stage. She wore an aquamarine sequin gown in a mermaid silhouette. Molly wondered if the woman had plans to reopen the joint and whether she might need childcare. Molly'd seen her at the grocery store, toddler twins belted into the cart, a baby strapped to her chest, everything seemingly together except for the bra that hung off the back of her sweater.

Molly placed the corn on a plate and rummaged through her purse for a card.

"Xavier," she asked, not finding one. "Have you seen my business cards?"

"The babysitting ones?"

"They're the only ones I have. They had a blue hair elastic wrapped around them."

Xavier slid down from his chair, bracing the side of his face with his hand. He disappeared under the table and returned with a blue pony-tail holder pinched between his fingers. "Is this it?"

Molly held the elastic in her palm. "Where are the cards?"

Xavier shrugged. "I think I might have seen Malcolm playing with them earlier. Before he went with Dad."

"For fuck's sake," Molly cursed. "Where are your brothers? They were supposed to be watching him."

"It was a while ago."

Molly searched the room for her two oldest sons. The hall was quiet, drawn into the performance, into the music, the song hopeful in tone, as if it was the soundtrack to an adventure, a great expectation. Soldiers going off to war, a first pregnancy. She didn't know the artist, only that the song was about bravery and overcoming obstacles. It was every song written by a woman, sung by a woman, cried by a woman. It was a woman. No one got up to refill their coffee or punish their child. No one adjusted his ball sack. Even the ceiling fan whirred softer than before.

"They're up on the balcony," Xavier whispered, flicking a niblet.

Molly followed Xavier's gaze. The balcony was supposed to be off-limits. It could only be accessed through a tiled corridor that ran behind the kitchen and a winding staircase that made anyone over forty too dizzy to climb. The upper railing was loose, and Clarence hadn't had a chance to fix it since one of the Mains brothers' weddings two weeks ago. The last Molly had seen, the railing was held together with gun tape.

"Stay here," she said, ducking away from the table before Xavier could respond. She carried her shoes and slipped through the kitchen, the air flavored with condiments and sweat. She kicked a hairnet out of the way, nodding at one of the line cooks who sat on an ice cream bucket eating a sandwich.

The corridor light was on, the bulb red: a ship's boiler room. She took the stairs two at a time, clutching the rail, remembering when she'd had to climb it in her wedding dress to throw her micro-bouquet of forget-me-nots and rosebuds.

She reached the balcony to find the boys kneeling in a circle with a dozen or so other teens. "What are you doing up here?" she demanded.

Cole, her eldest, threw up a hand but kept his eyes fixed on his phone. "Clarence said we could come up here," he said, then nudged the boy beside him. "Check this out."

Molly wondered what it was that he was showing off. Likely a meme that she'd never understand: a meatball holding a Kalashnikov, whole sentences without vowels. The latest Tik Tok challenge. Her dress pinched under her arms and she tugged at the boning.

"Yeah," one of the only girls in the group chimed in. She sat cross-legged at the back of the circle, coloring the tips of her black Converse high-tops, her tube top stretched and fluorescent. No bra. "As long as we don't go anywhere near the edge he said it was fine."

Molly examined the railing. It was taped in three places. "Whatever," she muttered. "If Clarence said it was okay. Dylan"—Molly nudged her other son's knee with her foot—"have you seen my business cards? Xavier said Malcolm was playing with them earlier."

Dylan, hyperfocused on a shooting game, nodded, his muscles tense and head cocked like he might have a stroke. "I think he left them on the book sale table."

"Is that your vape?" She noted the instrument resting beside him.

"That's mine," the girl said, snatching it away and sticking it inside her top.

"Don't vape," Molly said to everyone and no one. "They cause lung damage."

"Depends on the oil," the girl retorted. Her hair was parted in the center, a tightrope, chin pierced and beige with concealer. "This stuff's safe."

"Cole? Dylan?"

Neither son responded. Molly might as well have been addressing the broken music stand and the upright vacuum huddling in the corner.

"Don't go near the railing," she warned, though she'd considered going over it herself.

The girl made a face and filled in the heart she'd drawn on her sneaker with green Sharpie. Dylan grunted. "Can I have some money?"

"I already gave you twenty bucks."

"Where's Dad?"

Molly sighed. "He's at the hospital with Malcolm."

She looked at the hall below. The woman dressed as a mermaid hit the final note of her performance, loud and a little off, a knife on a plate. Still, the audience erupted in applause. The MC crossed the stage, clapping before she regained the mic, swung her hair off her face, and introduced Brett. Molly glanced toward the partition where Brett should have been waiting, but there was only a woman with a plate of fries, shrugging and shaking her head.

"We're looking for Brett Farquhar," the MC repeated, hand on her forehead as if searching the horizon for an overdue container ship. "Anyone see Brett? He was here earlier."

Roxanne and Judge #2 huddled below in conversation. From Molly's viewpoint, the headlamp left Roxanne's hair a disheveled mess, the kind of nesting material one would use to make fire or lay an egg. Why could she not just leave a porch light on?

Molly thought of the last time she'd seen Dale. It had been through her rearview mirror. The smoke was getting thick and he rummaged through his trunk with one hand, the other holding his Corrections sweater over his mouth and nose. Molly had waited, the pill bottle denting the backside of her bare thigh where she'd hidden it from view, until he waved the red gas can, victorious and proud, no clue that the pill bottle and her tank were both full. That it was her who'd been empty. Depleted and dark, the fire of the century, a postpartum for the ages.

"You just shot me!" One of the kids tossed his phone.

Molly would learn that Dale was not supposed to have worked that day. Roxanne made sure the world knew it, at the grocery store, the bank, his funeral. *He was not supposed to work that day. He was supposed to be home.* And Molly knew that things would have been different if Val hadn't traded shifts with him. Val wouldn't have stopped for her, for anyone. Not unless she'd been waved down with a case of beer or a shot of tequila. If Val had just gone to work that day, Dale would be alive, winning karaoke, and Molly would be a picture hung in the kitchen, frozen in time with a dated hairstyle.

Roxanne waved at the MC and Judge #2 added a similar gesture, flask open and balancing on his lap.

"We'll come back to him," Roxanne hollered.

"All right then folks, we're going to skip Brett for now and move on to our next contestant." The MC shifted a cue card to the back of her pile and announced an unfamiliar name. The woman who'd been eating the fries set down her plate, wiped her hands on her printed leggings, adjusted her pilot's cap, and tripped up the steps.

"Up two," the contestant murmured, referring to her chosen song's key. The DJ fiddled with the controls, and after a short delay, "Leaving on a Jet Plane" taxied into the hall. The woman sounded more like a helicopter. Molly flinched.

Where the hell is Brett? Molly scanned the audience below. She searched for Caroline Leduc and was relieved to see Brett's onetime mistress alone, forking a piece of cake. The backs of her arms were fleshy and flushed and still bore the name of her ex-husband in a tattoo of vines. Caroline's marriage had ended abruptly because of the affair. One moment with Brett had undone twenty years of marriage. It seemed wrong. Like serving a life sentence for stealing a loaf of bread.

Brett wouldn't miss this. She had seen the desperation in his face before the bird shit on his head. The opportunity to rise, to be the best, to be a Dale in a world of Bretts. Molly navigated the winding stairs, flew down the corridor and back into the kitchen. She asked the line cook, "You see Brett anywhere?"

The line cook wiped his face with the corner of his apron, stood, and slid the ice cream bucket under a prep table with his foot. "He fainted."

"Fainted?"

"'Bout ten minutes ago. Out in the hall." He brushed crumbs from the table with a dry cloth, ate a swath of wilted lettuce. "One of them come in here and grabbed some water."

"Is he still out there?"

The line cook shrugged. "Hey, Molly?"

Molly waited.

"I think you look real lovely tonight. Not, not, not in a perverted way," he stammered. "Like in a rock, rock star kind of way. Like a real singer."

"Thanks," Molly said. "That's very sweet." She turned, yanking up her sagging dress, and charged into the hallway. Scattered among the books on the sale table were her business cards. All of them had been defaced with a combination of pinholes and Malcolm's terrible rendition of a horse: a giant circle with legs that could hold up a pier. She assembled the wrecked cards into a pile and jammed them into her purse.

Molly scuffed down the hall. "Brett?" She stuck her head into the office, where blue-coveralled Clarence was emptying a wastebasket. She continued on, stopping in front of the men's room. "Brett?" she called. A urinal flushed and seconds later a man in a pinstriped suit came out, air-drying his hands.

"No one else in there," he said.

Molly nodded and headed for the front doors. She shook the handles to make sure they were still locked. The glass rattled as she pressed her face against it, squinting into the evening sun. No sign of Brett. She fished through her purse for the keys. A cigarette had snapped and flecks of tobacco and crumbs were embedded beneath her fingernails.

"Hey, Clarence," Molly yelled toward the office.

Clarence pushed a large wheeled garbage can into the hall, his mullet lifting in the resulting breeze.

"I'm going to unlock the deadbolt for a sec. There was an escape at the prison and Gary told me we should keep the doors secured, but I'm worried I locked someone out. Can you just watch the door? Keep it open until I come back in?"

Clarence parked the bin, cranked the deadbolt, and opened the door. "Heard the prisoner used a high jump bar to escape."

"A high jump bar?"

"Blanchard was out in the yard teaching 'em track and field."

"They teach that in prison?"

"In Crow Valley they do. You know Norm's an Olympian."

"Huh?" Molly leaned on the door. She did not know Norman was an Olympian though he was tall and svelte and quietly charismatic like one. She didn't know much about the people whose kids she did not teach how to hold scissors or peel an orange or zip up a coat. She scanned the parking lot again for signs of Brett. "Norman went to the Olympics for high jump?"

Clarence used his elbow to buff out a smear on the glass. "Javelin." He chuckled. "But he ain't allowed to teach that at the prison."

"Hold the door for me?"

Clarence nodded and Molly slipped outside. She paced the front of the building and then checked around the corner where the pigeons roosted and the smokers gathered near the pop machine. No one. She peered inside the hall shed, with its lawn mower, signs, and road salt, the floor bathed in grass cuttings and diesel stains. Empty. It should have been locked. She rushed back around front and stopped abruptly in Roxanne's vacant parking spot, the one marked with a handmade sign, the block letters red and menacing.

Clarence leaned out the door, a fresh garbage bag hanging from his pocket. "All good?"

"No," Molly said, walking the length of the parking spot. "Roxanne's truck is gone."

Chapter 27

ROXANNE

A heavy-chested woman in denim wedges and plaid leggings sang "Total Eclipse of the Heart." A french fry had followed her onstage and she attempted to punt it away. A calm had settled over the hall. The prisoner hadn't arrived to take anyone hostage. Satellite trucks weren't loitering in the parking lot with their lights and dishes and complicated microphones. There was no state of emergency and all of Crow Valley had overeaten.

Roxanne closed her eyes and listened. The contestant's voice was raspy and desperate, a right Bonnie Tyler. How Roxanne sounded for weeks after Dale's death, as if her throat had been soaked in gasoline and set on fire, her words blackened whispers.

"I can't stop yawning," Silas yawned, his posture collapsing. "If I hear one more ballad, I'm going to stab myself with a pen."

Roxanne crossed her arms. "Then I'd have to put you in the *HELL* column."

"We're in the *HELL* column." Silas swept his arm across the pile of score sheets. "This is it."

Roxanne rolled up the song codebook and smacked him across the back of the hand. "Crow Valley's not that bad."

"I was referring to the competition," he said, examining the red mark flaring across his knuckles. "We haven't heard anything particularly good or original since that firefighter, Babar."

"Kabir."

"Same thing."

Roxanne tried to focus on the stage, forcing her face into a look of engagement. She'd spent several of Dale's competitions staring down the judges, making sure they were paying attention. Had they caught his smile during the guitar solo? Understood why he turned his back for the refrain? Had they noticed the subtle way he'd thrust his pelvis during the bridge?

The bridge. Draped over Cougar Creek with its broken capstones and crumbling concrete and graffitied abutments. CLASS OF '88, CLASS OF '96, 2005, '18. BRETT LOVES VAL. How could she have forgotten the bloody closure signs? If the mayor drank too much he'd take the Halo Trail home and he'd see the bridge empty of signs and maybe one of the railings would have collapsed and a motorist fallen through. By Monday he'd be requesting a meeting in the boardroom and the HR man would be there with his coiled manual, blue shirt, and sympathetic but serious eyes.

Molly Chivers climbed the stairs.

"What's happening?" Silas whispered.

Roxanne concealed her score sheet. "She's going to ask for a re-sing. You just watch. She'll have some excuse about why she forgot the words, like her kid was having a meltdown or her fibromyalgia was acting up. Or postpartum. She's used that one before, even though her youngest is almost five."

"It's a real thing," Silas said.

Roxanne raised her eyebrows. "You speaking from experience?"

Molly closed in.

"Give me your notebook," Silas said.

Roxanne snatched it from the table and hugged it to her chest. "Here she comes. You deal with her."

Molly tiptoed up to the table, body language apologetic.

"Can I help you?" Silas asked.

"I actually have a question for Roxanne."

Roxanne straightened. Molly leaned in smelling of drugstore perfume, her eyes wide, lashes bent, and for a moment Roxanne felt a rush of sympathy. She hadn't made eye contact with Molly since rejecting her at Dale's funeral, even though she'd left her boys in Molly's care a hundred times since then. Molly's face, the sag of her dress, showed a familiar sadness that Roxanne recognized as grief but of a different nature. The grief of living.

"Did you let anyone borrow your truck?"

"Of course not," Roxanne replied. "No one's allowed to drive it but me." She nudged Silas. "I wouldn't even let Dale drive it." She placed her hands protectively over the lump of keys beside her empty iced coffee cup.

"You drove it here tonight?"

"Yes, I drove it here." Roxanne muttered, "Why are you asking?"

"'Cause your truck's not in the parking lot."

"Of course it is," Roxanne argued, showing off the keys. "It's in my spot."

"I know where your spot is," Molly snapped. "And your truck's not in it."

"Someone stole my truck?" Roxanne's heart beat in triple time. "Did you call the police?"

"I'll phone Gary. I just wanted to make sure you hadn't lent it to someone."

"Can I get a wave from the judges that they're ready for our next contestant?" the MC asked, her voice playful, oblivious.

"No," Roxanne barked. "We need a minute."

"Are you okay?" Silas placed a hand on Roxanne's arm. "You're shaking. It's just a truck."

"It's not just a truck."

Molly punched numbers into her phone. "Gary?"

"It's a safe space," Roxanne whispered. "My safe space."

"What's the license plate? Gary's at the hospital but he'll phone it in to dispatch."

"One four one B-E-X."

"What do you mean, a safe space?" Silas noticed Molly's score sheet jutting out from his pile, aggressive X's all over the margin. He slid it out of view, buried it with his elbows.

Roxanne waited for Molly to retreat back to the floor. A granola wrapper was stuck to the back of her dress. "Don't make fun of me," Roxanne said.

"Never."

"I sense Dale when I'm in that truck. Like I feel him next to me. I don't know why. It's the place where I most feel he's still with me. And I talk to him and I know it probably sounds crazy but I think he can hear me."

Silas nodded. "And this only happens in your truck?"

Roxanne whispered, "Mostly, yeah."

"Huh," Silas replied.

The MC paced the stage, thanking sponsors, promoting the town's remaining summer camps. A man circled his arms behind the partition. The DJ cracked a beer. One of the town's bank managers stumbled drunk into the wall. Kids were removing balloons tied to chairs and relieving them of their helium. Someone yelled, "Go fuck yourself!"

"Why do you think it mostly happens in the truck?" Silas pulled out a smoky bottle of gin and refilled his flask.

"Dunno. But after they put out the fire, after they put up the caution tape and covered him with the sheet, I crawled back to my truck and on the side of the road I found his Tic Tacs. The box was a bit melted but they were his."

"And then?"

"I felt him get in the truck with me. I could smell him. I felt every kiss he'd ever given me, I heard every sigh. I could taste his aftershave."

"And the Tic Tacs?"

She lowered her voice to a bare whisper, "I use them to channel him."

Silas slumped back. "A spirit portal."

"You know this?"

"Sure. Mediums use them all the time to connect with the dead."

Roxanne contemplated Silas's perfect complexion, the treble clef tattooed behind his ear, his sharp jaw. His mother's jaw? "Have you ever tried to reach her?"

"My mom?" Silas shook his head. "She's in the music."

Roxanne liked that answer. She folded her hands over her keys and looked down at Molly.

Silas passed the flask. "They'll find your truck," he said. "I just know it."

"They have to."

"They will."

"Molly," Roxanne yelled.

Molly looked up from the bottom of the stairs, Xavier hanging off her arm. In her hand, a stiletto, the heel broken and dangling.

Roxanne cleared her throat. "You can sing again," she said. "You can sing."

Chapter 28

VAL

Val sat in the Crow Valley Correctional staff parking lot, decompressing, drinking a no-name ginger ale left over from Brett's last ball tournament. A filmy layer of sweat formed on the can, and she wiped it on her chest. She stared through the windshield at the prison with its cheerful paint and sprawling bricks, then at the endless stack of trees in the rearview mirror, a stairway to heaven. Where had Marcel gone? How far could he go, in a cop car?

She started the ignition, turned on the AC, and thought about what Norman said. That Marcel wasn't ready. That without some sort of metamorphic prison experience, a program, a note on his file, a bloody certificate of completion, a GED, he'd set someone else's father on fire and end up back in prison, reading books about Stalin and small animals, fatherhood and trigonometry, alternately jerking off and rocking himself to sleep. No one left Crow Valley Correctional transformed. Not really. Benedetto had been proof of that.

She pulled out of the lot, passed through the gate, and arrived at the T intersection. There was no way she could go straight to the hall. She had to shed her work pants before her bush ignited. Why couldn't the prison switch to a lighter summer uniform? What did zookeepers wear in July?

She headed toward town, passing an RCMP cruiser, lights spinning, sirens wailing, speeding in the opposite direction. The driver was not Marcel. At the bottom of Crow Mountain Road, as Val signaled, something caught her eye. She made the turn, pulled over at the base of the hill, and got out. The gold and purple handlebar tassel from Daphne's bike lay on the ground like a discarded New Year's Eve accessory. Val scooped it up, dizzy, adrenaline wobbling her legs. Oh my God. She hyperventilated and dialed Brett.

"I just found part of Daphne's handlebar on the road," she cried.

"Her handlebar?" Brett replied.

"The little dangly thing that hangs off the handles. I found one on the road."

"Oh, the tassels. Probably fell off the last time she went for a bike ride."

Val searched for anything else suspicious. There was an empty motor oil bottle in the ditch, a faded ChapStick. Hip-height dandelions, bedraggled and bowed, lined the roadside like hitchhikers. "I brought her bike in last night because she left it in the middle of the driveway again. Both tassels were on it."

"I let them go to Al's for Slurpees earlier. It probably fell off then. I wouldn't worry about it."

"You let them go to Al's? They were supposed to stay home. There's a goddamned murderer on the loose!" She switched to speakerphone. "Are you in a car?"

"No," Brett replied.

"Because I hear road noise or something. Like a *shhhhh* sound. Aren't you up soon? I thought you were up."

Brett said, "It's the hand dryer. I'm in the bathroom, nervous. Anyway, gotta go. It's almost my turn."

Val separated the twisted gold and purple streamers. "Are you really in the bathroom?"

"Yes." He sighed.

"Is she there?"

"In the bathroom?"

"At karaoke?"

He sighed again.

"I will always ask."

"Yeah. She's here."

Val kicked a rock into the ditch. Silence. The loudest silence. The soundtrack of their marriage. She exhaled. "I was going to go home and change, grab a bite, and then come down with the girls."

"Don't."

"Don't go home first, or don't bring the girls?" Val spotted a beer can. Molson. Dale's favorite. She missed the days when a beer after work was just a beer and not ten, not passing out in the laundry room on a heap of Brett's logging pants, not calling out for water in the middle of the afternoon.

"I already got the girls."

"They're with you now?"

"Not in the bathroom, but with me, yes. Molly Chivers offered to pick them up. They were begging to come. Whole town's here."

"Bullshit," Val scoffed. "Molly only probably did that so Liv could babysit her herd of boys. You know she sent her youngest, the chubby one with the block head, what's-his-name, on a ride-along? That's how the whole escape happened."

"Malcolm?"

"Yes, Malcolm. I think he might be a bit off."

"Really gotta go now."

"Fine." Val paused. "Do I hear sirens?"

"Nope, not here," Brett said. "You're the one outside."

"I feel like I can hear them from here and through the phone."

"There are probably sirens everywhere right now. Hurry up."

"Brett?"

"Yeah?"

"If I don't get there in time for your turn, don't sing too loud. Sometimes you yell the lyrics. And keep the dedication short. Say like, *This one's for Dale*, and then you might want to point upward, to heaven. Or just look up. Yeah, that's even better. Do that."

"Love you."

"Love you too."

Val ran her fingers through her sweaty hair and carried the bike tassel back to her car. She was relieved the girls weren't going to be home. She could take a few minutes alone. Sit on the couch without even turning on the TV. Crack a beer. Brett thought he'd been clever hiding them in Daphne's closet. Did he think, at seven, Daph did her own laundry? Val put on her seat belt and drove up Crow Mountain Road.

A quarter of the way up, she passed the cabin with the rain barrels and the blind corgi that barked out the window. She passed the sign for Molly's daycare. She could still hear the corgi when she reached Roxanne and Dale's A-frame, with its thick lawn and overgrown shrubs. Another year and it would look haunted. Despite all the town's men offering to help, arriving with their hedge trimmers and clippers and threshers, Roxanne insisted on doing the maintenance herself, carving unsightly zigzags as though she'd used a bumper car instead of a lawn mower. It looked like she'd given up on the backyard entirely. The path to Dale's workshop was almost indiscernible. The family sign at the front of the drive was missing. When had Roxanne taken it down?

Val shook her head, ears popping as she ascended the mountain. It had been Brett's idea to live near the top. *Above the trees,* he'd insisted, having spent so much time below them, killing them with his harvester, carting them off to China. It was a great idea, until winter hit and they had to put chains on their tires.

The road turned to gravel and Val opened the top two buttons of her uniform shirt. "Frigging air-conditioning," she mumbled, fiddling with the controls on the dash. "You were working five minutes ago." Val turned the dial from blue to red to blue and slammed on the brakes. Ahead, no more than fifty feet, a man stood at the side of the road where a man shouldn't be. In a panic, Val honked the horn, pressing the steering wheel with all her might, her elbow hyperextending, face scrunched, eyes closed. When she looked again, he wasn't there.

"I'm going crazy," she said, waving her hands in front of the vents, the air warm enough to pop corn. "Why is it so freaking hot in here?" She flapped her shirt and rolled down the window. *That was not Marcel,* she told herself, easing off the brakes, inching forward. It could not be him. No inmate in his right mind would go up a mountain. When a person was in hiding they went down, they went underground. With the worms and the rabbits, the heathens and the whores. But then Marcel was never in his right mind and a little piece of her wondered, hoped, that maybe he had indeed gone up.

Chapter 29

BRETT

"Fuck, that was close." Brett hugged the phone to his chest and looked at Kabir. "I almost got busted." He playfully hammer-punched the glove compartment.

Kabir found Roxanne's sunglasses in the cup holder, the frames round, rhinestones on the hinges. He slid them on his face. "She believed you?" he asked.

"Hell, yeah." Brett raised a hand for a high five.

"You do this often?"

"Do what?"

"Lie to your wife."

Brett frowned, dropped his hand, turned to face the window. "Come on, Kabir. Not you too. You know how hard I've worked to regain her trust?"

"By lying to her?"

"Sometimes, yes. If she knew the girls were at Al's right now she'd freak out. This way she can go home and get a little time to herself before karaoke. She says she never gets time."

"Val needs your time too."

Brett's mouth gaped. "I always give her time." He snatched the Tic Tac box from the dash and folded his arms, slumping deeper into his seat. Last week he'd sat with her through three episodes of a terrible show she liked. He'd even helped make pierogies for fifteen minutes. He was trying to give her time, his time, but he had five years to make

up and there were other things he had to do. The tub needed recaulk-
ing. He'd promised Liv he'd take her stand-up paddleboarding before
the end of the summer. Roxanne's deck had a loose plank. Time was
short and there was always a fire. Kabir, of all people, should know that.

Kabir slowed to a stop behind a line of cars six to eight deep and
halted at the checkpoint. "Should we be worried about anything?"

"No." Brett waved, surprised. "They're just doing their job. Probably stopping everyone looking for that shithead who escaped from
Crow Valley Correctional."

Kabir nodded. Brett texted the girls again, reminding them he was
only five minutes away and to stay inside Al's. He told them not to call
their mother. Olivia responded with a selfie, painted eyebrows raised,
a Slurpee the color of a nightclub and the size of a gas can in her hand.
In the bottom half of the picture, he could make out Daphne's forehead
and mangled center part, just like Val's. He smiled.

They crawled forward, third in line. Brett watched the officer shine
his flashlight into the rear of a Jeep. It wasn't even dark out. Another
did the same from the passenger side. After a brief conversation at the
driver's window, the officer stepped back and waved the Jeep through.
The scenario repeated for the vehicle in front of them, a small pickup
plastered in snowboard bumper stickers. One of the officers came
around to the rear of the truck, examining the bed. She had a tidy bun
at the nape of her neck, slim shoulders. She knelt down by one of the
back tires, then stood and peered into the passenger seat. After a few
gestures between the police, the first officer sent the pickup through.

"I'm nervous," Kabir said, rolling forward.

"What for?" Brett hadn't thought to be nervous. They were looking
for an escaped prisoner. But then he wondered if he should be nervous.
Maybe they had done something. Maybe Kabir had been speeding or
had driven through a stop sign and Brett hadn't noticed because he was
telling lies to his wife. Again. Why couldn't he stop lying?

"What do I say?" Kabir asked.

Brett thought Kabir's eyes looked sort of crazy, the way they were
darting about. "Just answer the questions."

"Gentlemen," the officer said, approaching. "How are we doing tonight?"

"Yes, sir," replied Kabir.

Yes, sir? A wrench of confusion furled Brett's brow. Had the Mountie asked a yes or no question? He was certain all he'd asked was how they were doing. The kind of question that required a specific type of answer. *Not bad. Good good, All right, all right, all right.* "No," Brett blurted.

The officer moved closer, his head nearly inside Kabir's window. Brett could smell his aftershave, count the acne scars on his face. Seven. "No, what?"

"No too bad," Brett replied.

"What's your name?"

"Brett Farquhar, sir."

"You speak English, Brett?"

"Yes, sir."

"And that's your first language?"

"Yes, sir."

"And that's all you speak?"

"Yes, sir."

"Well, let me tell you something Brett. Your English is no too good."

"Yes, sir."

The female officer shone her flashlight in Brett's face. He flinched. The first officer looked at Kabir. "This your truck?"

"Yes, sir," Kabir replied.

"You like *Star Wars*?"

Kabir said, "I've never seen it."

The officer gave the bobblehead a flick with his pen. "Then who's the Princess Leia fan?"

"My wife, sir."

"Your wife's got good taste." He straightened and stuck his thumb in his belt. "Where are you two headed tonight?"

"Karaoke," Brett said.

"I heard about this," the officer replied, making a clicking sound with his teeth. "Big night over at the town hall. Is it true the top prize is ten grand?"

Kabir cleared his throat. "And a spot in the National Championships."

"Impressive." The officer glanced into the back seat. "You haven't seen an inmate running around in your travels? Tall, skinny guy, French accent, scars all over his neck? Got one of those fancy circus mustaches."

Kabir shook his head.

"He'd be wearing prison-issue jogging pants. We think he's probably on foot by now."

Brett drummed his thighs nervously. "Haven't seen him."

The female officer's radio squawked. "Hey," she shouted, summoning her partner.

The first officer moved to meet her. Brett heard the female cop murmur, "We got a report of a stolen blue Chevy Silverado." And then she turned her back, the pleats in her pants curving toward a peak, an exit arrow. Brett could only hear the first few plate letters.

"She thinks we stole the truck," Brett muttered.

Kabir tossed Roxanne's sunglasses into the back seat. "We did steal it, you idiot."

"Not on purpose. We borrowed it."

"What do we do?" Kabir looked boyish and desperate, a dismembered action figure.

Brett thought of Kabir's three brothers and whether they were really dead, buried in a mass grave with other people's brothers, never to grow up, never to be identified, or if they'd survived, like his sister, and were somewhere out there practicing dentistry.

"Brett," Kabir called, but Brett only read his lips. "What do we do?"

Brett's heart was a stampede. He had a pain behind his left eye. Was this what an aneurism felt like? Was he about to die? Had Dale experienced the same sense of doom seconds before the gas station exploded? "Drive!" he yelled.

"Drive?"

"Drive!" Brett seized the handle above, his head slamming into the seat back as Kabir, eyes dark as a night op, put the Silverado into reverse. It smashed into the car behind them and then Kabir accelerated like there was a fire in a galaxy far, far away. On a mountain in Iraq. In a Crow Valley marriage.

Chapter 30

MARCEL

Marcel dropped to the ground, hips and hands crashing into the stiff earth, a desperate sprawl, shoving his face into the dirt as if every millimeter of depth was lifesaving. It tasted like his childhood basement before he'd set his house on fire and watched it blaze from the playground, eyes fixed on the front door with fingers crossed that it would not open, that his father remained safely inside. It wasn't until his mother arrived on the scene, collapsing at the foot of where the steps once stood, until he saw her face, anguished and pleading, that he understood: he'd killed her too.

How had he not heard it coming? A minivan, too. Must have been one of those silent hybrid motherfuckers. He searched for cover. The empty shell casing of a tampon balanced on a twig by Marcel's left ear. Had someone changed a tampon up here? The thought both disgusted and exhilarated him. The roadside offered only a small depression, a shallow grave. He wrestled the backpack off his shoulders and tossed it to the side, yanking the steak knife from the front pocket. He had no idea how exposed he was. The last time he dared look up, the van had started moving again, creeping forward like a Google Street car mapping the universe.

There was a small embankment to Marcel's right, blanketed in a tangle of roots and branches, leaves unwieldy and heavy as soiled sheets. He could climb up, disappear inside the trees, but he'd be seen in the process. Alternatively, he could stay, tongue in the dirt, rock pressed into his liver, and hope the van wouldn't see him as it lumbered past.

Fuck it. He lifted his head. The driver was a woman, alone. She drove with caution, neck long, both hands on the steering wheel like she was operating a bus. Marcel's brain was pixelated. Was it her? He pushed up for a better view. He recognized the prison gray of her shirt, the frizzy hair, her steadfast expression. She was fixated on something outside the passenger window. Marcel knelt, scrambled up the embankment, and threw himself behind a tree.

The woman blasted the horn, once and then twice. Marcel stayed hidden. She'd honked earlier, before he'd dropped to the ground. Maybe she'd think it was all in her head. Marcel adjusted his feet, slipping on a toadstool the texture of casserole. He'd left the backpack. She was close now, the van's engine rumbling. She screamed from the open window, "Bear!"

"Bear?" Marcel thought about it. He hadn't seen any evidence. No scat, no trails. Though, he supposed, this was bear country. He stepped into the open. Across the road, a black bear stood on its hind legs, pawing at a tree, its back to the road. *Berries*, Marcel thought. He'd seen bushes. Could he outrun a bear? It was only a juvenile. He thought of all the people he'd outrun in his life: the Montreal police, his seventh grade gym teacher, Monsieur Pettipas, after Marcel had been caught smoking under the uprights. His father. Would he have been able to outrun Jepson had their encounters taken place outside the prison?

"Get in the car," Val shouted, causing the bear to turn.

Marcel stood at attention, debating. The bear didn't seem the least bit interested in pursuing him as it snouted its way deeper into the woods, batting away unacceptable vegetation with the discernment of a toddler. What would happen if he accepted the ride? Would Val turn him in? Seduction didn't work as well on the outside. He no longer needed her to sit on his face.

"Get in," she waved. "He'll eat'cha."

Marcel guessed the bear was a girl. Its face was narrow and it moved with the confidence of a female athlete. All lip gloss and sports bra and fuck you.

"I'm not going to turn you in," Val said.

The bear retraced her steps and stood facing the road, nose on alert.

"You're bleeding."

Marcel touched his head, stared at the blood on his fingertips, smelled the garlic from the guacamole he'd eaten earlier. "I have a knife," he said.

"You stab yourself in the eye?"

Marcel held the knife up and licked its serrated edge.

"Bravo, El Chapo." Val clapped. "I always had you pegged as some kind of madman. What's up with your tiny pants?"

Marcel grabbed his nuts.

"All right then, good luck." She pulled forward. The bear dropped to all fours.

"Wait," Marcel said, skidding down the embankment and swiping up the backpack. "Where will you take me?"

"Can't take you anywhere. Cops are combing this place. But I can get you cleaned up."

Marcel threw the steak knife over his shoulder. It bounced off a tree and dropped out of sight. The bear started across the road. She was beautiful, fur rich and glistening. Marcel went around to the passenger side and collapsed into the van.

"Cut looks pretty nasty." Val accelerated, tires coughing up debris. "Don't get your blood on nothin'. And don't pull any Houdini shit. I'll get you some better pants. Then you're on your own." She paused. "What the heck did you do to your mustache?"

Marcel made scissors with his fingers.

"You look like a bloody communist."

He shrugged.

"Better shave the rest of that off."

The road transitioned to gravel where Marcel had missed the turn and flipped the police car. They drove a half kilometer in silence.

"Duck," Val cautioned. "House up here on the right."

Marcel crouched forward, slamming his head against the glove compartment. Blood from his knees was seeping through his pants.

"Clear," she said seconds later, the car making a sweeping turn to the left and then stopping.

"Thank you," Marcel said, unfolding himself, observing the bungalow in front of him. It was pale green, remnants of girls in the front yard: a fuchsia skipping rope knotted at the end of the drive, a skateboard decorated like Valentine's Day.

"Thank Norman. He's the one got everyone feeling sorry for you."

He followed her out of the vehicle and around to the back of the house. There was a gray deck with a skirt of sun-faded lattice nailed sloppily beneath. The steps tilted to the left.

"Never mind the steps. Brett's fixin' 'em next week." She opened the door. "Leave your shoes out here. And no funny business." She held up her cell phone, threateningly.

Val pulled an elastic off her wrist and gathered her hair into a ragged bun on the top of her head. A bag of green beans lay open on the counter. Above the dining table hung a pair of eight-by-ten photographs. The girls. He recognized the younger one, her straggly hair, cheerful shirt, and tooth gap. The one who'd asked to see the scar on his back. The older one looked different without her makeup.

Val noticed him staring and moved swiftly to block his view. "Bathroom's over there." She pointed toward a hallway off the living room. "I'll get you a towel." She grabbed a plastic bag from a dispenser under the sink. "Put your clothes in here."

Marcel took the bag and crept through the hallway. He'd like to have a house like this. With halls and carpet and pictures on the wall. Pretzels on the floor. Tiny butterfly clips with pink ladybugs. He stopped and stared at a photo collage. *Jepson?* That son of a whore was in every photo, posing with another man. This must be Brett. They looked like they could have been brothers, Brett the uglier of the two, with his unsightly curls and fast-food stomach. They smiled side by side in baseball jerseys, in Search and Rescue shirts, in tank tops, in snow pants, in Ray-Bans. In Halloween costumes with kids at their sides. Daughters, sons.

Marcel noticed Val watching him from the kitchen. He pointed at the framed collage. "What happened to him? He get transferred?"

"Jepson? He got dead. Died in the forest fires last summer."

Marcel was drawn back to the images. Jepson didn't look dead. In fact he looked so alive in the photos, with his likable smile and open stance, he seemed immortal.

"How did he die?"

"Gas station blew up."

Val disappeared and returned with a pair of industrial pants, a towel, and a T-shirt. Marcel slipped into the bathroom. A Lego figure smiled at him from the rim of the sink. Globs of toothpaste dotted the counter. The tub was full of forks. He took off his bloodied clothes and slipped into Brett's. He washed the blood and dirt from his face. He tied off the plastic bag Val had given him and carried it down the hall, pausing again to stare at the collage.

"People liked him?" he asked.

"Everyone liked Dale."

Marcel remembered Dale's piss pooling in his ear, trickling down his neck. He remembered Dale describing all the ways he was going to fuck Marcel's mom. He tossed the bag of soiled clothes at Val and washed his hands in the sink.

Val leaned against the kitchen table. Her cheeks were pink, tits heavy. She bent to set the plastic bag on the floor. He looked down her shirt. The material, though stiff, gaped open and he could see the curve of her left breast, her skin unevenly flushed, vaguely freckled, not particularly nice. He stepped closer, and then, with his finger, traced a line from her chin, down her neck, which she obediently exposed by tipping her head back. At her clavicle he could sense her heart beating, slapping. He thought about her getting wet. He hooked his finger at the top of her shirt, gently pulled it away from her body, and rubbed his face into her chest.

Her breath skipped like a record, and then she grabbed the back of his head, pulling his hair, burying his face deeper inside her shirt, his severed mustache a cat's tongue.

Chapter 31

====

MOLLY

A re-sing and she didn't have to ask. Molly looked back up at Roxanne, hunched behind the judges' platform, a lost miner, and felt a surge of gratitude. A second chance and the privilege of going last. Everyone would be drunk by then, and if she chose the right song they might riot or weep or dance in the aisles shouting her name, confessing their sins, begging for mercy, begging for more. She would have to win, and when she did, Roxanne might forgive her. Maybe Dale would too.

Molly's thoughts turned to Malcolm, his leg, barely a leg at four years old, and stooped to whisper into Xavier's ear. "I'm going to the hospital to check on your brother. You're staying here."

Xavier tore open a stamp-sized salt packet, emptied it onto a small hill of pepper, and flicked the garbage onto the floor.

"Pick that up," she scolded, bending to retrieve it as the town librarian glared from the adjacent table.

"I don't want to stay here. It's boring." Xavier sighed and kicked the underside of the table.

Molly rested a firm hand on his leg. "What about the girl you were playing with earlier?"

"She had to go sit with her grandma."

"Well, the hospital will be more boring."

"But there's machines and stuff."

"Machines and sick people."

"I like sick people."

Molly slid into the chair next to Xavier as the MC introduced a stranger to the stage. Molly had seen the woman at the drugstore earlier that morning, half the woman's cheek a deep shade of plum.

"What's wrong with her face?"

"Nothing. It's just a birthmark. She was born that way."

"Does it hurt?"

She lowered her voice. "If you need anything, your brothers are up on the balcony. Don't touch the railing."

"When will you be back?"

Molly stood. "An hour, probably? You know what hospitals are like." She crouched again and whispered, "Don't go anywhere with anyone."

"What if I'm hungry?"

"You just ate a Ring Pop." Molly rifled through her purse, handed him a crumpled ten-dollar bill, and kissed him on the forehead. "Be good."

She gathered her car keys, which were partially buried under a heap of used napkins, and laced her way to the isolated rear exit, where no one could judge her for leaving. She stopped short of the door and sifted through the lost-and-found bin until she found a hoodie covered in tiny silkscreened diamonds to cover her sagging strapless dress. She pulled it over her head, ignoring that it smelled like a litter box and a high school dance. Molly popped open the back door and used her body weight to ram it shut.

Outside, it was still warm. It seemed hotter than it had been in the afternoon, the air dense, as though beaten into stiff peaks. She flapped the hoodie and kicked through the pine needles that lined the path toward the side of the building. She thought of the escaped prisoner and whipped around in a panic to make sure he wasn't behind her. Gary would lose his mind if he knew she'd left the hall. If she'd told him she was coming to the hospital, he would've protested. He would've reminded her of all the women he'd found without IDs or addresses or next of kins. All the women without pulses.

Molly reached the family's navy blue Yukon and unlocked it with the remote. The hospital was a ten-minute drive. She'd park down the street behind the A&W and tell Gary she'd gotten a ride. He'd be relieved thinking she hadn't come alone.

She turned out of the parking lot and pulled up beside the town notice board. A sign warned of a sloth in the area. Her daycare poster was torn. Main Street was abandoned. The parking stalls were vacant and the window of J-Dawg's food truck was sealed shut. The town cat, a fat-cheeked American shorthair, perused the scribbles on the second memorial bench that bore Dale's name. Only the bakery was still open, because the owners didn't believe in karaoke or, it appeared, in lockdowns either. Maybe they could give the prisoner a gingerbread man.

Molly made a right turn at the end of the strip. The hospital sign, which one of the Mains brothers had knocked with his plow last year, leaned at a forty-five-degree angle. Ahead was one of three level crossings in Crow Valley. As if they knew Molly was coming, the lights cued and the bar creaked to its downward position.

"Ah, come on." The train was still a notable distance away. She rolled down her window and listened, waiting for it to present itself while musing over what she could sing. If she'd successfully persuaded Brett to serenade Val instead of performing a Dale tribute, she could sing for Dale. A hero's song. A song for the dead. A song for those left behind. She turned on the radio for inspiration. All she got was news.

An alert warned of the escaped inmate. Molly still wished she could join him. His prison four walls, hers four boys. Old women told her to be grateful. She'd look back at these years as the best years of her life. *Children grow up so fast,* they'd say with nostalgia-tinted glasses and dreamy whispers. *One day they'll be all grown up and gone and you'll long for the days you rocked them to sleep in the wee hours of the morning.* Not true. She longed for the past when they weren't alive. She longed for the future when they were gone. She longed for anything but the present. She wanted the bookends and not the books.

The train drew closer, and Molly winced in anticipation. Across from her, a truck screeched to a hard stop, bumping the level crossing, sending the dashboard bobblehead into a holy dance.

Kabir? Molly squinted at the triangular mass in the driver's seat. His beautiful black cowlick and smooth forehead. She inched forward to get a better view. *Brett?* The train sounded its brute whistle and raged through the intersection, the cars alternating between wheat graphics and candy-colored graffiti. Molly put the Yukon in Park and got out. She cocked her head to the side to get a better glimpse of the truck.

Roxanne's Silverado. *The hell?* She texted Gary, the train blowing up her dress, the sun slick on her face. A used strip of paper caps flitted by.

Found Roxanne's truck. Cancel search. As she continued typing, her phone rang.

Gary said, "Where you to, Mol? Why's it sound like yer on the Polar Express? Tell me you didn't leave the hall?"

"I just came out for some fresh air."

"And the truck's there in the parking lot?"

"Roxanne forgot she'd parked around back," she lied. "She had to drop off the extra chairs from the elementary school."

"Geez, b'y. Dispatch going to think I'm stun. I'll call off the search. Listen, Malcolm's leg is right broke. There givin' him a boot."

"So, he doesn't need surgery?"

"Resident don't think so. Just waiting for a second opinion from the ortho."

A tumbleweed cartwheeled past. "Should I come relieve you?"

"And leave the boys at the hall?"

"The boys are fine. Kids are all playing together."

"Malcolm," Gary shouted. "Don't put that in your mouth, b'y."

"How's he doing?"

"Lard Jaysus, he damn near ate the ultrasound gel. Put that down b'y. The boy don't listen."

Molly could see the end of the train. "Did they find him? The prisoner?"

"Not yet, but got a call from a trucker who thinks he saw him at the Crow Valley Campground eatin' a Dilly Bar."

"That's almost an hour from here."

"Malcolm, fix your gown b'y, the nurse don't wanna see your arse."

"I'll be there in a bit."

"I don't like you being out of the hall."

"It's fine."

"Malcolm, come here b'y!"

Molly winced at the volume of Gary's voice.

"Sweet Jesus, he just asked someone if he could have a turn with his walker. Hurry up, would ya?"

Gary hung up as the last rail car passed. Molly was still outside, standing in the middle of the road, the Yukon idling beside her. The crossing lights blackened and the control barrier lifted.

Kabir cautiously accelerated.

Brett stuck his head out the window. "We didn't steal it," he said, thumping the exterior. "We borrowed it."

"Is something wrong?" Molly hollered.

Police sirens raged. Molly turned her ear toward the prison as Kabir cleared the tracks and pulled alongside her.

"Hey Mol," Brett pleaded through Kabir's open window. "Don't tell anyone you saw us."

"You missed your turn," she said.

"I missed my turn?" His face fell.

"They called you multiple times."

"No problem," Kabir interrupted. "I'll say we had a fire call." He turned to Brett. "You still on Crow Valley Search and Rescue?"

Brett nodded.

"Here." Kabir tossed something out the window. "My sister says they're bad for my teeth and I can't stop eating them."

The Silverado sped off, upsetting the gravel. Molly bent to pick up a scratched plastic container of Tic Tacs.

Chapter 32

VAL

Val stared up at the ceiling fan, its wooden blades slicing the air with an imperfect wobble, the dining room table pressing into her spine. She felt a Cheezie deflate under her shoulder blade. Olivia's pet rabbit, Bubbles, hopped into the room and stood on her hind legs, watching. Marcel's head, still wedged between her breasts, smelled like a locker room.

Val's phone rang, bumping out of her pocket and onto the table that once belonged to Brett's grandparents. She sat up, causing Marcel to retreat, and fiddled with her phone, unable to discern which way was up. "Hello?"

"Mom?"

"Liv?"

"Do you know where Dad is?"

Val straightened. "What do you mean do I know where he is? He's with you."

There was an exaggerated pause.

Val noticed someone had left a rotisserie chicken on the counter. "Olivia? Tell me you're at the hall with your dad."

"I'm at the hall with Dad."

Val slid from the table, placed a hand on her chest, the skin irritated as though she'd rolled in grass, and kicked a chair out of the way. Marcel sat cross-legged on the linoleum, stroking Bubbles between the ears.

"Where's your father?"

"Um . . . I think he just went to the bathroom. Yep, there he is. I think he's like, super nervous."

A faint *Yahoo!* chimed in the background. Val froze. *How do I know that sound?* She paced around the kitchen searching for her house shoes. "Liv, where are you?"

"At the hall."

Yahoo!

"No, you aren't. I know that sound. That's the lotto machine. You're at Big Al's, aren't you?"

"No."

"Yes, you are. I know it," Val repeated.

"That was Daphne."

Daphne yelled, "Yahoo!"

Marcel lifted Bubbles from his lap to his chest. The rabbit kicked. Marcel tried to wrangle the animal into a safe position.

"She doesn't like to be picked up!" Val hollered.

"What?" Liv replied.

Val covered and uncovered her mouth. "I said, I'll pick you up."

"Did someone try to pick up Bubbles?"

"No."

"She hates being picked up."

"I know that, Liv."

Daphne said. "Ask Mom if I can buy a scratch ticket."

Yahoo!

"You are at Big Al's."

Silence. "Maybe."

Val sighed. "I'm going to kill your father. Stay there, I'm coming to get you."

"Fuck, it bit me." Marcel examined his wrist as Bubbles sprinted down the hall, her ears stiff as cardboard.

Val flailed her arms angrily at Marcel. He shrugged, produced his forearm as evidence. She mouthed *Shut up.*

"Is Uncle Darrell there?"

Val heard customer laughter in the background.

"No."

Olivia waited.

"TV's on. I'll be there in five minutes."

Val found her house shoes near the washing machine, half-buried under piles of leggings. She jammed her feet inside and shuffled back toward the kitchen. Marcel stopped her at the end of the hall.

He held up his arm. "Fucker bit me."

"Because you picked her up. Rabbits don't like to be picked up. I have to go get my girls." Val pushed him aside. He resisted.

"I'm coming."

"No, you aren't." She madly texted Brett. *YOU SAID THE GIRLS WERE WITH YOU AT KARAOKE WTF??*

Marcel lifted Brett's drill from a stepladder. Brett was building a trophy shelf in anticipation of winning Crow Valley Heat's player of the season. Marcel turned the drill on and brought it dangerously close to his tongue. "But, they know me."

"What are you talking about, they know you?"

"Your seven-year-old. Daphne, right? Wants to be a bartender when she grows up. Sassy little thing. I like her. Went to school with a girl like that. Bitch put a sewing needle through my finger." He pointed to a scar below his nail bed and then tucked a piece of Val's hair behind her ear. "And your older one. Got the teen thing going on." He gestured to his mouth. "Braces. Those weird-ass eyebrows girls do now. She'll be real hot one day."

Val dropped her phone. Marcel picked it up, slid it into the front pocket of his borrowed pants. "Shall we go get them?"

Val felt like she had sleep paralysis. "I'll drive you to the edge of town. There's a logging road that cuts out to the highway, just south of the prison. Brett leaves a truck out there." Val's hands trembled as she crossed the kitchen to a pegboard of keys hanging beneath a family portrait from Disneyland. Daphne was just a baby, round, wild. Olivia was on Brett's shoulders, her Snow White dress bunched around Brett's neck like a travel pillow. Their smiles in competition.

The key to the GMC wasn't on the pegboard. It should have been on the third hook, the bent one. Val rifled through the other keys that were there. Why did they have so many keys? Keys to what?

Marcel whispered, "Is this the one you're looking for?"

Val whipped around, bumping Marcel, the GMC key dangling from his teeth.

"Yes." She was quiet.

Marcel removed the key from his mouth, pulled her face into his. She felt his huge thumb press into the back of her neck, the force of his bite on her lip. She tasted blood. Then he palmed the chicken that had been left out on the counter, tucked it under his arm like a newspaper, and said, "After you."

Chapter 33

ROXANNE

Silas leaned into Roxanne while the DJ performed a sound check. One of the Mains brothers had tripped on a cord, upsetting the audio and losing a container of fries.

Silas said, "I'm a bit buzzed up."

"You think?" Roxanne huffed. "You've been sipping on that thing all night." She gestured at the flask, nearly knocking it over. "Why do you drink so much?"

"Helps me manage my anxiety. It's always worse when I travel."

"I miss my truck."

"They'll find it." Silas massaged his temples and then flipped through the empty score sheets. "God, we're not even halfway through."

A fistfight broke out by the canteen. One of the Mains brothers and a stranger. Half of the Crow Valley Heat intervened, dragging the men apart, threatening them with angry fingers and swear words.

"How do you know they'll find it? They can't even find the escaped prisoner."

"It's a giant blue truck."

"He was in a police car."

Silas crossed his arms. A portly man with short limbs and a fisherman's vest heaved himself up the steps to center stage. His black hair was swept to one side, forming a peak above his left eye.

"Is that a costume?" Silas asked.

"Not really. Seasonal business." Roxanne leaned back in her chair.

"He takes Chinese tourists fishing. Says a few words in Mandarin and they all go nuts."

The jazzy opening of "Somewhere Beyond the Sea" sashayed through the hall. The contestant tipped the microphone and flicked his short leg with the finesse of a much lighter man.

"Love this song." Silas had a faraway look in his eyes.

"Your mom sing it to you?"

"It was my parents' wedding song. They had a barbershop quartet. You should see the pictures. Like something out of the movies. They'd dance to it on their anniversary."

Roxanne dropped her pen. The mayor's brother was getting married next weekend. Roxanne was supposed to have filed the permits and ordered the chairs. One hundred and fifty of them. How had she forgotten? She remembered talking to the rental place in Beggar's Creek. The man's voice was slightly hoarse, like Dale's had been, and he'd used the expression "all that glitters" . . . referring to the gold resin Napoleon chairs the mayor had suggested she order. Terrible chairs, the sales rep had said, recommending another model, but by then she'd been thinking about Dale's wedding band and how it still sparkled when the coroner handed her what was left of it in a tiny plastic collection bag. *I'm going to get fired.*

Silas's phone buzzed. Roxanne leaned over to look at the screen. "K. Jefferies," she read. "That your boyfriend? Or your partner?" She rubbed her weary eyes. "How do you call him?"

"It's my landlord."

"Why's your landlord calling? You got a thing with him?"

"No, I don't have a thing with him. Do you have a thing with your accountant?"

"I don't have an accountant. Didn't even bother filing my taxes last year. That was Dale's job."

The call ended without Silas answering. The contestant flounced across the stage, a far cry from the way he stood in the river as though he'd been planted there, hip waders strangling his crotch, line cast. The phone rang again. Roxanne spied a toddler eating the spilled fries off the floor.

"You better answer that," Roxanne nudged. "Maybe your house burnt down."

Silas bent below the judges' table, plugged his free ear. "Hello."

Roxanne circled a succession of threes on the contestant's score sheet, then dug through her purse for a Gas-X. She wasn't a fan of music from the forties. Too jazzy. Too "big band." Music unsuited for sturdy women. She and Dale had once taken a jitterbug workshop and the instructor told Roxanne she moved like a Winston Churchill statue. She circled a one.

"OMG," Silas held up his phone. "There's been a flood."

"What kind of flood?"

"What do you mean, what kind? A flood. There's only one kind of flood."

"Tell that to Noah." Roxanne scoffed.

Silas dropped the phone and grabbed his flask. "There's a foot of water in my apartment."

"It's okay." Roxanne touched his shoulder. "They've got special water vacuums that will suck it all away."

"But all my stuff. My mom's ashes."

"You've got your mom's ashes?"

"A portion. My dad gave some to me and some to my brother. I made a little urn."

"I put Dale in his thermos. He used the same one since the day I met him. Army green. He loved his coffee." Roxanne fondled the empty iced coffee cup. "Three cream, two sugar. Though lately he was putting butter in it. Imagine."

A frayed ball cap drifted to the floor from the balcony above.

"The urn have a lid?"

"A cork," Silas replied.

"Well, hopefully it was waterproof."

Roxanne tried to sound positive. She tried not to picture Silas's mother bobbing around his apartment, slowly mixing with the carpet fuzz and crouton crumbs and *Fuck, what if the neighbor's sewer had backed up?* She pawed at her headlamp, turning the dial to maximum brightness. "So, what did the landlord want you to do?"

The man two-stepped across the stage, the music trailing behind him.

"Someone needs to go to my apartment and decide what can be salvaged."

Roxanne touched his arm. An urge simmered to gather him into a hug, his long limbs and cosmopolitan scent and broken heart, but the connection would be her undoing. Her neural pathways might short-circuit, singeing her hair, fusing the headlamp to her face. Making her feel.

She withdrew. "You need to make some calls?"

Silas nodded, eyes glassy, his tall frame collapsing like a music stand. Roxanne waved at the MC, who did her own version of a two-step toward the microphone, her skirt bouncing, toes stubbing the wooden surface.

"It looks like our judges need a quick break before our next contestant," she said. "So, this is a great time to let you know the kitchen is all out of chili."

One of the Mains brothers booed. Silas exhaled, took his flask and phone, and descended the stairs toward the back of the hall. He looked dramatic, bent beneath the red glow of the exit sign. Below, the mayor pushed away from his table, straightened his jacket, and meandered toward the exit, his steps measured but unsteady, a last call gait. He would take the Halo Trail home.

Roxanne pushed her chair back abruptly and stood. The stage had been taken over by children playing tag. Boys in clumsy sneakers, the girls always faster, never getting caught. Behind her, Silas slouched against the wood-paneled wall, a hand sprawled across his forehead. The urn wasn't waterproof. Of course it wasn't, and now his mother was gone, again. A freak accident. He should have used a thermos, airtight and vacuum-sealed and handheld. He should never have left her behind. How could he have been so foolish? How could she?

Roxanne bolted.

Chapter 34

BRETT

Kabir parked Roxanne's truck behind the town's L-shaped elementary school, the once red brick now a muted brown. The peak of a hop-scotch pattern was visible from the passenger side. Dale had helped paint it when Olivia was five.

"Now what?" Kabir asked.

Brett rolled down the window, lifted his ear to the wind. "We need to think."

"Let's just take it back."

"The police are searching for us."

"They won't be for long."

Brett slung his elbow out the open window. The sun warmed his shoulder the way it should in July. "How do you figure?"

"We'll call the police and tell them we saw the prisoner. They said he had an old-time mustache."

Brett's eyes ballooned. "Where did we see him?"

Kabir stroked his chin and turned up the radio. Van Halen rang from the dash. "By the tire place."

"Up on the highway?"

"We have to draw them out of town."

Brett considered this. Mains Brothers Tire was five kilometers north. It doubled as a lot for private sellers to advertise their used cars. At any given time there were half a dozen vehicles angle-parked and polished by the road, their FOR SALE BY OWNER signs strategically arranged.

"Tell them he had a gun," Brett added. "And that he was stealing one of the cars." He shifted forward in his seat, excitedly. "And that he had a hostage, a woman, and he was dragging her around the parking lot by her hair." Brett attempted to demonstrate.

Kabir glared.

"Too much?"

Kabir handed Brett his phone. "You saw him near there. That's all."

Brett waved his hand. "I'm not calling."

"You have to."

"Why?"

"They hear my accent and they'll assume I'm a terrorist."

"Come on," Brett countered. "That doesn't even make sense."

Kabir dropped the phone onto his lap. "Do you know what happened when I first moved here and tried to open a bank account?"

Brett shifted in his seat, the sun now a burden.

"The manager cried, 'Please just let us go. We have families.'"

Brett twitched. "Well, were you dressed like a terrorist?"

"I was wearing a Penguins jersey."

"Oh. Crow Valley hates the Penguins. No one likes Sidney Crosby." Kabir shook his head.

"Fine, give me the phone." Brett dialed 9-1-1.

A skateboarder whizzed by, knees bent as he approached a ramp, green hair unmoving. He missed the landing. Kabir cranked the AC.

"Yes, I think I may have seen the escaped prisoner," Brett started. "Looked like he was trying to steal a car up near Mains Brothers Tire."

There was long pause. Kabir waited, nodding encouragement.

"He may have had a hos—"

Kabir snatched the phone. "A hotdog," he continued in his best North American accent. "He may have been eating a hotdog."

"What?" mouthed Brett.

Kabir hung up the phone. "I told you to keep it vague."

"I tried."

"If they believed you, we should hear sirens in about two and a half minutes." Kabir checked his watch and then gestured north. Brett, arm still hanging out the window, drummed the truck's exterior.

The skateboarder geared up for a second attempt at the ramp, pushing harder this time, adjusting his stance. He executed a kick flip and turned a hard right to avoid a bike rack.

Kabir counted down, "five, four, three . . ." and then snapped his fingers. A cacophony of sirens rose in the distance as though summoned by a conductor.

"Yes." Brett fist-pumped. "Now we pick up the girls and get back to the hall. I'll use the whole fire call excuse and they'll have to let me sing." He turned to Kabir, an idea blooming, the best idea of all time. And it was his. "If anyone asks about the fire call, can you say it was me? Can you say I did the saving?" He practically whispered. "Can you say I was the *hero*?"

Kabir maneuvered the steering wheel with the heel of his hand, running over a juice box in the truck's path. "But there was no one to save," he said.

"We can make it up. Say it was a stranded motorist."

Kabir raised his eyebrows. "Who had a handful of pills—" He stopped. "Who ran out of gas on the side of the road?"

Brett sighed. "You make it up then. You do this stuff all the time. What's a believable story? Something really . . . heroic."

"Animals or babies."

Brett's eyes dilated. "What about a baby animal?"

"Like a fawn?"

Brett punched the dash. "You've taken all the good ones."

"You know, there's more than one way to be a hero."

"Please, Kabir?"

"You can be a hero to your kids or to the environment. Your neighbors, immigrants, poor people, stray dogs. Your wife."

"Just this one time."

Kabir pulled cautiously out of the school parking lot onto Second Avenue. "Fine," he said. "Leave it with me. I'll come up with something."

Hope washed through Brett.

"Siri, play 'Hello' by Adele. Karaoke version."

"Ah, come on." Brett complained. "Not again."

"Hello," sang Kabir. "It is me." He turned up the volume.

Brett crouched, checking the rear window to ensure they weren't being followed before joining Kabir for the chorus. They carried the duet to Big Al's. Kabir parked around the side, where Crow Valley's only homeless man pumped air into his bike tires. The bike had been outfitted with a makeshift cart to haul his belongings. A shaggy guinea pig rode shotgun in a basket attached to the front. Kabir nodded at the man as Brett got out of the truck.

"Be right back." Brett lightly thumped the hood and went around front, a rainbow of oil glistening beside the curb. "Jody," Brett said, addressing the woman behind the counter. "Girls here?"

"At the back," she gestured, flipping the channel on the tube TV mounted above the cigarettes. "I told them they could have a burrito."

"Thanks," Brett said, striding to the rear of the store, where he spied Daphne kneeling on a stool. Olivia was parked in front of the microwave checking her reflection.

"Dad?" Olivia turned. "Aren't you supposed to be singing?"

"Not without my two favorite fans."

"Mom's on her way to get us."

Brett's face fell. "You told her?"

"Not on purpose." Olivia removed the burritos with a second remaining on the microwave's display.

"That one's mine," Daphne pointed.

Brett ran his fingers through his hair and strained to see out toward the parking lot. "She's going to kill me."

"That's what she said." Olivia squeezed a packet of salsa onto her burrito and licked her finger.

"Come on." He helped Daphne off the stool and picked up her burrito. "You can eat it in the car."

The girls shrugged. Brett grabbed a handful of napkins and started out of the store, Olivia close behind, Daphne stalling to kick a box of Ritz that had fallen off a shelf.

"Leave it," Brett said, pushing through the door. "Thanks, Jody. If you see Val, let her know the girls are with me at the hall."

"Will do," Jody replied, hand in a chip bag, eyes fixed on the TV.

Brett rounded the corner to find Kabir bent over the homeless man's bike, fixing it with a hex key. "That should do it," he said.

The homeless man folded his hands in prayer. Kabir tousled the guinea pig's head and turned.

"Here," he said to Olivia. "Take a selfie of us and send it to Mom so she knows you're with me."

Olivia rolled her eyes, but obliged. "Why are we taking Roxanne's truck?" Olivia asked.

"Never mind," Brett sighed. "Just get in."

Chapter 35

MARCEL

Marcel loathed the expression on Val's face, the way she gripped the steering wheel. Her entire body was rigid, scaffolded to the seat. It was regret. He knew because women always felt guilty. That's what girls were made of. Sugar and spice and guilt and shame and doubt and fear. But had it been *that* bad? He'd been deliberately gentle even though he pegged her as someone who liked things a little rough—hair pulls, handprints. Prison sex. But he'd used only the tips of his fingers, the tip of his tongue. He'd stopped things from going any further than lying on top of her, inhaling her skin, her worry. Didn't she know how hard that was for him? To use restraint? To be tender?

Sunlight poured through the windshield. Marcel closed his eyes, felt the warmth on his face and a flash of giddiness. If all this worked out, this getting out of Crow Valley, he could eventually buy a bed. He'd never slept in anything bigger than a sleeping bag, a bunk, a bench, a doorway, a cot. No more. He'd buy a king-sized mattress. A frame made of steel. Expensive sheets from Egypt with enough thread to choke a camel. Ten thousand threads! And a bed skirt. And pillows. Jumbo ones, square ones, round, gel, feathered, soft, bolster. And he would show his lovers that they were not made of guilt or shame or doubt or fear, but of power and manners and magic and vanilla. Of love.

Val's phone pinged in his pocket. He ignored it, placed a hand on his growling stomach. He spread the rotisserie chicken across his lap while Val continued to steer the family van down the driveway, avoiding the red wagon weathered pink by the sun, a rogue rake, a flip-flop.

"Want some?" he asked, holding up a swath of skin he'd fashioned into a tube.

Val shook her head.

"Worked at St. Hubert for a month. When I was sixteen. Know it?"

She stopped at the end of the drive, straining to see if anyone was coming down the mountain. Her expression was grim, her mouth an underscore, eyes wet as a bathroom mirror.

Fuck, he thought. She better not cry.

"I don't know St. Hubert," Val replied.

A flotilla of airborne dandelion seeds drifted past the windshield. Marcel perked up. "Never?" He dismantled a wing. "It's fast-food chicken. They're all over Quebec."

"Like KFC?"

"KFC's fucking . . . they cook their chickens live. With their beaks and shit still attached." He paused. "Can't believe you've never heard of St. Hubert."

"What was your job?"

Marcel's ears popped as they descended the mountain. "Mostly cash." He smiled, reminiscing. "But I also had a thing with the franchise owner's daughter." He wedged his hand between Val's clenched thighs. She might have winced, and then her legs went slack.

"Is that why you got fired?'

"What makes you think I got fired?" He pulled his hand away, tossed a bone out the window. He watched it arc and then fall.

Val shrugged. "Then why'd you leave?"

"I got fired."

Val made eye contact.

"Not for reasons you think."

"You steal somethin'?"

"Nope."

"Mess up the till?"

"Punched a customer in the face." Marcel drove his fist into his hand, upsetting the chicken, causing a gelatinous scrap to fly up and land on the gearshift.

"You can't punch customers."

"You can."

"What, did you forget his coleslaw? Not give him enough ketchup?"

"He wouldn't let his kid go to the bathroom. Went off on him for having to go because he didn't want to lose his spot in line. Told him to hold it. Told him he should've gone before they left the house. Kid was begging. *Dad I got to go pee.* He was like four, five? Maybe three? No one else did anything. They just stared at the menu board contemplating their order, pretending like everything was fine, that it was normal to yell at a kid for having to go pee, that there was no need to intervene. Finally I just yelled, *Take him to the fucking washroom*, and when he got in my face to protest, I broke his fucking nose. Piece of shit."

Val tensed again. Back like drywall, eyes damp, blinking.

Marcel clenched his teeth. *For fuck's sake.* "I'm not gonna hurt you, okay? Just don't get all emotional and shit. I can't fucking stand when women cry. My mother. Always crying. Like she's scared of me. Her own son. Can you imagine being scared of your own kid? You know how many pictures I colored her? How many times I got her ice or Advil or Polysporin?" He wiped his hands on his pants, leaving behind greasy prints. "You know how many times I got in between?" He pointed to a scar on his forehead.

The van halted abruptly. Marcel recognized that they were at the bottom of the hill where he'd encountered Val's daughters. He thought he could see the exact spot where they'd crashed their bikes, a skid mark, the gravel disturbed. A police car zipped by.

"Go that way," Marcel gestured in the opposite direction. "I got to get the fuck out of here." He still carried Val's phone in his pocket and its sudden ringing startled him. He threw the remains of the chicken, including the plastic tray, out the window and wiped his hands on his shirt. He pulled the phone out and held it up. "N. Blanchard."

"Norman," Val reached.

"My Norman?" Marcel hugged the phone to his chest.

"Give it," she ordered, snatching it away.

"Don't answer."

"I have to answer."

"He'll be mad at me." Marcel frowned.

"He'll be suspicious if I don't."

Val turned onto the road toward the prison. "Norman?"

The van's Bluetooth kicked in and Norman's voice filled the space as though it was a cloud that had slipped in through the window. Marcel enjoyed the soothing weight of it on his shoulders. He wished he could take Norman with him wherever he was going.

"You'll never guess what just happened," Norman said.

"Nope. Probably not," Val replied, motioning for Marcel to keep his mouth shut.

"Came home to get ready for karaoke, let the dog out, and she comes back quilled. Val, she's covered in them." His voice dipped.

"Ah, Norm. Did you call the vet?"

"She's out of town. Running a marathon." He paused. "Come here, girl."

The dog whimpered. Marcel squirmed.

"Should I pull them out?"

No, Marcel tensed. *You'll wreck her. She'll get fucking gangrene and look like that sonofabitch in Cell Block A with the red hair and stumps for hands.*

"Geez, I don't know." Val adjusted the visor.

"Didn't your old dog get quilled before?"

"Nah, she got skunked. Can't you just Google it, Norm?"

"Wi-Fi's down. She backs away whenever I get close."

"Sedative," Marcel shouted. "She needs a sedative."

Val nearly drove off the road. She swerved and backhanded Marcel. Norman was quiet.

"Can't you just try and pull them out real gentle?" Val asked. "Give her a treat and while she's distracted, carefully pluck them. I gotta pick up the girls and get to the hall."

"They're all over her face. She couldn't eat if she tried."

"You can't just pull them out," Marcel burst. "They've got barbs. Sometimes they snap. Has to be done a certain way."

"Sorry, Norman. Picked up a trucker. Blew a tire so I'm giving him a lift to the garage."

"The Mains brothers are all at karaoke," Norman said.

"Well, he can wait for them to finish. Gimme a second?" Val put Norman on hold. "What the heck are you doing?"

"What?"

"You can't be sittin' there talking. He'll recognize your voice."

"You think so?" Marcel was pleased. He wanted to be memorable. When he'd first met his infant daughter, it was at a bus stop in downtown Montreal. He'd never held a baby before. She was smaller than he'd imagined. Wrapped in a peach blanket. Tiny fists and baby ears and thimble socks. Her scent like a pecan, sweet and earthy. He'd held her up close to his face, cheek to cheek, and whisper-begged, *Please remember me.*

"That's not a good thing," Val said. "You'll get us both in trouble."

"But I can help."

"Your dog also had a run in with a porc?"

Marcel looked out the window. "My mother."

"Your mother got quilled?"

"I took care of her when my dad hit her. Treated her wounds, gave her her meds." Marcel recalled his mother's sunken eyes, the slump of her shoulders. The way she jumped whenever a car pulled into the driveway or a door slammed. Marcel slapped himself.

"Stop it," Val yelled. "You can't keep hitting yourself like that."

"Marcel?"

"Norman?" Val responded, hands shaking. She tore at the vents as though her coworker was speaking from inside them.

"Is that you?" Norman repeated.

Val stared at the screen. Marcel leaned in, the phone clearly not on hold.

"I know how to fix your dog," Marcel said. "But you got to keep her real calm." Marcel ended the call and looked at Val. "Where's the vet clinic?"

Val thumbed over her shoulder. "Just outside town."

Marcel jammed his hand between her legs again, her pants awash with his fingerprints as big as a bear's, the scent of Safeway on his lips. He buried his face in her lap and inhaled until her breath skipped.

"Drive," he commanded. "I owe Norman."

"If we get pulled over, you took me hostage."

"Is that what you want?" He covered her mouth.

The van lumbered forward.

Chapter 36

MOLLY

Molly slumped over the Yukon's steering wheel, summer spilling from the vents, Roxanne's truck, the train, long gone. What had they been up to? Kabir driving at attention, Brett a hot mess begging her not to say anything. She sighed, advancing over the tracks toward the A&W. Gary didn't like hospitals. Once he got over that she'd left the hall, he'd be relieved to see her.

She passed the crooked cedar where they'd first met. Before then, Molly'd wanted out of Crow Valley, away from the blue-collar men who worshipped her, the corporate types who shunned her. The bank teller jobs and the seasonal cafés that flogged "seed" this and "vegan" that, their reusable straws and chalk menus. Gary was new to town and off duty the first time she saw him, halfway up the cedar, saving a cat. His dress shoes were impeccably polished. She remembered the way he gaped at her after he'd climbed down, bloody claw marks all over his forearms, hair like an unmade bed. He'd made her feel rare as a white peacock. And for a girl who looked about as thrilling and exotic as a character in a picture book, feeling rare meant a quick marriage. It meant staying.

In her daze, Molly drove past the A&W and the hospital, forcing her to turn right by the old tennis courts and the town library with its peaked roof, pride flag, and muraled siding. She headed back toward the hall. She sped up only to reach Crow Valley's second level crossing, the same train she'd stopped for minutes earlier barreling down the tracks as though it was late for an appointment.

Come on, she urged, reaching for the box of Tic Tacs next to her. She flicked open the tab and shook out a couple. Across the street was the pool hall with its mint-green stucco, slot machines, and low ceilings. Molly had a sudden and vivid memory of Dale. He and a bunch of other prison guards were shooting pool. Had to have been April, because it was spring, but there was still snow on the ground and the guards' winter uniform coats were heaped all over the barstools and piled on hooks. Val was drunk, Norman was not. And Dale was . . . different. Not his usual life-of-the-party self. They'd spoken briefly, at the bar while Dale was paying his tab, settling up because he had to go home and feed his goldfish. He'd looked so withdrawn. Familiar. The way Molly caught herself in the microwave's reflection when she was answering questions about why the sky was blue or what happened to the dinosaurs but was thinking about ways to not wake up the next morning.

The back of the train came into view and Molly crept forward. When she reached the hall to turn around, Roxanne was clutching her purse, pacing her empty parking space as though it were a loved one's burial plot.

Molly tried to continue unseen. She made a sharp turn to escape, but the parking lot was a mall at Christmas, and she had no choice but to back up. When she completed the trek, dizzy and overheated, Roxanne was there, waving her in like an air traffic controller.

Shit, Molly cursed, watching Roxanne circle around to the passenger side. Gary was waiting and she still needed to pick a new song.

"I need a ride," Roxanne said, brushing a fry from the front seat and climbing in. "I have to get Dale."

The thermos. Molly had heard rumors that Roxanne kept him inside the old military relic. Sometimes Roxanne would pull up to the house to pick up her boys and Molly would catch her, headlamp on, thermos in hand, mouth frantically moving, alone. *Who's our mom talking to?* Roxanne's boys would ask as Molly zipped their coats and assembled their backpacks. *Heaven*, she'd tell them, always the same answer. *Your mom's talking to heaven*, and then she'd send them out the door, eyes twinkling with hope, unknowingly lost, so young they still wore their shoes on the wrong feet without noticing. But one day they would. One day their shoes would feel incredibly wrong and they'd stop believing in heaven, they'd stop remembering their father.

"Just up Crow Mountain Road," Roxanne said, teary-eyed, stiff.

"I know," Molly whispered. The Yukon lurched forward out of the parking lot, the windows open, Roxanne's hair lifting.

"Thanks, Molly." Roxanne adjusted her headlamp. "I didn't mean to leave him."

Molly nodded. Dale hadn't meant to leave either. He was on his way home and that was the worst part because was there anything less homey than a gas station with its cold pumps, cracked pavement, and stale snacks? Was there anything more pitiful than a man with a gas can in the middle of a fire? She was the only one who'd intended to go. Why hadn't she just gone to therapy or become an alcoholic like Val, like everyone else?

"I'll be quick," Roxanne added. "I know exactly where I left him."

Molly thought of Xavier, alone at the table, his older brothers ignoring him, the contestants traumatizing him with Southern rock. "Yes, we should hurry." Her phone rang inside her purse and she slowed to fish it out. It was Gary.

"Geez, Mol, you get lost? The boy got too much energy. B'y breaks his leg and he still turnin' cartwheels. When you gettin' here?"

"I'll be a bit longer." She signaled to turn up the mountain.

"Got a report of de prisoner at Mains Brothers Tire. B'ys up there stealing cars and eatin' a hotdog."

"Eating a hotdog?" Molly asked.

"Dat's what de report says."

"I gotta go."

"Where you at?"

"I'm driving Roxanne to her house."

"You take her truck?"

Molly pressed the phone against her cheek to muzzle Gary's voice. She'd only been to Newfoundland once, but they all shouted like they were on a fishing boat.

"Someone stole my truck," Roxanne blurted.

Molly frantically hung up and slid the phone under her seat. "He was kidding," she said. "He knows about your truck. He just has a terrible sense of humor. You know Newfoundlanders. Their favorite instrument is an ugly stick, they drink something called Screech, and they show up at people's houses wearing burlap masks. Before Christmas! I mean, who does that?"

Roxanne stared straight ahead, sullen and withering. Molly could barely stand it.

"I miss my truck," Roxanne said.

Molly tried to make eye contact, swerving. She corrected the Yukon's course. "They'll find it," she offered, reaching for Roxanne's leg, her crepe-paper office pants.

"It's not even the truck," Roxanne confessed. "It's the Tic Tacs."

"Tic Tacs?"

"Orange ones. In the truck. Special ones."

Molly could still taste the tang of citrus on her tongue. *Oh my God*, she thought, searching. Where had she put them?

"They were Dale's."

Molly rifled through the cup holders finding only sticky nickels, a pen top, Dylan's eye drops. Then she saw them, perched on the dash, masking the speedometer. Molly needed Roxanne to keep talking so she could retrieve them.

"What makes them special?" Molly asked, not wanting the answer.

"Oh, Molly," Roxanne broke. "Dale talks to me through those Tic Tacs."

Fingers grazing the dash, Molly froze. She waited for Roxanne to continue.

"Silas called it a spirit portal."

Molly leaned out the window and spat. Roxanne was now staring at a picture of Gary in his full RCMP Red Serge, swinging like a pendulum from the rearview mirror.

Roxanne pointed to the photo. Her voice cracked. "I have no one to love me."

Molly opened her mouth but didn't know what to say. *Your kids love you* wasn't the correct response. Roxanne had meant romantic love. She meant the microscopic-hairs-in-the-sink love, snow-boots-on-the-doormat love, change-your-oil-and-lick-your-neck love. I've-known-you-forever love. And though Molly'd been with half the men in Crow Valley at one time or another, there weren't many available bachelors and certainly none who could fill Dale's shoes. Roxanne had to start over. From scratch. She was no longer the exuberant sunflower she'd been when Dale was alive. No longer the jokester, the party host, the rowdy fan with the face paint. No longer young. What man could possibly get by the headlamp? The spirit portal? The rage? The grief?

"It's just . . . I never thought I'd be alone. I mean maybe when I was old, because women generally outlive their husbands, but not by decades. Not because my husband got blown up! Do you know that not once did I imagine Dale not coming home from work? Not once did I imagine I'd be a widow. No one warns you that you might be alone."

Molly offered Roxanne a sympathetic smile. "Life doesn't come with warnings, because if it did, we'd probably not bother, but if we didn't bother, we'd miss out on all the good stuff, like—"

Roxanne was staring at her anxiously and Molly squirmed. She was a fraud. Who in the hell was she to be convincing anybody that life was worth living when the pills were still in her glove compartment, right now, invisible, but directly in front of Roxanne? How could she possibly admit that Dale died in vain because even on her darkest days she'd found reasons to smile. The way Gary nuzzled her neck in the morning or sang folk songs in the shower. The joy she got from watching her boys eat—God did they ever eat!—or sleep or figure out how to do something hard like talk to a girl or fix a TV. Bear cubs, the smell of coffee, wildflowers. All of it made her feel something, even if it was only for a moment. Especially if it was.

"Well?" Roxanne said.

"Love," Molly choked. "It's all around. Even if you can't see it."

Roxanne tweaked the dial on her headlamp. "I can't see anything,"

Her A-frame came into view. *Thank God*, Molly thought. She was running out of advice.

"I'll be quick," Roxanne said, hand already poised to open the door.

Sweat formed on Molly's hairline as she creaked into the driveway, the house a shriveled mushroom, as though Dale had been the only one keeping it alive.

Roxanne slid out of the Yukon, the Tic Tacs undiscovered on the dash. Molly exhaled and shoved the plastic container into Roxanne's purse. Roxanne bypassed the front door and circled to the rear of the house, the grass lengthening with each step. A broken tire swing full of rainwater dangled from a chain. When Roxanne disappeared from view, Molly called Gary.

"Why'd you hang up?" he asked against the backdrop of rattling dishes.

"Are you in the cafeteria?"

"Ortho sent us down for dinner. Malcolm, use a fork! You comin' then?"

"As soon as I get Roxanne back to the hall."

"Ain't she supposed to be judgin'? And why'd she not take her own truck? You said she just forgot where she parked it."

"I don't know. She was having a moment. I didn't ask. A grief thing, I guess."

"Lord lumpin'. It's been over a year."

"It's been almost five since Malcolm."

Gary was silent. Molly checked her lipstick in the mirror. All she saw were laugh lines. Cry lines.

"I do think of me mudder sometimes and it guts me like she died last week. Happened the other day in the hardware store. My mudder loved nails." He paused. "You're okay though, right? It's not a little easier now dat the boys are more grown?"

Gary didn't get it. Many things made him a man. Many things made him *Gary*. Cop. Newfie. Dad. Molly was just Mom. And because she couldn't fight that, she became the town's mom. Like a closeted American Republican who fought against gay marriage while secretly blowing every gay man in his state, she fought her own identity; she fought motherhood with more motherhood. Opened a daycare. Converted their yard into a playground. She might as well get a tattoo of a goldfish cracker swimming across her heart, the cast of *Paw Patrol* on her neck.

"I'm trying."

"Never stop," he begged. "I know it's hard, but you're de best mudder. The boys and me'd be a dinghy in de North Atlantic without you."

Floating in a dinghy in the North Atlantic sounded like a vacation to Molly. She might drift all the way to Greenland or some tiny uninhabited island where kids didn't exist and she could die off the land. Or perhaps a rogue wave would flip the dinghy over and dump her into the freezing waters. She was already numb. How cold did the ocean need to be to freeze her entirely?

Molly watched from the window, lowering her phone as Roxanne ran from the house, arms flailing, legs buckling, her face a portrait of hysteria. What had she seen?

"Mol?" Gary shouted. "You still there?"

"I gotta go."

"Molly!" Roxanne shrieked, breathless and stunned, crumpling to the ground on all fours, grass in her face.

Molly climbed out of the truck. "What is it? What's wrong?"

"He fixed the deck," she panted. "Before I left tonight I yelled at him because he was supposed to fix it ages ago and he didn't and I almost fell through and now it's fixed. He fixed it."

"Who fixed it?"

"Dale."

Molly opened her mouth to speak, but what was she supposed to say? Roxanne's headlamp had twisted and her blouse was rumpled but her face contained all of life's joy: childbirth, Christmas morning, true love, first place, whipped cream. How could she squander that by telling Roxanne dead men didn't fix things? How could she tell her she was crazy when she herself was crazy too?

"How do you know it was Dale?" she finally muttered.

"The sign," Roxanne whispered, eyes pleading.

"You saw a sign? Like from heaven? What was it?"

"Literally, the sign," Roxanne pointed to a tree.

"I don't get it."

Roxanne stood. "Come."

It was getting late. Molly started to worry. "We should get back."

But Roxanne had already turned the corner. Molly staggered behind, dodging an engine, a sandbox, a rollerblade missing its wheels. When she reached the deck, Roxanne was on the top step, bent over.

"See?" Roxanne said, running her finger along the board.

"The Jepson Family," Molly read. She didn't comment on the shoddy workmanship. The sign had been used to replace a deck board. It was angled and splintered and six inches too short. Not bad for a ghost.

"See?" Roxanne repeated. "He fixed it." She traced the letters.

"But . . ." Molly began. She couldn't say *he's dead*.

"He must've just torn it off the tree and banged it into the deck with a rock or somethin'."

"A karaoke miracle," Molly offered. "Now grab him and let's go. The mayor's going to wonder where you are."

At the mention of the mayor, Roxanne's face fell. She clambered across the deck toward the barbecue and slowly turned. "He's not here."

"Who?"

"Dale." Roxanne was pale as a Newfoundlander. "I left him on the barbecue."

"Well, maybe . . ." Molly struggled. "Maybe he's gone to look for you." She erased from her mind the image of a thermos strolling down the street on tiny metal legs. She was now complicit in another woman's crazy. The entire town knew Roxanne needed to grieve and yet no one knew how to tell her. No one could find the words. They'd all been lost in the fire.

"Do you think it's possible?" Roxanne squeaked.

Molly shrugged. "Anything's possible." She hadn't killed herself, after all. And she'd been granted a re-sing. "We should go."

They walked back to the Yukon in silence. Roxanne looked small in the passenger seat.

"If the mayor says anything," Roxanne started.

Molly cut in. "I'll say you were helping me."

"I'm sorry."

Molly didn't know what Roxanne was apologizing for, but she forgave her. Postpartum aside, Dale died because of her. Roxanne's boys were fatherless because of her. Roxanne wore a headlamp because of her. Because of her, Roxanne had no one to love her.

"Me too," Molly whispered, turning down Crow Mountain Road, her thoughts on the spirit portal in case Dale was listening.

Chapter 37

BRETT

"What if someone sees us?" Brett asked.

Kabir and Brett were parked a block from the hall, idling between a dumpster and a pyramid someone had built out of discarded furniture. Brett guessed it had come from the Crow Valley Green Apartment Complex after the last bedbug infestation.

"I don't see anyone," Brett replied, straining in all directions. "If we go right now, no one will notice."

"Are we trying to be sneaky?" Daphne asked, unbelted in the back seat, remnants of burrito on her chin.

"No, we're not trying to be sneaky," Brett corrected. "We just want to be respectful of the other contestants."

"Where are they?" Daphne asked, shifting to a window. "Is the karaoke competition outside?"

"He's lying," Olivia said.

"Liv?" Brett replied. "Why would you say that?"

Olivia ignored him, fixing her gaze on her sister instead. "He's just saying that because Roxanne doesn't know we're in her truck."

"Not true," Brett said. "We borrowed it and now we're returning it."

A cardboard air freshener smelling of bathroom cleaner dangled from the rearview mirror.

Olivia rolled her eyes. "Everyone knows that Roxanne doesn't let anyone drive her truck."

"And that's why we're being sneaky," Brett added, airing out his shirt.

"Because Dad stole it."

"No, because we borrowed it." Brett turned to face his daughters. "And since we're the only people she's ever let borrow it, we have to return it without anyone noticing."

"Translation: Dad stole it."

"I did not." Brett reddened. "Kabir did."

"That's it." Kabir gestured. "Blame it on the Arab."

"In fairness, you were the one who hot-wired it."

"I've always wanted to ride in a stolen car."

"Daphne, we need to talk about your life goals."

"She also told the cop she wanted to be a bartender." Olivia twirled her gum around her finger.

Brett shifted in his seat. "Don't tell people that, Daph. Especially cops. Gary's gonna think we're alcoholics."

"Mom is an alcoholic," Olivia whispered.

"No," Brett exhaled. "She's a *recovering* one. Can we not talk about that?" He turned to address Daphne. "Next time someone asks, you tell them you want to be something respectable."

"Like what?"

"Like a nurse or a prison guard."

"What about running a pet store?" Olivia asked.

"When I was a boy, I wanted to be an actor," Kabir offered. "Like your dad."

"I don't wanna be an actor," Brett frowned.

"Sure you do. You want to be Dale. To some degree, we all do."

Brett's mouth gaped.

Olivia snapped her gum. "No one could ever be Dale."

"It's true," Daphne said, moving to the edge of her seat. "Mom said there'll only ever be one Dale."

"Your mom said that? When?"

"The last time you were pitching and you guys lost like ten–nothing."

"Put your seat belt on," Brett ordered, his face flushed. "We have to make this quick. Does anyone see anyone?"

Brett scanned the parking lot. Daphne crouched, pressed her face against the rear window.

"Nobody," Kabir declared. "Should we go?"

Brett's eyes darted.

"Yes?" Kabir asked, revving the engine.

"Girls, you see anyone?"

"No, Dad." Olivia sighed. "Just hurry up before someone comes out for a smoke."

"I'll tell you if one does," Daphne offered. "And if they do, we could just, like, hit them or something."

Brett spun in his seat. "Daphne, that's a terrible thing to say."

Daphne shrugged, eyes wild, smile crooked, the way Disney might animate a meth addict.

Kabir pulled forward, leaving the cover of the dumpster and accelerating onto the open street.

"Still no one," Daphne announced.

"Go straight," Brett gestured.

"Over the curb?" Kabir asked.

The front tires were already climbing onto the sidewalk, an ice cream wrapper flitting by. They were fifty feet from the parking lot, Roxanne's empty spot sunlit and square.

Brett could hardly stand it. "Go faster," he said, clenching his fists, his jaw.

"This is as fast as I can go." The speedometer needle hovered at 10.

"Can we get a dog?" Daphne slumped in her seat, legs in the air, flip-flops on her hands like mittens.

"Get your feet out of my face." Olivia scowled, pushing her sister's leg. "You don't even help look after the rabbit."

"Rabbits are stupid."

"Girls," Brett cautioned.

"Bubbles is *her* pet," Daphne whined.

Kabir cleared a second curb, the truck now safely in the hall parking lot, albeit far from the front door. Daphne kicked Brett's seat.

"Come on, Daph. Sit properly." Brett leaned forward, staring out the windshield.

Kabir coughed. "I played Jesus once. In a passion play."

"Isn't that appropriation?" Brett replied, his mouth dry as sawdust. The truck advanced. "I think you can go to hell for that."

"Jesus was brown, Dad." Olivia rolled her eyes.

Brett didn't know much about brown Jesus. The concept fascinated him. Were there two Jesuses? Because if there were, then that meant there could be two Dales.

"What else have you played?" Daphne asked.

Kabir counted the roles on his hand. "A doorman, hotdog vendor, terrorist number one, cop number three, a Reno passer-by-er, and pall-bearer number five."

"Our dad was a pallbearer at Dale's funeral," Daphne said. She was twiddling a hangnail.

"I remember," Kabir replied, wiping sweat from his brow. "It was a day very much like this. Hot and humid."

"He cried the whole time," Olivia added.

"We all did," Kabir said. "Dale was a good man. He helped me find an apartment when I first moved to Crow Valley. Gave me an impromptu karaoke lesson once, too, because I was singing in the wrong key."

Brett frowned. Dale had never given *him* an impromptu karaoke lesson. Marital advice, yes. Pitching tips, recipes, investment strategies. Maybe Dale just thought his singing was good enough. Brett felt an ache, heavy as a coffin and so sudden he held his hand to his chest as if it might crumble otherwise.

"Isn't that Molly's Yukon?"

"Where?" Brett swung around in his seat, contorting to see where Olivia was looking.

"There," she pointed. "Where we crashed our bikes." Olivia showed off her skinned elbow, her bruised cheek.

Brett lifted her arm and examined the scabby mess. "Brown Jesus, Liv. That looks bad. Gary didn't give you a Band-Aid?"

"Gary's sick today. It was his backup." Daphne twirled her flip-flop on the end of her finger. "The French one with the mustache."

Chapter 38

VAL

The vet clinic stood on the edge of town, between a gravel pit and Mains Brothers Tire. It was a narrow building, log cabin in the front, warehouse in the back. It had been both a restaurant and electrical shop before the vet arrived in Crow Valley with a harem of whippets and an oversized lab coat.

"Anyone going to be up there?" Marcel fiddled with the radio.

Val swallowed and tightened her grip on the steering wheel. How in the hell had she gotten herself into this? Why had she picked up Marcel when she could have kept driving? The bear might have eaten him and she could have driven home, enjoyed a secret beer in the hot tub, and shotgunned a box of Kraft Dinner. She could have shown up at karaoke, fashionably late and perfectly buzzed. Fuck, she might even have offered her services as a backup dancer. Instead, she'd let Marcel rub his strong chin all over her.

"Shouldn't be," she replied, turning up a winding road. "The pit shuts down at five, the Mains brothers are at the hall, and the vet's runnin' a marathon in Reno." The quarry, with its loping piles of gravel and sand and crushed aggregates, came into view.

"My grandpa worked in a quarry," Marcel said. "In some shit New Brunswick town. That's where he met my grandma. Where my dad was born. My dad's not even a real Frenchman."

Val stared, unblinking, out the windshield. She should've gone straight from the prison to karaoke. Who picks up a murderer, invites him into her home, and gets aroused by the anticipation of his felonious breath in her face, his youth on her skin? What kind of deviant whore mother was she? A mother whore. At this point, she might as well stage a carjacking and drive into a tree.

"My mom's family came from Paris after the war," Marcel said.

"As soon as you fix Norman's dog, you got to leave," Val blurted.

Marcel hugged the backpack to his chest and frowned. "I was in the middle of telling you something."

"Your dad's not real and your mom's from France. I get it, bon appétit. You gotta get out of here. Just look." She slammed on the brakes and gestured. "There're at least three cop cars up there at the tire shop beside the vet."

Marcel gnawed at his knuckle and stomped his foot. "You said no one would be here."

"Maybe someone saw us." Val swallowed, looking down the embankment. "Can't even turn around. We're trapped."

"I'm not trapped," Marcel said. "Move." He climbed into the back, his foot catching on the netting of the center console, Daphne's goggles crunching under his knee.

Val unbuckled, slid out of her seat, and awkwardly crossed the console, bumping the dash with her hip, her head scraping the ceiling. She plunked into Marcel's spot, tossing his backpack behind her. She was a passenger now. A prisoner? Would it change anything if they got pulled over? Would the cops believe her if she told them he'd forced her into the van at knifepoint? She checked the glove compartment for a weapon, kicked at the garbage around her feet. She uncovered a plastic spoon. She'd have to say he'd threatened her with a coloring book or a packet of sweet-and-sour sauce.

Marcel maneuvered himself behind the wheel, elbows bent, knees in his face. He adjusted the seat and straightened, cranking the gearshift like a stock car racer. Sirens wailed. "Which way?"

"Go back," Val replied. As though it were that easy. As though she could unfeel Marcel's teeth on her collarbone, his hands in her hair, his junk on her thigh. Maybe this is what Brett meant when he said *I can't go back*? What their marriage counselor meant when she said *He can't go back.* What all of Crow Valley meant when they said *You can't go back.*

Marcel shifted the van into reverse, twisting in his seat, straining to see behind him. Val studied his neck, scarred and branded, his youthful cowlick and boyish expression. She wondered if he'd felt the same after he'd poured the gasoline, after he'd lit the match and his house, his father, became engulfed. At what point did he know his actions could not be reversed?

"I can't go back," he said, righting himself. "There's nowhere to turn around. We'll get stuck or go over the side."

"Go down the embankment," she said. It was either that or walk away. Abandon the van, the old booster seat and coloring books and ketchup stains. The road trip to Sandpoint, Idaho. The acorns in the cup holder and the fastball equipment in the trunk. They could just climb out and go their separate ways. Val leaned into the window, analyzing the steepness of the drop, the depth of the weeds.

Marcel switched the gearshift into drive and accelerated, traveling fifty feet or so before driving down into the ditch, grass thick as rope, scraping the undercarriage.

The van jerked, lurching side to side, Val bracing herself against the window with both hands, her wedding band quietly knocking. They drove in silence until a road appeared, perpendicular to the ditch. Marcel gunned it up the hill, the van jostling with dizzying effect until the tires met pavement.

"We did it!" Marcel cheered, pumping his fist, smile charged.

We, Val thought.

Accomplices.

Lovers.

She gagged.

The peaked roofs of Crow Valley's wealthy side were visible in the distance, the water tower, robust and robotic, its pale blue drum noble and proud. Brett had helped Dale paint the town's name on the side in white cursive. She started to cry.

"Fuck, not again," Marcel said, swerving to avoid a dead raccoon.

Val covered her face. "I just got to get to the hall."

"I just got to get to Quebec," he snapped. "But Norman needs us."

Us.

"If my instincts are correct, this road should get us there." He turned left.

After a mile, Val spied the dull red plastic of Mains Brothers Tire's cloud-shaped sign, the aluminum siding of the vet clinic, and the quarry's moonscape lot.

Marcel turned off onto a range road and parked in a tangle of bushes. "We walk from here."

They got out of the van, careful not to slam the doors. Val listened for sirens but they'd stopped. All she could hear was the telltale hum of summer insects, the imagined buzz of the evening sun. It had been years since she'd been on this road, the last time when she drove out to pick up Brett after his truck broke down. She'd had to haul the girls out of their beds to fetch him. When she found him, he was carving their initials into a tree.

They walked single file, Marcel leading the charge. Val considered running or at least dropping off the pace, buying herself space to find a hiding spot, but then she thought of Norman's dog, face skewered and body barbed. Norman was always there for her. Through shifts she could barely finish, timeless weekends and late nights and silent phone conversations. She hadn't even been there for him when Marcel escaped. She carried on.

"That it?" Marcel pointed to a squat aluminum building through the trees.

Val nodded.

He veered onto the shoulder and kicked an old fence post draped in unruly barbed wire. "You gotta knife?"

She didn't tell him she'd already looked. He scanned his pockets for her phone. Maybe he'd left it in the van. "Could be one in the trunk," she said, retreating.

Marcel eyed the clinic. "Hurry up."

Val jogged down the road, a hot mess of middle age, her thighs groping each other with each stride, her eucalyptus and rosehip deodorant staining the air and her shirt. When she reached the van, a concert of wasps was swarming the front bumper. Inside, her phone was ringing. She climbed into the back seat and answered in haste.

"Val?" Norman whispered from the phone's speaker. "You there?"

"I'm here," she panted, pretending to search, in case Marcel was watching.

"Police are at Mains Brothers Tire," Norman said. "Someone called in a tip."

"I know that. We almost drove right up on them. We're on a back road now, hiding. At least the sirens seemed to have stopped."

"You and Marcel still together?"

"Yeah, we're just out here buying snorkels and planning our retirement in Palm Springs. Come on, Norm. You think I could get rid of him?"

"Sasha keeps trying to lie down, but she can't. Porc got her on both sides. She keeps staring at me for help. It's killing me, Val. Almost enough to make me . . ."

"Drink. Tell me about it. We're coming." Val hung up, quickly glanced at her messages, A selfie from Olivia with Brett looking over-groomed and nervous as a new prisoner. She tucked the phone into her bra and scrambled out of the van. She ran.

"Any luck?" Marcel, bleeding, had found some way to remove the barbed wire and it was wound around his wrist.

Val shook her head.

The area behind the vet clinic was sparsely wooded. They wove through the spindly trees as if searching for a place to set up camp. A single window the width of a movie poster broke up the siding. Behind Mains Brothers was an altar of worn tires and a pair of Camaros on blocks. No sign of the cops.

Marcel stripped off his shirt, revealing his soft and scarred torso, an indiscernible branding below his rib cage. A chicken-scratch tattoo over his nipple: *Isabelle.* He wrapped the shirt around his hand like a boxing glove and punched the window. It shattered on impact, the sound ricocheting off Val's teeth, making her cringe.

Marcel cleared the frame, hoisted himself, and slithered shirtless into the darkness of the clinic. Somewhere in the building, a fan whirred. No alarm. Val leaned against the building, her head the weight of a globe, and dreamed of alcohol.

Chapter 39

ROXANNE

"Could you drop me off around back?" Roxanne edged forward in her seat. "I didn't tell anyone I was leaving." She wondered if anyone was looking for her. What they'd think if they'd known she'd run out on the competition. If they acted like they knew, she'd give them zeros. Raise their taxes.

Molly made an abrupt turn toward the rear of the hall. "You have your key?"

"Not for the back door." Roxanne tucked her hair into the head-lamp strap.

Molly pulled up beside the rear metal door and shifted the Yukon into park. "I'll go 'round front and let you in."

Roxanne slid out of the passenger seat. "Thanks again for the ride," she said, climbing the curb.

Molly nodded, maneuvered the steering wheel with the heel of her hand, her arms slim and tanned the color of Kraft Dinner. Roxanne thought her lipstick looked as though it had been applied with a restaurant crayon. Her nails were a bit much, all metallic and pointed, but at least they matched her dress. She'd give her that.

When the Yukon was out of sight, Roxanne slumped against the siding. *Am I crazy? I'm crazy.* She shook her head. Were miracles real? Could dead men fix things? Did ghosts carry tool belts? She laughed hysterically, acknowledging that her unresolved grief might finally have mutated into madness. The kind of batshit crazy Dale used to describe the inmates at Crow Valley Correctional as being. Inmates who ate paper or talked to ants or jerked off to *Jeopardy!* Inmates who punched themselves in the face.

But the sign. She remembered when Dale had brought it from work, how he'd handpicked the inmate to make it because of his impeccable cursive. The boys were little then. Roxanne had just had her tubes tied and watched from their bedroom window as Dale dragged the stepladder, the boys in their late spring digs of underwear and rain boots and muddy knees, leading their dad around the yard until they found the perfect tree. She'd closed her eyes, the clap of the hammer a lullaby, her family complete.

I'm nuts.

She rooted through her purse for a Mentos. Instead: Tic Tacs. She pulled out the warped box, cupped it in her hands like it was something delicate and feeble: a baby bird, an organ ready for transplant. Some of the candy was missing. She was certain the box had been half full this morning. Half empty. She flipped over the container, stroked the blistered plastic, then flicked open the top. Roxanne brought it to her lips, as if it were a prison walkie-talkie. She spoke quietly, though she was alone.

"Did you fix the deck?" she interrogated the Tic Tac box, then brought it to her ear like a conch shell. She closed her eyes and counted. One one thousand, two one thousand, three. Silence. The only thing she heard was time, and it was lonely and cruel and moving.

"Of course you're not going to answer," she mumbled, sliding the Tic Tacs back into her purse. She hated that he'd gone quiet in his last year, or few months, or whatever. Maybe not in public. Out there, he was still the town mascot, a Macy's parade balloon, the one and only Dale, the man of the hour, of all the hours, but at home, he was different. Distracted? Troubled? Consumed, and by what she hadn't been able to figure out and that was perhaps the worst part.

Maybe love really was all around and she might find it again. Or something like it. A role model for the boys, a part-time lover. Someone to put up the Christmas lights, or to split the dinner bill, or to vent with about work or parenting or living. Someone to go to Vegas with. But never knowing what had been bothering him in those last few months was torture. It gnawed at her. Slow death by the unknown.

She zipped her purse and stared up at the mountains in the distance. There was still snow on the glacier. She imagined Dale standing at the top of it waiting for a gondola to heaven.

Beside her, a rattle. Roxanne corrected her posture, hovered in front of the door, waiting for Molly to let her in. If much more time lapsed someone would come looking. The MC could only delay the competition for so long. The door swung open and the mayor stepped out, his eyes approaching bloodshot, his tie loose as a lei. Roxanne froze.

"I just—needed some fresh air," she stammered.

The mayor staggered, opened his mouth, and vomited into the cedar mulch. "I think there's something wrong with the poutine."

He remained hunched, hands on his knees and head down, heaving.

"I think it was the gravy," he droned, the gravy part discharging in lumps.

Sure, Roxanne thought, her nose twitching, the smell of beer, sour and hot, rising from the mulch like sauna steam.

"Yes," she agreed, "it tasted a bit off." She wondered if she should touch him, whether she should place a comforting hand on his back, offer a few warm strokes of encouragement. Was there a more universal response to barfing than rubbing the barfer's back? She studied the mayor's knurled spine through his pinstriped shirt and held out her hand. She thought of her boys when they got sick. How their bodies went flush and limp, boneless. They practically made love to the toilet seat. Even Dale, when he'd had too much pie or sun or whiskey, climbed half inside the bowl. She shivered.

"Hold my hair," the mayor whispered.

"Huh?" Roxanne replied.

"My hair." He lifted a stubby finger toward his head. "Hold it," he slurred.

Roxanne stared at the back of his head. His hair was an inch long, an inch and a half at best, and it was gelled. At his feet, a wet pile of fries.

"Please," he said, but it came out as a growl.

Where was Molly? Roxanne looked expectantly at the door. *Where was Dale?* She opened her hand, stared at her palm apologetically, and then cupped the mayor's head.

"Oh, yeah," he drooled, stumbling to the side.

This was good, Roxanne thought. The mayor couldn't share a moment like this and then fire her. This was her opportunity to make things right.

"You got this," she whispered.

She couldn't hold his hair without sort of tugging it the way one might during sex, so she sort of stroked his forehead instead.

"You're almost done," she added, this time with authority. And then she placed her free hand on his back and softly rubbed.

The door clicked open behind them, a metal slingshot. "Oh," Molly said.

Roxanne motioned aggressively for Molly not to say anything, noticing for the first time that one of Molly's shoes was held together with duct tape. "Molly," Roxanne commanded. "Go to the canteen immediately and tell them to stop serving the poutine."

"They're out of poutine," Molly replied.

"Good," said Roxanne. "Because there's something wrong with it."

"Right. I will let them know." Molly fished a rock from the mulch bed and stuck it in the door. "They're waiting for you," she said. "They just called the next contestant to the stage."

"Tell them I'll be right there."

"You too," she said, nodding toward the mayor. "The garden committee was hoping you'd make an announcement about volunteers to weed the flower beds."

Sweat pearled on Roxanne's chest. Her underwear itched. "Got it," she replied. "We'll be right there."

Molly slipped back inside. The mayor straightened, his face wet and red as a Valentine.

"Do I look okay?" He careened.

Roxanne winced and then used her blouse to wipe the mayor's

drunken face. He cleared his throat, adjusted his tie, and stuck out his chin. A soldier ready for battle.

"You're good," she said brushing a bud from his shoulder. "Now get in there. I got a roll of mints in my purse. I'll bring you one."

"Roxanne," he slurred, "I know I should do this onstage, in front of all of Crow Valley, but I don't think I can." He clutched his stomach. "Because of the poutine. So, um, I just wanted to thank you for your service." From his pocket, he retrieved a pin. It was cumbersome, round, silver. EXCELLENCE was engraved across the top, IN SERVICE at the bottom, and in the middle, the number 25. A cluster of stars filled in the background. It was gaudy and heavy. Excellent.

"Thank you," she said. "I know . . . I know I've been . . . a bit distracted . . . sometimes. On the job. It's just, I—"

He held up his hand to stop her, swayed as if trying to reclaim his sobriety, and then looked her straight in the eye. "I knew Dale," he said, raising a pointed finger. "I never told you this before, because, well, I never told anyone and you can't tell anyone, but once I drove drunk, really it was only the one time, and I crashed. On the Cougar Creek Bridge. It was years ago, but that's why it needs fixing. And, well, Dale found me and he didn't tell anyone. He gave me a second chance. That's why I don't drink and drive anymore. I mean, it only happened once, but I don't. I don't do it anymore."

Roxanne nodded.

"My point is, I think Dale would want you to have a second chance too. That's why I keep giving you chances—second chances, third chances, fiftieth chances, anniversary pins—because he did that for me. And I think . . . I think he'd want you to have a second chance too. At living."

Roxanne clasped her hands in front of her chest, a mix of gratitude and defense.

The mayor's expression darkened. "But here's the thing about chances. They expire. Tick, tick." With that, he dry-heaved and staggered inside.

Roxanne took a cleansing breath and closed her eyes. The mayor's

words burned and she could smell his stomach on her sleeve. She
rolled the offending part to her elbow and plucked the errant pine
needles that had collected in her socks.

The eight o'clock sun was made to order, the temperature warm
bread, the light majestic and turning everything to art. Roxanne bathed
in its pink glow, but a flicker of panic flared in her chest. Even if she
wanted to start living, she didn't know how. *Not* living is what she
knew. Standing knee-deep in grief is how she functioned. She believed
Dale would come back with the same fervor a Christian believed in
the second coming of Christ. It was the only way. But the thermos was
missing. How could she possibly move on when he was missing? She
dug the Tic Tacs back out of her purse and squeezed the container until
it cracked. *WHERE ARE YOU?*

A seagull, beak hooked and yellow as a hard hat, swooped and
landed on a signpost across the parking lot. *Dale?* she whispered into
the breeze. *Is that you?* The gull flicked a wing and turned its back. She
asked the same of a squirrel, scampering up a tree with video game
speed, its tail black and exaggerated. Then a wasp, then an ant, then a
Popsicle stick stained orange. Finally Roxanne swiped her hand through
the air, eyes squeezed with concentration, searching for an anomaly:
pressure in her fingertips, heat in her palm, weight on her wrist. She felt
nothing, only grief, shackled and chained to her ribs, holding her prisoner in the bowel of a ship.

Chapter 40

MARCEL

Marcel stood in the vet clinic's examination room, distracted by an avian anatomy chart pinned to the wall. In the corner, a metal cage housed a fancy bird the size of a pigeon. Marcel studied the poster and then asked the bird, "Is that you?"

The bird showed its crimped feet.

"You're a nice boy," Marcel said, transfixed by the bird's tiny black eye. It reminded him of his mother's sewing pins.

Marcel moved closer, his nose practically wedged between the cage bars. "Hi, little bird."

The bird bowed its head.

A sign on the counter read: PLEASE KEEP YOUR FINGERS OUT OF ROLF'S CAGE.

"Rolf," Marcel whispered. "Who's a good boy?"

Rolf tilted his head to the left. Marcel tilted his head to the right. Marcel stared into the creature's little pin eye. It seemed to be alive now, swirling, and churning. A storm on a weather map. No, it was something even more powerful. As if the entire solar system operated inside Rolf. The sun, the planets and moons, the asteroid belts. Marcel closed his eyes and felt a rush of solar wind pass over him, warming his lashes, electrifying his brows.

"You almost done in there?" Val called from outside, her voice hoarse.

"I think I met Jesus," Marcel replied.

"Jesus?" Val appeared in the broken window, hair on alert, annoyed. "If that's the case, then ask him where the medicine is. Hurry up."

"I feel warm."

"Tell me about it." Val fanned herself.

"And immense love. Just like the chaplain described."

Val gave him the side-eye and stared at the cage. "Rolf made you feel that way?"

Marcel nodded.

"Christ, we don't have time for crazy." She plucked a shard of glass from the window frame, heaved herself up, and climbed into the vet clinic. A goldfish poster hung above a sink. She placed a hand on Marcel's forehead. "You don't feel warm."

He frowned and put his shirt back on.

She studied a row of tidy white cabinets fixed to the wall. "Think you'll find what you're looking for in those?"

"I've never felt love like that before."

Val raised her brow. "I've seen the picture of you and your mom back in your cell. She loves you hard."

"I'm hard to love."

"Nah," Val waved, opening a cupboard. There were rows of compact glass bottles, four deep, all neatly labeled. "Everyone's lovable. You just got a lot of baggage. Trauma, they call it nowadays. We all have it in some form or another. That's the price of living."

Val opened a drawer and held up a packaged syringe.

"My mother loved me," Marcel choked.

"Of course she did," Val replied. "You looked after her."

"I washed her hair when Dad broke her arm."

Val nodded.

A cage lined with shavings rested on the counter. Marcel said, "I used to read this book called *La Souris Noire*."

"The Black Mouse?" Val rested her hand on a stack of pilled towels.

"It was about this boy whose father was a sniper in World War Two. Russian." Marcel paused. "Did you know that the Soviet Union had the best marksmen? They were the only country that specifically trained sniper units in the decade before the war. Anyway, so this boy's father goes to Stalingrad. Mom's dead, kid's twelve, looks after himself. Every time the father kills someone, his son sees a black mouse."

"Sounds cute," Val said, eyeing the wall clock.

"But the mice don't leave and they start eating all the boy's food and crawling all over him. At first it's not a big deal. There are only four. Dad is only average in his unit, but as the battle continues, his shot gets better, and the mice multiply. By the end of it, Dad comes home and is awarded the Distinguished Service Cross, but finds his son dead, eaten alive by four hundred and fifty-three mice."

Val's mouth gaped. "And this was a kid's book?"

Marcel shrugged. Rolf squawked.

"God, Marcel. Who in the hell writes books like that for kids? *La Souris Noire*, by Giant Asshole. No wonder you're fucked up."

"I thought I was fucked up because of my dad."

"There's also that. Look, we gotta get out of here. If I don't get to that karaoke competition soon, police are going to send a search party. And don't forget Norman's dog, right? Why we're here."

Marcel snapped into action, removing bottles at random from the cabinet and tucking them inside his shirt.

"I already took some syringes," Val said, holding up a sample. "That all we need?"

"Grab some of those towels," Marcel pointed.

Val took the entire stack. "Let's get out of here."

Marcel got a charge. Guard Val was back, barking orders, direct and strutting. She tossed the towels out the window, hauled herself up on the frame like a sea witch and turned her head. "You coming?" she asked.

"Yes!" Marcel hollered, rushing across the room.

"Shhh . . ." she warned.

He stopped in front of the sink and pointed at the fish poster. "Why does that goldfish have black fins?"

"Beats me," Val replied. "Maybe it went to a funeral."

The bottles clinked inside Marcel's shirt, a tiny wedding reception.

He halted short of the window. "What about Rolf?" he asked, touching the cage.

"Leave him," Val called from outside.

"But he loves me," Marcel countered. "I felt it."

"He belongs in a cage," Val argued, half-whispering. She looked over her shoulder and then back at him. "He won't survive out here."

"Val?"

"What?"

"You think I can survive out here?" He swallowed.

Val exhaled. "Anyone can survive. You just gotta stop hittin' yourself in the face. Get your GED. Work real hard. And Marcel?"

He waited.

"You gotta forgive."

Marcel noticed her breath catch as the words came out.

"You too," he said, followed by a moment of silence so powerful Marcel felt his knees give until a bottle dropped from his shirt, shattering on the floor. His shoulders slumped.

"Let's go," she said, back to business.

"At least let me say good-bye."

"Sweet mother of 1918. You ain't being shipped out to France. Should I close my eyes so you can give him a nice big kiss?"

"Would he let me do that?"

"No!" She started counting in German.

"Fine."

Val turned away, a hand still on the frame. A bee flew in the window.

Marcel leaned his head on the cage. "'Bye, Rolf. Thanks for everything."

The bird hopped to a dowel next to a food tray and pecked at a sunflower seed.

"I love you." Marcel sniffled and, clutching the vials in his shirt, rolled out the window, narrowly missing the barbed wire he'd wrangled earlier.

"Let's get this done," Val said, wiping sweat from her forehead. "We go straight to Norman's and then you do whatever."

"Go to Quebec."

"Right, Quebec; St. Hubert; vet school; Anchorage, Alaska. Don't care, but you gotta go." Her hand gestures we~ ¸ intense. Poses from a feminist protest poster. A pussy march. It made him hard. He loved feminists, with their angry uteruses, handmade clothes, and half sleeves. Maybe he'd marry one and she could turn him into a submissive little bitch. It would be a good way to reinvent himself. No one would suspect him as a criminal. They could have children and he'd vacuum and take care of bedtime. He'd buy all the groceries, make all the dentist appointments and Halloween costumes. Sign all the permission slips. He'd do all the invisible labor. He'd learn to knit and he would make her the finest pussy hat and at night when she was done being a feminist, he'd tie her up and make love to her so hard. He'd fuck her like it was still 1802.

Marcel grabbed his junk but abruptly stopped. Rolf might be able to see through the window and he didn't want the bird to think he was a pervert. He needed to do better if he was going to make it out here.

He followed Val back through the woods, skimming the adolescent trees, awkward and eager. At least one more vial dropped, disappearing into a circus net of ferns.

Val was out of breath by the time they reached her van, the family-ness of the vehicle striking: roof rack, handprints, dashboard sunflower. He dumped the bottles onto the floor of the passenger seat, carefully placing the barbed wire coil on his lap.

Val plunked beside him, adjusting the steering wheel like she'd never driven before, and exhaled, disrupting a curl of hair above her brow. "What's with the barbed wire, anyway?"

Marcel put on his seat belt. "In case I have to kill myself."

Chapter 41

BRETT

"Go, go, go," Brett encouraged, his eyes searching the hall parking lot.

Kabir accelerated toward Roxanne's open spot. A quick turn and they were in.

"We did it!" Brett whooped as Kabir inched to a halt and jammed the gearshift into park. Brett made victory fists, drummed the dash, then slapped Kabir's back. "We freaking did it."

"Yay, we stole a car," Olivia said with the enthusiasm of a server working the continental breakfast. "So proud."

"Olivia, where's all this negativity coming from? We did a good thing here."

"What good thing? Get your feet off me!"

"Daphne, put your feet down," Brett cautioned. "That's the second time I've asked you to stop."

Daphne retracted her legs and then slowly, methodically, let them fall back in Olivia's general direction like a minute hand.

Kabir turned to Daphne. "You know, listening is an important skill if you want to be a bartender."

"She's not going to be a bartender," Brett intervened. "Girls, grab your stuff and go inside."

"What about our bikes?" Daphne asked, biting her T-shirt collar.

Brett pondered. "What about them?"

"They're still at Big Al's."

"Olivia, why didn't you tell me that earlier?" He covered his face with his hands.

"How do you think we got to Big Al's?"

How would he explain the bikes to Val? The more he tried to fix things, the more lies he told. *I'm a filthy liar.*

"I had to ride a bicycle when I played cop number three."

"I see someone!" Daphne squealed.

"Where?" Brett scanned the front of the building. Molly scuffed alongside the wall in her crumpled dress, legs skinny as a malnourished teen, a sweatshirt tied around her waist. A cigarette dangled from her lips.

"Nobody panic," Brett said, his neck muscles cable-tight.

"Nobody's panicking," Olivia replied, pinching a Tic Tac between her thumb and finger.

Brett stared. "Where'd you find that?"

"On my seat."

"Don't eat it."

"Here she comes," Kabir said.

"Go seduce her," Brett ordered.

Daphne collected her flip-flops. "What does 'seduce' mean?"

Kabir placed his hand on the door. "Watch and learn," he said getting out of the truck.

Brett moved to the edge of his seat and sat tall. How did he have less swagger than a man who grew up in a refugee camp?

Kabir tilted his head, just a touch; Brett guessed no more than ten degrees. He copied. Then Kabir ran his hand through his hair, his shoulder chiseled as a Swiss mountain. His hand was beautiful, tanned and strong, without being clownish. A scar below his knuckle indicated some past atrocity.

Molly stopped in front of him, lips fidgeting. She tapped the ash from her cigarette, clutched a tiny lock of hair and twirled it around her finger.

"Ah, come on," Brett hollered.

Kabir stepped closer to Molly, his hip bumping hers as he gestured toward the truck, his eyes a sad puppy rescued from a dogfighting ring.

Brett ran his hand through his hair, and then remembered a bird had pooped on his head earlier.

Molly seemed to laugh as Kabir placed his hand on her bare shoulder. Brett didn't remember the last time he'd seen Molly really laugh. Grade five? Two? "What's so funny?" Brett asked.

"No idea, but this looks easy." Daphne replied. "Can I try to seduce you, Daddy?"

"Okay, we're done here." Brett got out of the truck. "Let's go."

"That is so disgusting, Daphne," Olivia whined. "Don't ever say that again."

The girls followed Brett onto the sidewalk.

"Everything okay here?" Brett asked. "Geez, Kabir. Never realized how short you were." Brett used his hand for measure, bringing it from the top of Kabir's head across to his nose.

"One does not reach one's full height on refugee camp rations."

Molly pouted and then turned her attention toward Brett. "Roxanne's around back. You get inside now, and she'll never know you stole her truck. Go, quick!"

"Told you Dad stole it," Olivia said.

Kabir clapped Molly's hand between both of his and whispered, "Thanks." His eyes said it in French. And then he slipped through the front door like someone's space heater had caught fire. Molly followed, then the girls. Brett trailed behind. Last place.

Chapter 42

VAL

Norman Blanchard lived in a brown A-frame a mile west of the vet clinic where the wildfires had ripped through last summer. His house had not been damaged. Just when it appeared he'd lose everything, the wind shifted, taking the flames with it and leaving behind the fawn that Kabir saved and took a selfie with.

Val turned on her blinker. She wished she'd checked the vet staff room for a fridge on the off chance there was a beer hiding inside. Her hands jittered.

Norman was in the window. He was wearing a plaid shirt, colonial red, his hair loose at his shoulders, when Val pulled into the driveway. He motioned for Val and Marcel to park around back near his retrofitted minibus.

"Norman," Marcel shouted.

"He can't hear you." Val scooped up the pile of syringes she'd dumped in the center console. "Come on." She waved. "Grab the medicine."

Marcel obliged, hurriedly collecting the vials and trailing Val to the back door.

Through the tightly woven screen, Norman was a Picasso version of himself.

"Welcome," he called, throwing open the door. The hinges creaked and Val was reminded of her grandparents' hunting cabin, with its bloodstained doormat and yellow stove.

Val shook her head. "Don't judge me."

"Judgment is not the job of men," Norman replied. "Marcel," he said extending a welcoming arm.

Marcel went in for a hug.

"What have you done to your mustache?"

"Wrecked it, didn't I?" Marcel pulled at it with a violence that made Val wince. He wound up to punch himself, but Norman intervened, calmly taking Marcel's wrist. "It can be fixed, but first, please help my dog. Come, Sasha."

A distressed shepherd-lab mix pattered into the room.

"Holy shit." Marcel dropped the vials onto Norman's kitchen table next to a plate of fried eggs and tomatoes. "It's worse than I thought." The dog whimpered. "I gotta wash my hands."

Norman showed Marcel to the sink. Val ate a tomato off Norman's plate. Her colleague lived simply, except for his big-screen TV and collection of violins.

With the water running and Marcel's back turned, Norman whispered, "What were you thinking?"

"I told you not to judge me," she hissed. "He almost got eaten by a bear."

"A bear?" Norman leaned back in an office chair that doubled as a dining chair. "Where?"

"Crow Mountain Road." Val flicked a tomato seed from her collar.

"What was Marcel doing there?"

Val slouched into a chair beside him and threw up an arm. "He was coming around the mountain."

They stopped talking as Marcel shut off the tap and dried his hands on a dishtowel.

"Norman, I'm going to need your help. Flat-jawed pliers and a pair of tweezers."

"Yes," Norman replied, jumping from his chair, which rolled away in the excitement. "I've got both." He disappeared down the hall toward a linen closet and returned with the tweezers.

"They clean?" Marcel asked.

Norman shrugged. "I don't really use them."

"Pliers?"

"In the toolbox. Give me a minute." Norman slid a toolbox out from under the kitchen sink and placed it on the linoleum floor. He sat in a straddle and rummaged through layers of screwdrivers and nails before yanking out the pliers, their rubber handles yellow and peeling.

Marcel sorted through the vials of sedatives and antibiotics he'd lifted from the vet. "Acepromazine," he read with crossed eyes. "This'll do."

Val watched him prepare the syringe with fascination. She enjoyed his hard focus, the way his mouth opened slightly as he drew back the plunger with an expert touch.

Norman knelt beside Sasha, cradling the dog awkwardly. "Easy, girl."

Marcel got down on one knee. "Cover her eyes," he instructed, the syringe loaded.

Norman did so with the dexterity of a hypnotist. Sasha didn't even squirm. Val buried her face, unable to watch, opening her eyes only when Marcel whispered, *"Bonne fille."* Good girl. *Too late for that*, she thought remembering the weight of Marcel's hips on hers, his white-hot chest. There wasn't an alcohol strong enough to drink herself or her marriage back to good.

The dog slipped into what Val hoped was a dreamy sleep. With precision, Marcel started removing quills, careful not to snap them. When he moved to Sasha's face, Norman hummed. It was a tune Val had heard him play on the violin. Bach? Did Bach do violin stuff?

She rested her elbows on the table, exhausted, and fixed her eyes on the salt and pepper shakers. They were porcelain, black and white, smooth and phallic, with arm stumps and simple faces. The salt and pepper shook from their eyes and mouths. Val had noticed them the last time she was over when Norm needed a boost. When nestled together, the shakers hugged. They were separate now, the pepper presiding over Norman's neglected plate of eggs, the salt with her no-good arms outstretched, nothing in front of her.

"Got any peroxide?" Marcel asked, after forty minutes of focused work.

Val jumped.

"Val, grab the peroxide from the bathroom. It's in the medicine cabinet."

Val eased herself up and went to the bathroom. Framed photographs lined the hallway: Norman in his Olympic tracksuit, his daughter dressed for prom, and a dated picture from a charity golf tournament: her, Norman, Dale, and Trevor. They'd come in first and were posing around a trophy. And friggin' Dale had sunk a hole in one. She took a step closer, examined her face in the photo. She looked . . . happy?

The medicine cabinet was nearly empty. A box of Q-tips, nail clippers, and a bottle of calamine lotion were the only things inside other than the peroxide. She snagged a handful of cotton balls from a fishbowl on the back of the toilet.

"Can I help?" she asked, setting the supplies on the kitchen floor.

Marcel ignored her and continued treating the dog's wounds.

"Paayikw, niishu, nishtu," Norman said, standing. "I'll get her favorite blanket. It's in the bus."

Val followed Norman outside. "Now what do we do?"

"Beats me," Norman replied. "You're the one who picked him up."

"I saved his life."

Norman climbed into the bus, Val at his heels. "What do you do in here, anyway?" she asked.

"It's my fishing bus. Or camping one," he said, collecting a multicolored quilt from the front seat. "It's whatever bus I need it to be."

"We can't go back in there without a plan. What are we going to do?"

"First, I'm going to make him dinner."

"Next, you're going to take him to a movie? Tell him how beautiful he is?"

Norman stopped, a laundry bundle of quilt in his arms. "What exactly did you do with him, Val?"

Val reddened.

"Then I'm going to clean up that terrible mustache." Norman snapped the bus door shut and meandered up the path back to the house.

"Fine," Val caught up to him. "But after that. How do we get rid of him?"

Norman opened the screen door with his bare foot. "I have an idea."

Inside, Marcel, all limbs, lay stretched out on the floor opposite Sasha. He sang to the dog while stroking a patch of her head that hadn't been quilled. Norman went to the fridge.

"Forty days," Val mumbled. "Just make it to forty-one." The salt shaker fell from the table.

Chapter 43

BRETT

Brett led the girls to his table and motioned for them to sit. He kept his head down, but caught a coworker's wink. He ignored it. The MC crossed the stage as his onetime lover, Caroline Leduc, returned to her table in the shadows. He'd not only ruined his marriage, he'd destroyed hers. Even Dale hadn't been able to persuade Caroline's ex-husband to take her back. Brett had a sudden desperate longing for Val. The old Val who laughed too loud and took an extra running start before she slammed onto the Slip 'N Slide. Now she just sat on the deck like a person twice her age. He ordered a beer.

"When's it your turn?" Daphne asked.

Brett frantically fingered through the karaoke program searching for Caroline's name. "Molly said I missed my turn," he said, distraught.

Olivia rolled her eyes for the tenth time since they'd sat down. Daphne swung her legs and ate cold fries off a stranger's plate. She dipped her thumb in a ramekin of clotted gravy.

"What am I going to do?"

"Call Mom," Olivia said, not looking up from her phone. "She'll know what to do."

"Where is your mom?" Brett asked, looking for a watch he didn't wear. "She should've been here by now."

"Text her."

Brett set his phone on the table but was distracted by the man onstage singing "The Fight Song." He looked like he'd escaped from prison, arms covered in tattoos and a scar on his cheek, angled like war paint, a missing tooth.

"Who is this guy?" Brett asked, scrolling to find the Messages app.

Gravy glistened from Daphne's hair. She'd moved on from the fries and was eating the crust of a BLT.

Olivia sighed. "I think that's Jenna Fisher's dad. Or brother."

Brett flattened the program in front of him. "Says Tyler Fisher." He mumbled the song title under his breath, "So is it her dad or her brother?"

"Same thing."

"No, Liv, it's actually not the same thing."

"Geez, relax. Why do you have to be so judgy all the time?"

"Liv, I don't even know what you're talking about." He looked to Daphne for assistance. "I just said that being someone's dad and being someone's brother are two different things."

"Are you saying that a guy can't be both a dad and a brother? Because you're my dad, unfortunately, and you're also Uncle Darrell's brother."

"That's not what I was saying."

The hall hushed as Tyler Fisher staggered across the stage as though fighting a Siberian blizzard. Brett marveled and took mental notes. Val had advised him that a strong physical performance could give him an edge. He understood what she meant.

"Why are you standing?" Daphne asked, face reddening.

Brett froze. "I don't know." He sat down, nearly missing his chair. He hit his elbow on a plate, pinging a fork onto the floor. Kabir was coming from the bar, and picked it up.

"What do you think?" Kabir nodded toward the stage, pulled a chair from the adjacent table, and sat.

"Dad thinks a man can't be both a brother and a father."

"No, Olivia. You've got it wrong. I never said that."

Tyler hit a high note, a hard one for a dude, sharp and feminine. Kabir whistled. Brett frowned.

"He's one of my apprentices." Kabir smiled, covering a tablecloth stain with his Sprite.

"That guy's a firefighter?" Brett gaped. "Looks like a crack dealer."

"Crack's not so popular in Crow Valley," Kabir replied, helping himself to some fries. "Fentanyl, coke, a little bit of meth."

Olivia looked up curiously from her phone.

"And no, he's not a firefighter. He's one of my voice students."

"Voice students?" Brett crossed his arms over his chest. "Since when do you have voice students? Are you even qualified to do that? Let me guess, the refugee camp had a boys' choir."

"Anyone's qualified to do anything if someone will pay for it."

"But I asked you a month ago if you'd listen to me sing and give me some tips. You said no."

"You offered me a cooler bag as payment."

"It was a nice bag!"

"You got it free from the liquor store."

"That's true." Daphne said. "Remember when I broke the zipper and you said not to worry because it was free and you could probably just go and get another one as long as that bitch Terry wasn't working."

"I never . . ."

"I like Terry," Kabir offered.

"Question," Olivia said, resting her elbows on the table.

Brett noticed Olivia was wearing lipstick that she hadn't had on a minute ago. It was far too bold for a thirteen-year-old. It was Anna Nicole Smith. It was the entire Dutch red-light district. He thought he should tell her to tone it down. Any responsible father or brother would, but behind her scattered freckles and flushed cheeks, the tiny turquoise ice cream cone earrings she never took off, her scrawny tree-climbing arms, was a girl more terrifying than Satan.

"As I was saying," Olivia continued, "is Tyler Jenna Fisher's dad?"

Kabir took a swig of his pop and reset the can over the stain. "He definitely has a kid," he replied. "Don't know if her name's Jenna, but he did leave a lesson one night to pick his daughter up from softball."

"That's totally Jenna," Olivia said, beaming.

"He does have a brother, too. Not a very good singer, though. Little too nasal," Kabir mocked.

"See?" Olivia said, directing her eyes at Brett. "Dad and brother."

"Oh my God," Brett covered his face, his hands so tense he thought his fingers might snap. "I never said that."

Kabir smacked Brett congenially on the back. "It's okay. You're raising a strong daughter. And strong daughters grow up to be strong women. That is a good thing."

"My tooth came out!" Daphne held out her hand. Floating in a pool of blood and saliva was a little tooth. Everywhere else, dirt.

Brett plucked the tooth from her palm, wiped it on his pants. "Olivia, take Daphne to the bathroom and help her wash her hands." He asked with caution, expecting a fight, expecting Olivia to tell him how unsupportive he was, or that he didn't understand her because they didn't have Instagram or Snapchat in the olden days.

"Daph, let's go wash your hands." Olivia grabbed a napkin, wiped Daphne's chin, and guided her sister toward the bathroom.

Brett texted Val. *Where r u??*

Stopped at Norm's. Dog got quilled

Oh no. She ok???

Think so. Just cleaning her up and then I'll be down. You good? You sing yet?

I missed my turn

Talk to Roxanne

K

That it?

Olivia's mean to me

Yeah, she can be mean sometimes

Do you think she might be bipolar?

She's a teenager. I wouldn't worry about it.

K. Miss you.

Miss you too.

I'm sorry.

Val didn't respond. Brett put his phone away and exhaled. Across from him, Kabir was pensive, spinning a ceramic sugar packet holder around the table.

"You want a singing tip?" he asked.

Brett moved to the edge of his seat.

"Two things. One, you have to pick the right song."

"I did that, but someone else already sang it."

"Then sing something else."

"And two?" Brett asked, massaging his hands as though they were someone else's.

Kabir leaned in, pointed a finger at Brett. "You must sing with conviction. You must believe it."

"I don't have a good backup."

"You don't need one. Pick anything, as long as you sing it with conviction."

"I missed my turn."

"Then ask the judges to fit you in."

"Will you do it?"

"Must I do everything around here?" Kabir sighed.

"Ask Roxanne, please?"

Tyler finished "The Fight Song" on his knees.

"She doesn't like me," Kabir replied.

"Why do you say that?"

"I couldn't save her husband."

Brett sighed. "Good point. You should have tried harder." He thrummed the table as the MC flounced across the stage, stepping dramatically over the traffic cone stage right.

"Are we still in lockdown?" someone yelled from the audience.

"I need to let my dog out," added a woman in the front row.

The MC wrapped her hand around the mic. "The competition isn't over," she said.

"Get on with it." A man slammed his beer on the table and belched.

The MC introduced the next contestant, liquor store Terry. She was dressed like 1982. Legwarmers, rubber bracelets, tulle skirt, prosperity.

"You know," Brett continued, "you could ask judge number two."

Kabir paused to consider the suggestion, looking over at the judges' platform, at Silas's angular silhouette and ski jump hair. "You think so?"

"You're the actor."

Kabir's eyes shifted. Then he ran his fingers through his hair. Brett gulped.

Chapter 44

MARCEL

Marcel sat up, gathered the soiled towels and cotton balls, and collected the discarded porcupine quills into a tidy bundle. Norman dragged a diner-style stool into the center of the kitchen. Like the restaurant his father took him to whenever Marcel was discharged from the hospital. Bruised ribs, a broken arm, stitches twice. His father apologized in milkshakes.

"Have a seat," Norman said, thumping the vinyl pad with his hand. "You can leave all that stuff. I'll clean it up after."

Marcel shoved the pile to the edge of the kitchen, away from Sasha, who rested, her face half on a floor vent, in front of Norman's dishwasher. She was an old dog, Marcel guessed, at least twelve. He'd like to get a dog. Something benign. A lab or a poodle. A family dog. He could take it to the dog park and teach it to shake a paw. He blinked off a head rush and hauled himself onto the stool, noting Val hunched over her phone, typing manically and sucking back Gatorade at the table behind him.

Norman flipped open a straight razor, displaying it on his palm for Marcel to see. "Shall we clean you up?"

Marcel nodded.

Norman set down the blade and pumped shaving foam onto his hand, then massaged it liberally over Marcel's upper lip. It felt loving and pleasant. Fatherly.

"Okay," Norman said, wiping his hands on a dishtowel. "Let's do this." He placed one hand on Marcel's chin. The other held up the blade. The track lights interrogating them from overhead glinted off the blade. Marcel closed his eyes, reveling in Norman's extraordinary touch. The shaving foam smelled like wood smoke, like the prison yard at night. A forearm around his neck, the Crow Valley Hospital. It smelled like ligature marks, Tic Tacs, crushed ribs. He could taste it now. The spring snow, the piss, the blood. The humiliation. Jepson.

Marcel shot off the stool, tipping it backward, upsetting the bowl of warm water Norman had set out to rinse the blade. The razor flew out of Norman's hand, landing in the kitchen sink beside a thawing ham. When Marcel looked at Val, she was wiping her face with a napkin, orange Gatorade staining her shirt.

"It's okay," Norman said calmly. "You're safe, Marcel."

Marcel couldn't breathe. Adrenaline pumping, he thought he might fall over.

"Marcel," Norman repeated. "It's not real. Whatever you saw, whatever triggered you, the danger isn't here."

Sasha lifted her drowsy head. Marcel related. He felt like Will Ferrell in a Will Ferrell movie. Shot with a horse tranquilizer, on fire, drunk. He staggered to the kitchen sink, fished out the blade, and sawed off the remainder of his mustache. He didn't recognize his warbled reflection in the window.

He felt Norman approaching, his presence like a sanctuary elephant, generous and warm. Marcel collapsed.

"Val!" Norman shouted.

Val sprang from the table, as Norman eased Marcel to the floor. He wanted Norman to drop him. He wanted to smash his head against the linoleum. He wanted to feel the subfloor, the plywood and nails, reverberate through his skull like a viral story. A bridge collapse, a terrorist attack. A beheading.

Val hunched over him, her face in a tormented frown, chest flushed. She stuffed Sasha's quilt under his head. It smelled like a sleeping bag. A companion.

"Marcel, can you hear me?" Norman asked.

Marcel turned his cheek, an earthy mix of blood and shaving foam trickling into his mouth.

"Thatta boy," Norman soothed. "It's all good now. You're safe."

Somewhere an engine sounded. Val stood and crept to the window. Marcel cranked his head and watched her finger part the blinds to peer out.

"See anything?" Norman asked, dabbing Marcel's marred lip with his shirt.

"No, but it sounds like it's getting closer. Listen," she said, a hand behind her ear. "Who else lives up here?"

"Terry from the liquor store. But she's at karaoke."

"Her boyfriend?"

"They broke up. He wanted kids."

"Terry doesn't want kids? Good thing, if you ask me."

"She wants to breed those dogs that look like lambs."

Marcel lifted himself to his elbows and then onto his knees. Sasha had gone back to sleep, and he stretched his fingertips to stroke the top of her head. Norman had joined Val at the window and both hovered around a gap in the plastic blinds, as if waiting for Santa to arrive.

"Now, who's that?" Val asked, voice catching. She ducked behind the side of the couch.

It wasn't a pleasing image, Val hunched in a ball, her pants gathered tight, her face flushed like she'd tried on too many small dresses.

Norman followed suit, rolling away from the window to the adjacent wall. He whispered, "They turned in the driveway."

"Who is it?" Val repeated, gripping the sofa arm.

"I didn't see."

Val crawled back toward the window, squat as a hippo, and, moving the blinds an inch to the left, peered out. "It's a red Ford Explorer."

"I don't know anyone with a Ford Explorer," Norman said, repositioning himself under the window casing. "You sure it's red?"

Marcel slipped out of the kitchen. The hall closet was open. A row of Norman's Canada Corrections jackets, stiff and square, hung obediently, ready for duty. A frayed leash dangled from a hook. Sasha's name had been inscribed on it with a thick black Sharpie.

"They're coming to the door," Val said. "Marcel, hide!"

Marcel crept down the hall and pushed open a door. Norman's bedroom. Marcel scanned the room. A music stand, a violin, slanted walls, an unmade bed, king-sized, just the kind he'd been fantasizing about. Broad, manly, the frame like an altar. He pressed his hand into the mattress. Memory foam. He would have a bed like this someday. What had Hello Kitty said? He just needed to manifest it. Even if it he had to put it in the living room because his apartment was small and it wouldn't fit in the bedroom. Even if he had to put it on the front lawn.

Val and Norman exchanged fumbled words in the kitchen. Marcel looked down, finding an ant crawling up his arm. He didn't know where it had come from. How it got up to his wrist so fast from the floor. Whether it had suddenly materialized. He opened a window and flicked it off.

The mountain air had overtones of barbecue and family. The scent of potato salad drifted by. Maybe he should hide in the bus? He climbed through the window and jumped, leaving Val and Norman talking as though into a loudspeaker.

The backyard resembled a campground, and for a moment Marcel had a childish desire to explore it. The lumber clumped like a beehive behind the bus, the blueberries, potted plants, and ski boots. The hammock slung between a pair of trees like a worn bra.

From inside, Norman's voice boomed louder. A warning? Marcel cranked on the bus door, surprised by how effortlessly it bent open despite its age. A well-cared-for bus, a well-cared-for owner. Marcel sat in the driver's seat, a wedge of foam jutting out, and ran his hands along the steering wheel. A glint of its glory days was still visible in the shiny black coating.

Marcel had always wanted to drive a bus, his experiences with their drivers having been mostly positive. His grade eight bus driver gave him sandwiches, flakes of ham. They tasted so salty Marcel assumed they were expensive—the excess of an entire ocean. The number 10 bus driver, a woman with thinning hair and an ass that spilled over the sides of her seat like a melted ice cream cone, let him ride for the price of a cigarette. Even the man that drove the bus to the prison—his first prison in Quebec—was kind. He'd given a shackled and shuffling Marcel a nod. It had been two days before Christmas.

Marcel looked at the dash. There was no trace of dust. A picture of a young woman dangled from a green ribbon on the rearview mirror. She had a mole to the left of her lip, longboard lashes, tissue lips. Marcel guessed she was twenty.

He brushed a box of Tic Tacs away from under the accelerator pedal and pretended to drive. He pulled up to his mom's office. She skipped out of the building, the glass door jingling behind her, waving a check in her hand. She'd been given a raise. Her face was less gaunt. The staple scars above her brow had faded. She wore lipstick the color of a meteor shower. High heels because she no longer had to run.

Tears streamed down Marcel's face. "*Maman*," he whispered. "*Je suis désolé.*" I'm sorry. A gust of wind broke into the bus, blowing a piece of Norman's hair from the vent. The picture dangling from the mirror danced in a circle. Written in blue ink on the back was the name Theresa Blanchard. Norman's daughter?

There was movement near the back door of the house. Someone passed by the screen. Marcel ducked below the steering wheel, a child hiding in a cupboard. He wiped his eyes. With his cheek pressed against his quad, the other leg jammed up against the underside of the dash, he thought of Roberta Bondar back in Crow Valley practicing yoga. Contorting his squat body into feminine shapes, reaching for the sky as if the ceiling of his cell might dissolve into a soft cloud.

He searched the bus for a key. One would never leave a key inside a vehicle in Montreal. Actually, he concluded, that wasn't true. A mom had left her car running at Pizza Pizza while she dashed in for a Hot-N-Ready. Marcel had hot-n-stolen it, joyriding a good kilometer before noticing the row of booster seats in the back, stuffed with tiny knees and pink cheeks.

The rear door to Norman's house opened. Marcel recalled the shrill squeak of the hinges when he'd first arrived. He waited for the door to close. Someone held it open. Someone was looking. For him?

A minute passed, then another, before the back door slammed shut and the sound of conversation became muffled once again. Marcel unfolded himself, crawled back onto the seat. A car started on the other side of the property. The red Ford Explorer, he assumed.

Marcel was an excellent listener. He could differentiate between the whooshing sound of his father removing his belt and the grittier whooshing sound of his father dry-shaving his face. He knew the different prison guards' footsteps and gaits, the distinct jingle of their keys.

When he heard nothing, Marcel slipped out of the bus, yanking the door taut behind him. *Don't punch yourself in the face. Work hard. Forgive.*

Chapter 45

MOLLY

Molly's former seat had been taken. In fact, all the chairs had been dragged away from her table and reconfigured into a Stonehenge behind the DJ booth. Xavier and Daphne Farquhar had trapped themselves in the middle and were playing charades.

On the stage, the MC introduced the next contestants: a duet. Molly couldn't remember the woman's name, only that she lived in one of the townhouses by the fire station. The man, she'd gone to high school with. The DJ was in the washroom, so the couple rehearsed a snippet of choreography before taking the stage. Molly knew immediately what they were singing: *Shallow*. Hell.

When Molly was early pregnant with her first, Gary had taken her to Vegas for a whirlwind midweek forty-eight-hour getaway. They stayed at Circus Circus, with its worn candy store carpet and hallways that smelled of disinfectant. They used a coupon for a steak dinner. The karaoke was free. It was not a competition, but Molly knew she had won. She needed a song she could win with here too.

"Mommy!"

A yanking on her leg. Molly whirled around to find Malcolm, a soft cast up to his thigh, a bile-green sucker jammed between his lips.

"Malcolm." She crouched to hug him. He smelled like soiled laundry. "That's quite the cast."

"It's temporary," he replied, emphasizing all the wrong syllables. "Until I get the boot."

"I'm sorry." Molly ruffled his hair. "In the middle of summer, too."

"Dad said it means I don't have to play any more soccer."

Molly thanked Jesus. Malcolm's version of soccer was making "stew" out of the grass he picked, the ball occasionally smoking him in the face, while his teammates ran zigzags. "There's always next year." She looked over his shoulder toward the hallway. "Where's your dad?"

"In the parking lot, searching Roxanne's truck."

The meat-packing-plant table stared at Molly and Malcolm.

Molly whispered, "Why don't you join your brother over there and I'll be right back." She gestured to the mishmash of chairs where Daphne kicked into a handstand, flip-flop on one foot, the other foot bare. "I'm just going to say hi to Dad."

Malcolm licked the sucker, his tongue the color of algae. He nodded and dragged himself toward Xavier with the drama of a King Lear. Clarence was standing at the bulletin board removing old notices when Molly passed through the hallway. Molly smiled at the janitor, her heels clicking against the tired tiles.

"Gary find him yet?" Clarence asked. "The prisoner?"

"Think so," Molly replied, smoothing a flyaway. "I'm about to find out."

Clarence folded a lost cat poster in half. The cat belonged to one of the Mains brothers. The whole town had seen it dead just off the Exit 6 on-ramp.

A noise rumbled from the laundry room. Probably one of her boys getting high. Vaping was one thing, marijuana was another. It changed the brain. Made troubled men out of honest teens. She went back to look.

A man's ass, white and furred, quaked. Boxers stretched at the knees, hairy hamstrings. His pelvis crashing into the washing machine, crashing into a woman, her legs wide as a fifth wheel, ankles in the air. Molly could see the soles of her shoes. She cleared her throat.

The man looked back at her but continued to flex, continued to grind into the woman, who cooed like a dirty little songbird. She recognized him. A dad. One whose kids she cared for after school. A man who fixed smiles Monday to Friday and golfed on the weekend. Maybe he too felt numbed by the endless rows of child's braces and smiling hygienists. Predictable golf courses. Always eighteen holes. Why not twenty-one? Why not a blindfold instead of a pair of spiked shoes? Or just take the pills.

Molly turned and strode down the hall. The deadbolt was open. She shoved her shoulder against the glass door and stumbled into the parking lot. Gary hovered over the hood of Roxanne's sapphire Silverado, shining a flashlight at the windshield. It wasn't even dark yet, the sun holding its position like a stopped watch.

"Would you look at that, Mol," Gary said, pointing to the front of the truck. "She's damn near perfect." Carefully, he removed a yellow butterfly from the grille, its wings scalloped and the color of cheer. "But she dead. Poor ting." He placed the tiny body in the nearby hedge and wiped his hands on his pants. "You see the boy's cast?"

"It's huge," Molly replied.

"They didn't have the right size boot. They got to bring one in from another hospital." He thumped the Silverado's hood and then flicked away a seedpod resting near the right wiper. "Truck looks good. Little damage to the rear but I think that was always dere. You say it was parked 'round back?"

"Was."

Gary tried the doors. They were locked. He pressed his face against the window.

"Did they find him yet?" Molly asked. "Kids getting pretty rowdy in there. I want to send them outside."

"'Fraid not," Gary replied, switching off the flashlight. "Lots of sightings, but nobody picked him up yet. Tell de truth, he's probably long gone now." He placed a hand on Molly's shoulder and kissed her on the cheek. "Y'ask Roxanne for a re-sing yet?"

"She offered."

"She offered? Before youse had to ask?"

Molly nodded.

"That's right good of her. Why'd she do dat?"

Molly didn't reply.

"You got a song picked out?"

"No. I put everything into the one I already sang."

Gary placed both hands on her shoulders the way he did when he gave the boys a pep talk. "It don't matter what you sing, love, as long as it comes from the heart." He fiddled with his hat, swept his hair to the side, and brushed sweat from his forehead. "You know, my mudder never exactly said she was tired of being a mudder, but she did get right worn out. And when that happened, Pop would pack us up and take us to St. John's. He'd call it a boys' weekend. When we'd come back, she'd be all fixed up. Only now do I realize it was a mudder's weekend."

"I can't be fixed in a weekend, Gary. I need help. I need medication. I need a break. I need some sort of life outside the kids. I need to be more than someone's 'mudder.'"

"We'll get help. I'll take some time off work."

"And a song. I need a song." She gestured toward the hall. "They could call my name any minute."

"Okay, let's tink." He paced the stretch of sidewalk in front of the door, belly bulging over his belt. "What do you like?"

"Pills."

"That's not gonna work. What else?"

"Alcohol."

"Come on, Mol. From de heart."

"I don't know, Gary. My heart feels kind of small right now."

"You like to sing."

"Yes, I feel better when I sing."

"You should be singing all the time."

"What's the point if there's no audience? That's why this is such a big deal to me."

Gary stopped and grabbed her arms. "Your heart's bigger than anyone I know, Mol."

She studied his face, aware in that instant that he was getting old. He had lines on his face like a fisherman who'd spent too much time

on the water without sunglasses or a hat or a care on land. His hair was
flecked with silver, his nose bigger than she remembered, eyes sadder
in the way eyes appear when they start looking back instead of ahead.
When the past is thicker than the future, the fish stocks low.

"It's my fault Dale's dead."

"Sweet Jesus, Mol. Dale done got blown up. It wasn't your fault the
whole bloody forest was on fire and you run out of gas."

"I didn't run out of gas."

Gary put a finger to his lips and went to his car, an old Corolla he'd
driven west from Newfoundland. Patches of rust lined the wheel wells.
The windshield was cracked, the side mirror crooked as a smile. Someone must have given him a ride to the station to pick it up.

He popped the trunk. "Here." He handed her his mother's wooden
spoon.

She held it limply, a volunteer invited to assist a magician waiting
for further instruction.

"My mudder's spoon."

"Yeah, I got that."

He snatched the spoon and held the shaft to her face, making her
eyes cross. Four marks had been carved into the handle.

"You know what those are? Notches. For each time she tried to kill
herself."

Molly ran her fingers across the divots.

"To some, it was just a spoon, but to her, it was a reminder that she
made it." His eyes turned red, his lips quivered. "You're so much more
than a mudder. I know that because I knew you before you became
one." He cleared his throat. "You're going to make it too."

Gary leaned in and kissed her on the cheek, leaving the tang of his
summer sweat on her neck.

Molly stood. "You're not coming in?"

"I gotta go back to the prison. There's a shit-ton of paperwork waiting for me." He walked back to the car and closed the trunk. "Go find
a new song and sing like everybody in Crow Valley's watching. And

when you're done, we'll build a stage in the backyard. We'll string some lights and set up some chairs. Get you a real microphone. I'll be in the front row."

He started the car and pulled away. Molly watched him go. A billow of exhaust warmed her shins, the spoon dangling from her fingertips, her expression a blank sheet of music.

Chapter 46

VAL

Norman shut the front door and leaned against it, as if he'd just taken refuge from a child trying to sell him something. Val stood beside him with her face against the blinds. "Why in the heck would Wilson choose tonight, of all nights, to give you back your chainsaw?"

"I've been needing it." Norman gestured with his foot to the yellow chainsaw teetering on the sloping hardwood. "You see the size of that chestnut out back? It raps my window at night. I wake up thinking it might be Theresa."

"Why would Theresa be knocking on your window at night?"

"I miss her."

"God, Norm. She still got three more years."

"I didn't know she'd be training though the summer."

"Track and field ain't exactly a winter sport."

Norman bent to caress the chain saw. "Tomorrow, I'm putting you to work."

Val peered into the kitchen. "Where's Marcel?"

"I think I saw him go into the bedroom." Norman set a glass he'd been holding on the counter. "It's okay, Marcel, you can come out now. It was just a friend returning a tool."

Nothing.

Val stretched to look out the back door. "Van's still there, so that's a good sign. And your fishing bus, or whatever it is."

Norman checked the closet, which was open, and empty of a

traumatized Frenchman. He continued down the hall, checking the bedrooms, the bathroom.

"Come on, Frenchie," Val called, guessing Marcel enjoyed a good game. "Time to leave. The land of maple syrup and people in tight jeans making out on the sidewalks is calling." She sat down at the table, amused.

"I think he left. Bedroom window's open." Norman's face was unusually pale. "I think he made the bed."

Val straightened. "Are you sure? You checked everywhere?"

Norman swept his arm from one side of the A-frame to the other. "There aren't a lot of places to look."

Sasha batted a paw in the air and continued sleeping.

"He wouldn't have left without his backpack."

"How did he get a backpack?"

Val hadn't considered this. "He just had it when I picked him up. When I saved him from the bear. It's still in the van?"

Norman slid on a pair of rubber shoes and flung open the back screen door.

Val followed. "In the back."

Norman opened the van door, hauled the backpack onto the seat, and rummaged through it. "There's a bottle of Chablis in here. No one in Crow Valley drinks Chablis."

Norman fished through the unfamiliar clothes. "And there's cheese, too." He held up a partially wrapped crumble, examined the label. "Benton Brothers Fine Cheeses. Vancouver."

"Where in the heck did he get that?"

Norman pinched a sample. "Taste it."

Val waved the offer off. "Did you check the bus?"

Norman slid the van door closed, surveying the yard. The hammock hung undisturbed. There was a small shed ten feet from the drive, but the bells above the door hadn't chimed. The bus door was closed. Val assumed Norman had left it that way when they'd gone to get Sasha's blanket. The same blanket Val had used to support Marcel's giant head when he'd collapsed on the kitchen floor, his face distorted as though it was covered in plastic, as though he was being buried alive.

"Not on the bus," Norman announced, perched on the bottom step. "I think our boy's gone again."

Val threw up her hands. "That's perfect, we don't have to do anything." She danced in a circle and laughed hysterically. "We can just go to karaoke like nothing happened. 'Why were you late?' they'll ask, and we won't even have to lie. 'Sasha got quilled.' 'How about that last contestant? Sounded just like a young Michael Bublé.'"

"You broke into the vet clinic."

"Shit." Val stomped her foot. "Shit, shit, shit."

"It's fine," Norman said, raising a calming hand. "You haven't told anyone. We'll think of something else."

"I told Brett."

"That you broke into the vet clinic?"

"That Sasha got quilled."

Norman stroked his chin in a clichéd manner. "Okay, when you see Brett, just say it was a single quill. We were just concerned because it was close to her eye."

"You think a porc would shoot a single quill? I have a hard time believing that. I bet it's like peeing. Once you start, it's probably hard to stop. All the quills would be in the toilet."

"Fine, then just a few quills."

"But is that still what we're going with for why we're so late?"

"Less is more, when you're lying."

"So you don't want to say that we stopped for a hotdog?"

"Then someone would've had to have seen us buy one."

"Okay, so let's go through this again. I went home after work to change and grabbed something to eat, you called to say Sasha got seven quills in her face . . ."

"Too specific," Norman interrupted. "Besides, you're still in your uniform."

"A few quills in her face, we pulled them out, didn't have a hotdog, and went to karaoke."

"That works."

"Do we take two cars?"

"You drove because I forgot my glasses at the prison."

"Right, okay. Let's do this. Let's go listen to some karaoke!"

Norman left to lock up. Val slithered into the front seat a new woman and started the ignition. She kicked away a little bottle of pet sedative. Bananarama played on the radio. "Cruel Summer." Had it been cruel? Brett had received his first raise in five years. Daphne was finally sleeping in her own bed, and Olivia hadn't begged to wear a crop top like the rest of the grade eight skanks. Her marriage was a bit cruel, but marriage inherently was. Cruel and disappointing, like camping in the rain, hot pavement, warm margaritas, swimmer's itch, and forest fires. Nothing to do. She should drink to that.

Norman secured the back door. His hair was freshly brushed and dangled down his spine. He'd put on a quilted plaid coat. The same kind Brett wore to work. Val examined herself in the vanity mirror, car dancing, channeling eighties girl cool, red lips, and clothes that gave the finger. All of the worry about getting rid of Marcel and he'd gone off on his own. Problem solved.

Norman slipped into the passenger seat with a travel mug. "Hot water and honey," he said raising it for observation. "In case I decide to sing."

"You had to pre-register for this one," Val replied.

"There's always tomorrow."

"Cheers to that," Val said clinking Norman's mug with a vial of phenobarbital.

Chapter 47

MARCEL

"Cheers," Marcel whispered from under the cover of a damp Pinkie Pie sleeping bag in the back of Val's van.

Chapter 48

ROXANNE

Roxanne drew a score sheet from the pile and yawned. Silas drank from his flask, his eyes bleary and posture soft. He leaned over, scrutinizing the last duet's score sheet. "You only gave her sixes?"

"She was pitchy, and he was off-key."

"Eight pitchy, not six."

Roxanne shrugged. "Did you sort out your apartment? Your mom's ashes okay?"

"Yes, and no."

Roxanne straightened, a bolt of panic shooting up her spine. "You lost her?"

"She was already gone," Silas replied, quietly. "My neighbor managed to save some of my stuff and my landlord already has the pump going, but to be honest, it's kind of a relief."

Relief? Roxanne couldn't fathom.

"You know, sometimes I'd look at that urn and be so focused on her death, on the fact that my mom was inside it and had been reduced to something so meager and meaningless that she could fit in my palm, that I'd forget what she was like alive. The small things." Silas clasped his hands. "You should have seen the way my mom pushed a grocery cart. Aggressive and determined. Like she was trying to get to Hogwarts with it. Or her staticky hair. In the winter she resembled a cactus. Or the way she clenched her fists when flying or pointed her toes when diving. How she cried for a week when we put down our cockatiel." He snatched up his vape and took a desperate suck. "I don't care about ashes anymore. It's the memories I don't want to lose. And you may not believe this right now, but they fade. The memories."

Roxanne rubbed her hands vigorously on her thighs, mind racing. She imagined this is what the TV people meant by hate speech. Admitting to being relieved that your loved one's remains had gone the way of dust mites and cat litter. She would never find relief in Dale's goneness. His ashes were all she had left.

She stewed, speechless. She was about to make an adjustment on a score sheet when a memory materialized of Dale at the Crow Valley Pool. She'd challenged him to jump off the highest platform. They'd climbed the stairs together, past the springboards, all the way to the rafters with their sullen lights and antiquated championship club banners. Dale was scared of heights and wanted to go back down, but a line had formed, five, six deep, including some of the kids he used to coach. He had no choice but to jump.

Roxanne erupted into laughter. She clamped her mouth trying to keep the laughter in, trying to shove the memory back down to the pool deck where it had originated, but she couldn't.

"I pushed him," she blurted, hysterical now.

"You pushed who?" Silas asked.

"I pushed Dale off the diving platform at the Crow Valley Pool."

Silas covered his mouth. She could tell he was trying not to laugh because Silas was good. She'd already added him to the *HEAVEN* column and only people in the *HELL* column would laugh at the retelling of a story like this. A story of someone facing his greatest fear and losing. Dale, losing.

Silas cleared his throat. "Go on," he mustered, wrapping a scarf over his face.

Roxanne could barely speak. "Let's just say, he didn't point his toes." She snorted. "He sort of rolled like this boneless lump, or like a bag of trash when you've cleaned out the fridge, and landed in a bellyflop. From the highest platform." She was hyperventilating. "It was so loud, all of Crow Valley heard it."

Silas was convulsing.

Roxanne clutched her stomach. "He was so mad at me afterward."

They continued to laugh in silence. Silas, still hiding behind his scarf, Roxanne openly, until the laughter dissipated and tears formed. They both held their breath.

"Uh-oh," Silas said, tossing his scarf. "Crowbar is coming."

"Kabir," Roxanne corrected.

"What do you think he wants?"

"Not a date, if that's what you're hoping."

Silas whispered, "I was hoping."

Ascending the right side of the stairs was Molly.

"What does she want?" Silas asked. "And why does she have a spoon?"

Roxanne shrugged. The mayor took the stage.

"Quick update," he hiccupped. "Prisoner's still on the run."

Someone yelled, "How hard can it be to find one man?"

Very hard, Roxanne thought. She couldn't even find a dead one.

Silas paused to look down on Kabir and Molly. "Look, Kabir's smiling. Do you think he's smiling at me?"

Roxanne whacked Silas's arm and then hid her score sheets under a binder. "This all should really be computerized," she said before planting a fake grin on her face.

The mayor continued. "No one can go home until we get the all clear from the police."

"Fuck the police," a man yelled.

Another hollered "Get off the stage," before falling into the DJ equipment.

Kabir reached the judges' table first. "Sorry to interrupt," he said. "But my friend down there"—he gestured behind him at an area half the size of the hall—"he missed his turn."

"You mean Brett?" Roxanne asked.

"Yes," Kabir nodded, eyes like butter, an anime puppy.

"We called him three times," Roxanne said. "You know the rules, cowboy."

"If I always followed the rules, I'd still be in Iraq. I'd have nerve

damage, no parents, a house without a roof. My left leg would be missing just below the kneecap."

"Such specific details," Silas replied, shaking his head. "And so
tragic."

"May I?" Kabir asked, turning toward Silas with his hand outstretched. "You have something on your face."

Silas retreated. "Where?"

Kabir leaned in. Roxanne could smell him from two seats away.
The intoxicating scent of a man who'd grown up in a land of spice and
strife and rocket grenade launchers and black licorice.

"Is it gone?" Silas asked, wiping his cheeks vigorously with his fingertips.

"Not quite."

Molly had reached the judges' platform and watched as Kabir
swiped his thumb across the arc of Silas's cheekbone. He leaned away
to examine his work and exhaled a thousand-year breath from the ruins
of his diaphragm. Silas closed his eyes. Kabir leaned in again. This time
he ran his thumb along the right peak of Silas's lip. There was silence
around the judges' table as though the four of them, chairs and score
sheets and empty cups, had all been transported into another dimen-
sion, the air taffy-thick and spiked with lust.

"Now it's gone." Kabir placed a hand on his heart. "In the cover
of night I would walk to the river in search of water, my baby sister
strapped to my back."

Roxanne crossed her arms. "Thought your leg was missing below
the kneecap."

"I would crawl."

"Couldn't you get a wheelchair?" Silas flirted.

"Too expensive. And even if I could, there's too much rubble. The
streets of Mosul are largely impassable."

Below, the MC had made another costume change, a teal dress resem-
bling a mullet and the kind of shoes a Confederate soldier might have
worn. "I see some action up at the judges' table," she said, her voice more
liquid than before. Oily. "Does that mean we're ready to get started?"

"No!" Silas shouted.

"I'll take that as a no," the MC laughed, meandering toward the opposite side of the stage, where an arm-wrestling match was under way at a front table.

Molly tucked the spoon under her arm. "Roxanne, your truck is back."

Kabir and Molly exchanged glances.

Roxanne stood. "It's back?"

"Gary just dropped off Malcolm. Your truck was parked in your spot."

Adrenaline whipped up Roxanne's legs, causing her to lose her balance. She braced herself on the table. Silas placed a steadying hand on her back. "But . . . it was gone. You saw it when we . . . it was definitely gone." The weight of the headlamp pulled on her neck.

"It was." Molly agreed.

"I alerted the fire department," Kabir said. "They must have found it."

"It's a karaoke miracle," Silas offered.

Roxanne turned. "I told you Dale would come back." She began to laugh. "And you said he was gone."

Silas swallowed.

"A miracle." Kabir took Roxanne's hand, brought it to his lips, kissed it like it was the last hand on earth.

Silas presented his hand. Kabir kissed it too.

Roxanne sat down, pulling a score sheet from the stack. "You can tell Brett he's next."

"Next?" Kabir glanced at the table below. Brett was still flipping through the songbook, scratching his stomach with a butter knife. "That doesn't give him a lot of time."

"He would have sung already if he'd gone up when he was called."

"Someone sang his song."

Roxanne clicked her pen. "We're running behind. He sings now or he doesn't sing."

Kabir sighed. "So that's it? He has to go next?"

"Next or never," Roxanne replied.

Kabir turned and descended the stairs on a mission, as if he knew Crow Valley would always be on fire. That at any given time somewhere, something, someone would be burning. In this case, Brett.

"Brett," Kabir hollered. "You're up!"

Roxanne rubbed her weary eyes. Her truck was back, the deck was fixed, the thermos was missing. In the left side of her brain, the side Roxanne used to populate spreadsheets and calculate taxes and add up karaoke score sheets, she knew there had to be a logical explanation. She'd seen his body. She could see it now in her mind's eye, black and crisp. She'd touched the silky powder of him when she transferred his ashes into the thermos. But in the right side of her brain, the crazy side, she believed in all of it. The supernatural, the metaphysical, the unexplained. Ghosts, agoutis, miracles, headlamps. Dale.

Chapter 49

BRETT

"Me?" Brett dropped the butter knife he'd been using to scratch himself. What did Kabir mean by *You're up*?

Kabir reached the table and gave Brett an encouraging and somewhat painful shoulder massage.

Brett winced. "I have to go right now?"

"Next or never," Kabir replied, taking a seat, the chair's metal legs catching on the warped floor.

Brett gulped. "The girls aren't even back from the bathroom."

"You have to go."

The MC motioned for the DJ to cut the song he was playing in the interim. "All right, ladies and gentlemen, we are going to skip back in the program. Please welcome Brett Farquhar to the stage."

Someone shouted "Go Bretty," while a woman on crutches took a selfie with the DJ.

Brett stood too fast and knocked over a beer bottle. He whispered to Kabir, "What do I sing?"

"What do you know besides the one you were planning?"

Brett paused to think. What songs did he know? He knew lots of songs, of course. "Uhhh . . . 'Womanizer' by Britney Spears."

"I don't think that's a good choice," Kabir replied.

Songs, songs songs. "'Jeremy' by Pearl Jam."

"Too dark." Kabir shook his head.

"Once again, ladies and gentlemen, give it up for Brett Farquhar." The MC batted her orange lashes and shimmied like a bird in a bath.

"Fuck," Brett said. He took the long way to the stage, weaving between tables, stopping to pick up a soiled napkin. If Val had shown up he'd have asked her. And where were the girls? It seemed like an hour had passed since Olivia took Daphne to the bathroom. What were they doing? Making a Tik Tok video? Watching some idiot do rooftop parkour?

The MC waited for him behind the screen. "You still singing 'See You Again'?" she asked, her greenroom voice less playful than her onstage voice. Out there she was a Corvette, back here she was a flat-bed truck.

Brett shook his head.

"What, then, are you singin'? We gotta let the DJ know." She pointed to her wrist. "Tick, tick."

"I need a second."

Waiting with him was a voluptuous woman eating a turkey sand-wich. Her hair had been styled for another decade. The forties? Fifties? What was the decade of milkshakes? He eyed her sandwich. There must be a song about turkey. But nothing came. He twirled around. Fire alarm, flattened jellybean—might have been yellow—lady with a wart or skin cancer on her nose, baby, uglier baby, an M&M.

"Let's go," the MC said coldly. "You got ninety seconds to be up on the stage or you forfeit your turn." She pulled a little mirror from her bodice and studied herself. "Tick, tick," she said again, snapping the compact shut.

Brett cleared the stairs with one step, crossed to the other side, and squatted across from the DJ booth. He scarcely had time to retrieve the mic before the distinctive electro funk beat blasted through the speakers. The first time he'd heard "The Real Slim Shady," he was at a weekend-long baseball tournament in Saskatchewan. The weather had felt like a hair dryer. He'd hit an infield home run and eleven RBIs, yet Dale was still awarded the tournament MVP. All this before Val, the girls. He'd drunk too much and eaten a raw hotdog. He'd fallen over trying to have sex with a single mom behind a tree.

Brett's face turned poppy red as he thought of her, the last woman he'd been with before Val. Before Caroline. The sweet-ratchet taste of flavored vodka on her lips, the bleached bikini lines on her naked back. The horrifying scarecrow tattoo on her calf. How she pleasure-yelped like a chihuahua.

A woman in the audience catcalled as Brett immersed himself in character, rounding his shoulders, bending his knees, rapping, gesturing, perfecting the Slim Shady chop. The lyrics scrolled fast and furious, like the nut dispenser at the Safeway that always caused Brett to spill peanuts on his boots. He knew not to look at the screen. That's how you lost points. He continued to find inspiration packing his mind with cheese slices, jean shorts, wagon wheels, and dollar store lingerie.

Someone at the wheelchair table spun mechanical circles. An older woman raised the roof and shook her chest. Even Kabir seemed to have caught the vibe: he lay back in his chair, head grooving, manhandling his Sprite. Brett didn't dare look up at the judges' table. He gyrated and kept his mind focused, squirting out lyrics like nacho cheese. He thought of the color fuchsia. He thought of Budweiser, the New England Patriots, McDonald's onions, construction sites, tinsel, inspirational quotes, uncircumcised dicks, and apartment complexes.

Then he saw Olivia, frozen in the corner, trying to shield Daphne's eyes. Was he that bad? Was he unwatchable? Offensive? He had taken his shirt off at some point. The music called for it. He'd be awarded for choreography. His nipples were on the puffy side, but they were barely visible through the great swaths of hair that covered his chest. Maybe it was the lyrics. He tried to ignore his daughter, rapping instead to the folks at the wheelchair table. They all seemed to love him.

Brett filled his diaphragm with a desperate gulp of air. He was almost there. Just the chorus left, two times. If Val could see him now, maybe she would notice him. That was all it had taken for him to step out on their marriage. Caroline had noticed. Him.

He worked the stage from left to right. He shoved his crotch against the traffic cone marking the hole at the front. Crow Valley's pharmacist whistled. The chaplain covered his eyes.

Was Eminem *not* the real Slim Shady, Brett wondered? Spaghetti on his sweater, Missouri in his limbs, lawsuits in his pockets, Detroit in his scars, controversy in his teeth? Was Brett the real Brett Farquhar? Who even *was* Brett Farquhar? Brett didn't know. He'd spent most of his adult life trying to be Dale. The better man. The faithful man. The dad man. The rescue-pitcher-guard man. The man of all mans.

The final chorus was approaching. Olivia ran out of the room, leaving Daphne to build a tower out of empty beer cans. This was already his second chance. He ignored her and bellowed the lines with an edgy warble, like he was singing from the bottom of a dumpster.

Mic drop. It was over.

Brett got a standing ovation. People howled, whistled, whooped, threw cans. He soaked up the glory, arms spread, trying to suck in his gut.

"Well, thank you, Brett Farquhar," the MC said, having picked up the mic. "Some things are worth the wait, hey?" The audience cheered. The lights came up, and Brett felt a wave of embarrassment as he bent to collect his shirt.

"I think you roused everyone's inner Eminem, so thanks for that, Brett. Am I right, folks? Don't we all have a little Slim Shady in us?"

"I'm the real Slim Shady!" someone shouted from a back table.

"Well, I like my Shadys a little curvy," the MC responded, performing a seductive wiggle.

Brett entered the greenroom and yanked his shirt down over his head.

"You killed it," said turkey sandwich, brushing crumbs from her jagged red blazer. "So good."

"Thanks." Brett smiled.

The woman high-fived him and then proceeded to the base of the stairs, feet together, arms folded neatly in front of her as though she was waiting to read the Bible.

Brett flew out of the greenroom in search of Olivia. He could still hear the audience cheering behind him as he strutted into the hallway, past the men's washroom, past the mayor's office and the trophy case. Past the wall-mounted Rocky Mountain elk buck with the magnificent antlers.

Chapter 50

MARCEL

Marcel found the back of Val's van comfortable. In addition to the sleeping bag, there was a fluffy pillow—remnants, he decided, from a recent sleepover. He'd managed to stuff the pillow under his head just as Val had opened the driver's side door and climbed in. She'd sighed the relief of a hundred freed hostages. It hurt to know how joyful she was to be rid of him. He'd recognized it before—in his mother's smile, in his father's fist, in Jepson's boot.

He'd caught only fragments of Norman and Val's conversation on the way to karaoke. Theresa had come up. Norman's daughter was on a track scholarship. Ohio State. Pole vault. The young woman whose photo he'd seen dangling from the rearview mirror in Norman's bus.

They talked about indigestion, sawed-off shotguns, and AA meetings. New hires at the prison. At one point Norman must have made a joke because Val laughed and it sounded like fireworks, so dazzling and rare that he'd actually felt sorry for her. Not that he hadn't heard her laugh before. She was always carrying on at the prison. But this was different, like it had come from another Val, a previous one, a lost one. A box of roman candles buried on a garage shelf.

Dale's name had come up twice, and Marcel had strained to hear over the sound of the radio and a passing train. Once had been in relation to karaoke. Some past performance where he'd dressed up as Jesus? The second time in relation to his wife, from which he learned she was crazy.

Marcel felt his ears pop as the van wound down the mountain. The nylon of the sleeping bag made him think of the body bag used to collect his father from the ruins of his house. Couldn't the coroner tell that his father had been a bad man? Even burnt, didn't the firefighters see the size of his fists? The rage in his eyes? Eye anger was the scariest anger of all. And why did the reporters have to call him a victim?

The van stopped. "I hope I didn't miss Brett," Val said, over the click of a released seat belt.

"Singing's hard without fans."

So is living, Marcel thought.

Norman coughed. "If Brett's already sung, I'm sure he'll forgive you."

The van doors closed and he was alone again. It was so quiet he could only hear the faint inner workings of his body. The things keeping him alive. Organs, veins, cells. He thought about forgiveness. How did it work? Marcel had attended a few group sessions in prison. Forgiveness wasn't one of their themes. In order for him to make it out here, as Val had suggested, whom exactly did he need to forgive? Himself? His dad? Jepson? How did you forgive a man who taught you how to use the stove and then burnt you with it? How to build a fort and then smothered you with it? Tie a tie, and then strangled you with it? Even if he was able to forgive his father, how was he supposed to forgive Jepson? How did you forgive a monster?

He sniffed the sleeping bag, and his thoughts shifted to his daughter. He wondered if she had sleepovers and whether an imposter father made popcorn at night and pancakes the next morning. Even if he made it back to Quebec he couldn't make contact. He couldn't take her out for ice cream or buy her tiny woodland figurines or scratch 'n sniff stickers. He'd be reported and sent back to prison. Longer this time. His only choice was to start over and assume the identity of a better man. A man who was fatherly, sporty, handy, heroic.

He scooched an inch to the right, arched his back, and removed a golf ball that had been wedged under his hip. He would wait a bit, make sure the parking lot was clear, and then he'd leave. He'd rely on the criminal intuition he'd fought so hard to refine, selecting the unlocked doors, choosing the best victims. He fought sleep.

One of the side doors opened. Hard. The entire van shook. Marcel, still buried, jerked to attention. Someone got in the seat in front of where his shins were achingly tucked. He heard the unmistakable dialing of an iPhone keypad. A girl's voice.

"Hey."

A boy. "What's up?"

"My dad just sang Eminem at karaoke."

"Cringey," the boy replied.

"Super cringey. He like, twerked on a traffic cone."

"Isn't he almost forty?"

"I wanted to kill myself."

"You wanna come over?"

"Maybe," she replied. "My mom just got here, so I don't have to babysit Daphne."

"My parents aren't home."

"Cool."

The conversation paused.

"Shit, my dad's coming. I'll text you."

A minute passed and a door opened. The one directly beside Marcel's head. He held his breath.

"Liv," a man said. This must be Brett. "Why did you hate on me like that when I was singing?"

"Ew, don't ever say that. It makes you sound . . . just, don't say that."

"Don't say *hate on*?"

"Yes," Olivia barked. "It was embarrassing. I thought you were singing a slow song."

"Someone sang it before me. I didn't have a choice."

"So you rapped?"

"You saw how quickly I had to decide." Paper crinkled.

"I was in the bathroom," Olivia said.

"I didn't mean to embarrass you."

"I thought you were doing this for Dale? That's the only reason I came tonight." Olivia's voice transitioned to a whisper. "You still owe me forty bucks."

Silence. Breathing. Incoming text.

"I was doing it for Dale until I had to pick a new song."

"Why did you take your shirt off?" Olivia asked, her tone less sympathetic than it had been seconds before.

"I don't know, Liv. I was in the moment. When you grow up, moments are hard to find. You get up every morning and you got to go to work. Doesn't matter that it's four a.m. and you'd rather stay in bed. You can't. You make your lunch—the same lunch you made yesterday and your feet are cold and the drive is quiet and you think about whether you'll ever get the Visa paid off and if you'll ever take another trip to Disneyland and whether your father is really okay on his own or if you should be inviting him to live with you."

Marcel sniffed. The conversation paused. Had they heard him?

"Sounds stupid," Olivia said.

"Very," Brett replied. "You'll spend most of adulthood regretting your life choices."

True, Marcel thought.

"Like what you did with Caroline?"

Brett sighed. "Like Caroline."

"And that all made you take your shirt off?"

"I don't know, Liv. I've spent most of my life unnoticed. Never feeling like I'm enough. Like I don't measure up, and once I got going I just felt really good about myself up there. I felt seen. And I'm sorry if my feeling really good embarrassed you. Sometimes life makes you feel dead inside, and when it doesn't, when you find yourself in a moment where every part of you is buzzing and your cells feel like they're multiplying and exploding, you gotta embrace it. You gotta rip off your shirt and throw it down, and own it. You know what I'm saying?"

Marcel nodded.

"Obviously, I mean that figuratively." Brett spelled it out slowly as though second-guessing the definition. "I mean *you* don't rip off your shirt. Just embrace the moment, Liv. It's in your name to."

Seconds passed. Marcel pulled the sleeping bag down, exposing his ear. He didn't want to miss anything. He didn't want the conversation to end. He wanted to bathe in Brett's fatherly advice. Maybe he would become Brett. A faulty man with a good heart who never gives up. It couldn't be that hard. He was already wearing his clothes.

"What hairstyle do you like better?" Olivia asked, changing the subject. "The one in the first picture with the sort of half curls, or the second one with the more waves?"

Marcel imagined the hairstyles in question. He'd worked at St. Hubert with a girl who had sort of half curls. They were caramel colored and stuck out from the sides of her visor like cumulus clouds. He didn't know many women with wavy hair. His mother's hair was limp, his grandmother's cropped like a seaman's. Though his grade eight science teacher had had wavy hair. She'd been kind to him.

"Wavy!" Marcel blurted.

Chapter 51

ROXANNE

"I didn't think he had it in him," Roxanne said finalizing Brett's score with a swirl of red pen. "Not nearly as good as Dale ever was, but nice effort. Dale would have enjoyed that. He would have been proud."

Silas fondled his vape, which was perched on the rule book like a centerpiece. "The best performances are the unexpected ones. They're usually the ones I give perfect scores. Straight tens."

"I've never awarded a perfect score."

"Of course not."

"Why do you say that?" Roxanne asked.

"You keep a *HELL* list."

"People are hellish."

"People are human," Silas replied. "And so was Dale."

Roxanne pushed away from the table. "What's that supposed to mean?"

"Everyone's doing their best. You might need to cut the town some slack. Give out a few tens. Give people something to hope for."

"Cut the town some *slack*? Crow Valley killed Dale." She threw her hand toward the audience. "You want me to reward them with tens? You want me to give them hope? What about me? What about my hope?"

Rage began to burn inside her. Repressed and female. A pink Chernobyl. "I'm not responsible for their hope," she managed through clenched teeth.

"No, but you're responsible for your own."

Her mouth gaped. How dare Silas tell her to have hope as if she had none? She had plenty of hope. A thousand watts' worth pulsing from her forehead waiting for Dale to come back.

"Hope feels good." Silas said, taking a sip from his flask.

Of course hope felt good. She didn't need schooling by some avocado-loving millennial with nice hair and a side gig. She loved hope. It felt amazing. Like stepping in water after putting on fresh socks or sticking the mascara wand in your eye and brushing your cornea or every day passing the remains of the gas station where your husband exploded and left behind his essence in a sad shadowy pavement stain the size and shape of a cat.

"Let's go," she hollered down. "We don't have all night."

The mayor's wife delicately crossed the stage toward the mic stand. An ember of panic heated Roxanne's stomach. She looked down at the mayor's table. He was staring up, beady-eyes locked and loaded. She remembered his warning: *tick, tick.* Roxanne lifted her hand, a flicker of acknowledgment, the mayor tipping his head toward the stage, toward his wife. Roxanne swallowed.

Silas leaned in to Roxanne. "Song number?"

Roxanne swiped through the contestant entry list. "One hundred five."

Silas fingered his way through the songbook's index. "Ah. Sting. 'Every Breath You Take.' Creepy."

The mayor's wife closed her eyes and held up her hands like her voice was in her fingers and she was helping the music escape. She started to sing.

"Odd choice," Silas said.

Roxanne looked back down at the mayor. He sipped a colored drink from a red straw, half-facing the stage, half-facing the judges' platform.

She whispered to Silas, "He picked the song."

"Who?"

"The mayor picked the song."

"For her?"

"For me."

Silas rolled his pen between his fingers. "I think you're being paranoid."

Was there something else she'd forgotten? Bear warning, bridge signs, chair rental, botched party invitations. She unhooked her purse from the chair, set it on her lap, and searched madly for her agenda. Unsent mail, Pokemon cards, paper clip, Tic Tacs.

"Oh my God. I forgot to lock the shed. Someone'll steal the town's lawn mower."

The mayor's wife hadn't moved from center stage. She cupped the mic, body timber-straight, eyes still closed.

"No one's stealing a lawn mower tonight. Half of them are drunk."

"Exactly. Someone will try to ride it home." Roxanne's mouth was dry. No water. "It's the second time I've done this. Last time they cleared out the whole shed."

The mayor was gone from the table.

"Where'd he go?"

"Huh?" Silas squinted in confusion. "Who?"

"The mayor."

Her cell phone tumbled from her purse, a fledgling coal. A missed call from the boys. Her fatherless boys. It was too late to call them back. Too late to ask them what grandma had fed them for dinner or whether they'd seen any elk or if they remembered the sound of their father's voice and what it was he said at bedtime: *Dream big? Rest your head? Sleep tight?* Roxanne held her face, shoulders a tension rod. She pushed the songbook to the floor. Silas jumped. The mayor stood in the entryway, gazing up, up. Anguish, too, rose like a thermostat. She felt the headlamp might overheat and shatter.

"You okay?"

"I can't stand this," she squeaked.

The mayor brought the straw to his lips. His wife lifted her arm toward the stage lights, warm and white.

"I have to get out of Crow Valley. I have to get out of this hellhole and find another job. And I have to make at least what I'm making now because the boys want to play hockey this fall and Dale said if they're going to play hockey they got to do all the dry-land training and the camps." She turned to Silas. "There are camps in August. For ice hockey."

The mayor's wife bellowed the final lines.

"I could sell the house. Move to the Lodgepole Pine Apartments. Run a firing range or a call center or a laundry business." She shouted, "I have to look after the boys."

Roxanne's body shook, pain crept through her skull.

"Roxanne," Silas started.

From behind the platform, the mayor continued where Silas left off. "You have to grieve."

Crumpled in her hands was the karaoke poster. She held it to her chest.

Silas whispered, "Let go."

Chapter 52

BRETT

Brett turned to Olivia, squashing his knees against the seat in front of him. "Did you hear something?"

Olivia shrugged, an ad blasting from her phone. "So, which one?" She swiped the screen and showed Brett the competing hairstyles again.

"I'm going with curly." He pointed to the picture on the right.

"That's wavy," Olivia replied.

"Same thing." He reached behind him, ran his fingers atop the sleeping bag in the trunk. "This yours or Daph's?"

Olivia peeked over the seat. "Daphne's. It's been there since she slept over at Kylie's."

"Kinda gross to have it loose like this in the trunk."

"I think Mom was going to take it to the cleaner's. Remember Daphne peed in it?"

Brett pulled his hand away. "Sounds like something Daphne would do." He picked up a paper A&W bag at his feet and stuffed a pop cap and a drawing from last school year inside. "Whose backpack is this?" he asked, peeling back the zippered front pocket.

"Not mine," she said.

"Looks like there's cheese in here?" Brett sniffed his fingers.

"Oh, I think that's Norman's. Mom gave him a ride."

"Right," Brett replied. "Speaking of which, I need to find your mom. Tell her about my awesome performance. She's probably looking for me."

"She is."

He rezipped the backpack. "I'll bring it in for Norm. You good to go back inside?" He ruffled Olivia's hair. Too much. Her muscles tensed and she frantically pulled her fingers through it.

"Fine, but I'm not sitting with you."

"Deal," he replied, offering a hand.

"Don't do that." Olivia got out of the van. She walked a few paces and then slowed, waiting for him. He jumped out, swinging the backpack over his shoulder to join her. He would bask in her company even if it was only for fifteen seconds.

Brett held open the hall door. "Hey Liv," he whispered before she slunk off. "Don't say anything about us taking Roxanne's truck."

Olivia paused. "Can I get my eyebrows tattooed?"

"No."

She sighed. "I'm going to the balcony."

"Don't—"

"Touch the railing, yeah, yeah."

"Love you," he called as she slipped around the corner toward the back hall.

"Not here." Her voice faded.

Brett went to the washroom. It was empty but smelled like weed. He tossed the backpack into a corner, away from the urinal, and relieved himself. When he came back out, Val was pacing in the hallway.

"Hi," she said. It was a heavy hi, as if the letters were made of iron. "I guess I just missed you. Heard you brought the house down."

Brett cupped Val's face and stooped to meet her eyes. "I killed it, Val. Like *killed* it."

He loved her so much. That was the hardest part about the affair. Convincing her, convincing all of Crow Valley that he could literally love her more than the moon or a meal or an overtime win and still have put his hand inside another woman.

"That's what everyone's saying. You were great. *Dale* great," she whispered. Val looked around as though the *everyone* she referred to were milling about, but they were alone. Only the tip of Clarence's mop could be seen swooshing in and out of the main office.

"I wish you could have seen me," he said. "Why were you so late?"

"Told you, Norman's dog got quilled. Nothing too serious. Just a few . . . I think there were five or twelve quills in her face? Anyhow, he needed a hand pulling them out. I couldn't say no with all he's done for me."

"Is that why your chest is all scratched up?"

Val placed a hand across her collarbone. "Why were the girls at Big Al's, alone?"

Brett's ears pricked with heat. "They wanted to come watch." Another lie. He shouldn't tell lies.

Val raised her eyebrows.

"I wanted them to come watch. It was before the escape."

"Enough about that," Val said. "Tell me about your performance. Did you dedicate it to Dale like we planned? Did you look up, to heaven?"

"I took off my shirt."

"I left something in the van."

"A backpack?"

She paled, rubbed her shipwrecked eyes.

"Don't worry, I brought it in. Liv said it was Norm's." He pushed a frizz of hair from her face. "Didn't know he was back on the bottle." He paused to look at his wife. There was something different about her, but there was nothing different about her. She was the same. She was a stranger. He remembered the first time he'd seen her at the registry. He'd loved her instantly. He reached for her hand.

"Where is it?" she asked. "The backpack."

Brett felt his pockets. "Shit. Must've left it in the bathroom. Just a sec." He hurried back to the men's room, avoiding a CAUTION WET FLOOR sign near the entrance. The bathroom still smelled like weed and it was still empty. One of the taps was running. He turned it off. The backpack was gone.

Chapter 53

MOLLY

Molly climbed the twirling theatrical staircase to the hall balcony. Why did it seem like she was the only parent actually parenting tonight? Minutes ago, she'd found a toddler in the kitchen and no one else had been up to check on the tweens and teens since karaoke started. She squinted at the wall clock. That was nearly three hours ago.

If she made it until all four of her boys grew up, she imagined she'd still be running a daycare and mothering the town. It was her penance. For the times she bent over her boys' cribs and wished them away. Held them and felt nothing. For every birthday cake she set on the table, stared at the fat wax number candle, and thought *Is that all?*

"What's going on up here?" she asked, a touch out of breath.

"Nothing." Dylan shot up. He'd been crouching over something.

Molly surveyed the balcony. There were eight kids. Her oldest two, Olivia Farquhar, some of the Mains brothers' children, a boy she recognized from Cole's class, and a few ferals.

"You guys keeping away from the railing?" Molly tested it with a firm tug. The gun tape seemed to be doing its job.

"Yes, Mrs. Chivers," said the girl in the Converse high-tops she'd met earlier. Molly looked from son to son. Cole's arms were stretched unnaturally behind him, as if he was handcuffed. There was something behind his back. Olivia Farquhar looked the way she always had since Molly'd known her, uncomfortable, as if she was at the wrong table or on the wrong planet. It didn't help that her eyebrows had been filled in with a furry marker, giving her the appearance of a bison.

There was a clink behind her, a series of whispers. Molly whipped around and watched a bottle of wine roll to a stop at her feet. She scooped it off the floor and held it up to a wall sconce. "Petit Chablis," she read. The wine was warm. She held it by the neck like a slaughtered chicken and approached the group. "Whose is it?"

Dylan blamed it on one of the Mains brothers' boys. Molly recognized three of them, all easily identified by their scrawny limbs and unkempt hair.

"It's not mine," the youngest of the Mains trio replied, his head tilted so he might see through his greasy bangs. "But I'll take it."

"No, you won't take it," Molly replied. "It's alcohol."

"Yeah." The boy shrugged.

"You're what, fourteen?" Molly tucked the bottle under her arm and focused her attention on the kids she didn't know. "Do your parents know you're up here drinking?"

A boy in ratty jogging pants shook his head. "We weren't even drinking it." He spoke with conviction. Molly thought he might be the new cashier at Safeway.

"Not drinking it?" She held the Chablis up to the light. "That's not what it looks like."

Cole rolled his eyes. "We were daring each other to eat the cheese."

Molly scanned the floor. There was a Shop-Vac in the corner, a stack of unused chairs leaning against the paneled wall. A program from last spring's production of *Billy Elliot: The Musical* had been turned into a paper airplane. Molly recognized the cover artwork on the wing. "What cheese?"

Cole grabbed the backpack Dylan had been concealing, nudging it forward with his foot. It was fancy, as far as Molly could tell, aerodynamic design, probably waterproof, made of recycled tires and failed goals. Resting on the front pocket was a nest of plastic wrap and a crumble of stucco-colored cheese.

Molly bent down. "What kind is it?"

"Smell it," one of the Mains kids urged.

"No," she replied, though she'd already picked up the scent of abomination. It rivaled the spread Gary paired with bologna. She moved in closer. Had this cheese ripened in the laundry bin shared by her boys? She waved a hand in front of her nose.

"Dare you to eat a piece," said the girl with the Converses. She was propped up on her elbows, kid cleavage exposed, scars on her wrists. One of her fake eyelashes had partially detached.

Molly leaned in, took another sniff, gagged.

Classroom-style laughter erupted. A reminder that those around her were very much kids, though their scars and sex lives would suggest otherwise. She knew Dylan had already had sex. He was sixteen. She'd caught him going at it with a ballet girl, all limbs and leggings and Instagram poses. Now, looking down at Cole sidled next to the Converse girl, his shoulders worked like a varsity athlete, hair pasted, she guessed he was probably doing it too.

"What do you get if you eat it?" Molly nudged the cheese onto the discarded plastic wrap as if it were a baby rodent, blind and infirm. She observed it from all angles.

"The wine," Olivia replied, as if it wasn't obvious.

Molly considered this. A drink would be good about now. Below, people were getting rowdy. The hall was full of heartburn and heartache both. Things were slowly becoming unhinged and undone. Zippers, buttons, straps, marriages, thoughts, feelings, fists.

She separated a scrap of cheese, poking it with her finger.

"Just eat it," sighed one of the kids.

You can do this, Molly said in her head. *It's just a tiny piece.* She turned over the wrapper. Vancouver. She opened her mouth. The cheese went down like a teenage blow job, dutiful and foul. She gagged over the balcony railing, cupping her mouth so the morsel would stay inside.

"Show us your tongue," Converse girl heckled. "Doesn't count until we can see that you swallowed."

Molly braced herself against the rail. The cheese had the texture of wet chalk. She forced it down, brushed the remnants from her lips, and stuck out her tongue.

The tweens/teens stared back.

"Your mom's sick," said a Mains kid.

Cole smiled.

"You have to eat *all* of the cheese." Converse girl again.

Molly crossed her arms. "That wasn't the deal."

"Whatevs," the girl shrugged.

Molly wrapped up the remaining cheese and zipped it inside a front pocket. She swiped the bottle of wine from the floor, satisfied. "Whose backpack is this, anyway?" Only hipsters would eat cheese that tasted like hot underwear, and even then they probably would have made it by hand, with organic ingredients, in a tree house, while someone drummed barefoot in the corner. Besides, none of the hipsters in Crow Valley had kids over the age of five.

"His." Dylan pointed to one of the boys Molly didn't know. The boy shrugged. Pulled the backpack toward him.

"I think it's Norman's," Olivia offered.

Molly shook her head. Norm had been sober since before Malcolm was born.

"Can we have some food?" Cole asked. There was a hole in his Nike shorts. He'd picked the scab on his shin, leaving a smear of blood.

"I've already given you food."

"We're hungry," Dylan added.

Molly stormed off the balcony. Midway down the back stairs, she unscrewed the cap and drank from the bottle. It had a slightly metallic taste, a paper clip, a pistol. She didn't know her wines and wondered if this was simply a Chablis thing, or ignorance. The MC was sitting at the bottom of the stairs, doctoring a hole in her fishnets. She stood when Molly closed in.

"Second chance is coming up real soon."

Molly nodded and made a beeline for the bathroom. She took another swig from the bottle and set it beneath the sink, exposed. She blotted the sweat and flecks of mascara from her face and stared into the mirror. *Your last chance*, she chided. She ran the water, room temperature, dipped her fingers in the stream and wet-styled her hair. Beside the tap, a Tic Tac. She thought back to the day of the fire, the pills on her lap light as cotton, the theme park traffic, the weighty smoke. Dale. Had the steel in his boots melted when he caught fire? What about the keys on his belt? Why had she let him go off to the gas station?

She pinched the Tic Tac between her fingertips and dropped the candy into her palm. *What should I sing?* She'd already tried a confession. Maybe she needed a punishment song. The karaoke songbook didn't have a section of Songs for the Unworthy. And then Molly had a thought. Dale had saved her. She was alive in this gold dress, in this washroom cocoon, in broken stilettos, in the climax of summer, because of him. Maybe if she could save someone in turn, she'd free herself from the guilt. The guilt of motherhood, of survival. The guilt of living.

Who in Crow Valley needed saving? She closed her fingers around the Tic Tac and a song came to her.

Chapter 54

MARCEL

Marcel peeled the synthetic sleeping bag from his sweat-drenched face. His naked upper lip stung, each microscopic cut a tiny scream. He'd nearly blown it blurting out "Wavy!" the way he had. Now he was alone.

The sign out front of the Crow Valley Town Hall advertised the karaoke championships, both Ks installed backward, the O unmistakably a zero. He kicked through the hoard in the back of Val's van. Jumper cables, steel-toed boots, a birthday invitation ("Shelby's turning 7!"). He needed to find some sort of bag. Brett had taken the backpack.

Marcel crawled to the middle row of seats and found a soft cooler. Empty. He filled it with the barbed wire coil, a forgotten vial of pet sedative, pistachios, a Sharpie. He took a Green Bay Packers T-shirt that might have been used to wipe a windshield. A plastic name tag stamped BRETT was under the seat. He put it in his pocket.

Marcel pressed his cheek against the window. The sun was easing. Dusk was advancing like an army from a rival kingdom. You couldn't yet see it but you felt its presence, thick and ominous. He'd do better under the cover of darkness. All criminals did. His dad had come alive at night, a werewolf with blackened eyes and hands turned to cement. Dale too. It had been in the prison's dark corners in the single-digit dead of night when rage tugged at his fists.

Marcel needed a map to figure out where the hell he was. The glove compartment was stuffed with Barbie DVDs: Barbie and a skateboard, Barbie and a computer, Barbie and a sexy dolphin. He tossed the

DVDs. Scrunched in the back he found a paper kid's menu. One of the girls had drawn a self-portrait with green crayon. The menu had pictures of sand dollar pancakes and happy eggs. He flipped it over. A map, the tourist kind, advertising around the perimeter like properties on a Monopoly board. The street lines were soft, as if the whole town had been conjured inside a thought bubble, or resided on a cloud. The points of interest were printed in dreamy theme park letters. DONNA'S HARDWARE, BIG AL'S, HAIR CUTS 4 U.

This wasn't Crow Valley. Crow Valley was hard. Crow Valley was right angles and caution tape and cold cells. And much of it was still burnt. He'd seen the remains of an Esso gas station. Counted limb-less half trees, collapsed roofs, the shell of a Jeep. He saw the outlines of garage pads and playgrounds. A ghost motel. The people too were burnt. Burnt out, burnt in. Some of them still on fire.

Town hall was smack in the middle of the map. From it, Marcel traced all possible routes out of Crow Valley. He glanced toward the road bordering the hall parking lot where the girls had crashed their bikes. The prison, he concluded, was behind him. It wasn't labeled on the map, but Marcel theorized it was the shaded hexagon under his thumb. He needed to go east. It would take him through town, past houses and dog walkers and empty basketball courts. The hospital. An A&W.

He scooped things from the floor of the van and aimlessly rammed them into the cooler bag. Anything might be useful. Even the Barbie movies. He found a toque, yanked it over his head, and stumbled out-side. He checked the notice board on the edge of the parking lot and there again was that motherfucker Dale riding in a rescue truck, pitch-ing, smiling, glowing, posing like a town founder. A Hero.

Fuck him.

A hand-drawn sign warned that a large stuffed animal was in the area. Where was the bear warning? He'd seen her not far from here. Berry-eating whore. He pulled the Sharpie from the cooler and under the blue pen block letter WARNING added GIRL BEAR.

He went back toward the hall, ready to get the fuck out of Crow

Valley, when Olivia slipped out the door. She bent beside the tangle of red bushes that lined the front entry and looked back at the building, making sure no one had followed. Then, hunched over, she ran, head bobbing just below the windowsills.

What the hell was she doing, knowing an escaped convict was on the loose?

The boy. The one she had FaceTimed or Snapchatted or whatever it was teens used to love each other. The one with the parents not home. Didn't she know dusk was a terrible time for girls?

Olivia disappeared behind the hall. There was nothing but woods back there, as far as he could tell. He studied the map. Yes, woods and then train tracks, a farm maybe? Houses. What would a father do in this case? He imagined Olivia was his own daughter, sneaking out of karaoke. He fondled the name tag in his pocket.

Marcel slung the cooler bag over his shoulder and tugged the toque lower over his head. A fat woman stumbled out the front door of the hall. She wore cutoff jean shorts, her hair in braids. In the quiet of late July, her crying was the only sound, making it seem like Crow Valley itself was sobbing. The sidewalks and squirrels. The schoolyards and women. He paused a minute to absorb her sorrow.

Marcel crouched between cars and rushed to the corner of the building where Olivia seemed to have dissolved. He saw her in the woods, zipping through pine trees with the agility of an athlete twice her age. When she crested a hill, he followed.

The earth gave a little beneath his feet. Unlike those in the forest flanking the mountain, the paths were as worn as a trampoline bed. He reached the crest and slowed. Down the hill was a pasture. Probably the first farm in Crow Valley, its owners now a hundred and ten, holed up with their fly tape and rifles and memories of a time when their property wasn't surrounded by hybrid vehicles and dance studios.

Olivia stopped at a fence weathered as driftwood. She walked a good ten paces beside it before she ducked between the rails and broke back into a run. Marcel hurried down the hill in an effort not to lose her. At roughly the same spot she'd climbed through, he vaulted over.

The sun lowered. Marcel jogged, maintaining a safe distance. A train whistle blew in the distance. Was he making a mistake? He'd made many. Jepson went as far as saying he was one. And not a simple unplanned pregnancy or a missed pill or a broken condom, but that his very DNA was garbage. That instead of A and C and T and G nucleotides he had Fs and Xs. Born wrong.

Olivia reached the other side of the farm. A motion light triggered at the end of the driveway, but no dog barked, no one came out to investigate. When the floodlight flickered off, he followed. A car drove by. The occupants didn't seem to notice that Marcel was a mistake, walking down the road out of breath and in Brett's pants.

Up ahead, Olivia stopped at a house. A minute passed and a boy in a tank top came out onto the porch and wrapped his arms around her. His hair was an uncut lawn. A dog with a severe underbite barked from the front door. Marcel watched from the cover of a Trans-Am on blocks.

"Shut up, Logan!" The boy yelled, tugging Olivia across the porch to a bench lined with faded floral cushions. She sat on his lap sideways. A hanging plant dangled above them like mistletoe. The dog's nose pressed against the screen, black and hopeful.

Olivia and the boy kissed and Marcel looked away, conflicted. Their mouths had collapsed into each other, scandalous and mature. His heart started to beat faster. He flexed his chest, made fists. Heat coursed through Marcel's body. He watched.

The couple stood suddenly, the boy staggering backward feeling for the door, Olivia attached to him like a puppet. *No*, Marcel thought. *They cannot move inside.* Inside is where bad shit happened. Inside was where girls were dragged, mothers were punished, fathers were set ablaze.

Marcel charged toward the front door, where Olivia was now half inside. The boy saw him coming, his eyes swelling with fear, and fell backward into the entryway. Marcel wanted to put the boy's face through the screen, smash it off the milk jug on the porch, stomp on his sallow cheek, but Olivia stood over him.

"Stop," she said. "We were just . . ." her voice weakened, her eyes filled. "We were just going to feed the dog."

On cue, the dog appeared from around the corner, with his British smile and wagging tail. Marcel spied a piano at the end of the hall, glossy and black. The boy struggled to stand.

Marcel pointed. "Don't you fucking touch her."

"I won't," the boy stammered.

"He wasn't," Olivia agreed.

"You're too young to go around fucking up your life. I know your parents aren't home."

"We weren't doing anything, *Officer*," Olivia said, eyes narrow. She'd drawn out the word "officer," made air quotes when she'd said it.

Officer. The bikes, the girls, the bloodied elbow. Val.

Marcel straightened, cleared his throat. "The last time we met, you were supposed to be at karaoke, cheering on your dad."

"He already sang," the boy piped.

"Yeah," Olivia nodded. "Like twenty minutes ago."

"And does he know you're here?"

Olivia's shoulders collapsed.

"We were just hanging out," the boy offered.

"You know a prisoner escaped from Crow Valley Correctional earlier this evening?"

The boy shook his head, alarmed.

"And you had your girl sneak over here alone, so you could 'feed your dog'?"

"I didn't know," the boy said. "And it wasn't just to feed the dog."

"Yeah, I saw that," Marcel countered.

"Please don't tell my parents," Olivia said.

"I invited her over because I wanted to play her something," the boy blurted. He was trying not to cry, shifting his weight from one sport-socked foot to the other. He gestured to the piano. "Something I wrote for her."

"You did?" Olivia pushed a swatch of hair behind her ear.

Marcel crossed his arms, nodded toward the piano.

"It was kind of just for her."

"Play it, right now, or I'll put you both under arrest."

"For what?"

"For scaring me."

Olivia and the boy exchanged looks.

"Play," Marcel spat.

The boy shuffled awkwardly down the hall, tugging nervously at his fingers, and sat at the piano. Marcel and Olivia followed. He cleared his throat, hands hovering over the keys, eyes closed. The dog dragged his bum down the length of the hall rug.

The boy began to play, quietly at first, only a few notes, the pace tentative. Marcel thought of ice cubes clinking in a glass. Tiny hamsters. Tuning forks. Nickels. There was a key change. Minor? The music darkened. He thought of a dim forest. He thought of his hollow mother. The crushing weight of his father. The devastating malice of Dale Jepson.

Olivia sat cross-legged on the floor between the living room and kitchen. The dog stood at attention beside her. Marcel squeezed his eyes shut and listened.

The music became lighter, happier. The forest parted like the Red Sea. The hamsters sprouted wings and flew away. The nickels morphed into helium balloons. Everything was color.

The boy started to sing.

"Don't sing!" Marcel shouted. "Just keep playing."

The boy obliged, striking the keys harder, the music tumbling. The dog howled. The music didn't stop. It came at him like a freight train, a flying knee, a forest fire, and then it slowed again. Back to a few notes, high as stilettos, pleasing. Marcel fled. Down the hallway, barreling through the door, knocking over the milk jug, flooding the lights. He ran and ran and ran.

Chapter 55

VAL

Val scanned the room for Marcel's backpack, trying to ignore the alcohol on the tables, the empties and half empties, the Bloody Caesars, abandoned and cloudy, margaritas the color of pool water. She excused herself and snaked her way toward the back of the hall. One of the Mains brothers was passed out in the corner, body generously spread as if waiting for an autopsy. Daphne and two boys were taking turns jumping over him. Molly's boy Malcolm ambled toward the exit, a cast up to his hip, hair thick with sweat and disaster. What had she done with his Croc?

She ducked into the narrow hallway that led to the women's bathroom and there was Roxanne, melted into the wall, blouse rumpled, the strap of the headlamp half-covering her eye. *Christ*, Val thought, *she's finally lost it*. Val glanced over her shoulder for an escape route, but there was no turning back, no way to avoid the carnage in front of her.

"I can't do it anymore." Roxanne's voice was a whisper, excruciating and burnt. "People keep telling me to let go, like Dale was a balloon or a grudge or a pair of pants that don't fit." She gripped her pleats like gearshifts. "They keep telling me to move on. What does that even mean?"

How was Val to answer? The only thing that had helped her was the alcohol, and she'd been stripped of that privilege. The only thing that was helping her now was not to move on but to move forward, physically. Steps forward. One foot in front of the other, like a goddamn baby. She took one now toward Roxanne. She had to find the backpack.

"You know what the worst of it is?" Roxanne said, pushing off the wall.

Val didn't want to know. She'd been living in it. The worst. It was on her skin.

"Dale just wasn't the same in those last few months. He barely spoke, I mean, he talked to that stupid goldfish, but it's like, I don't know. Maybe I did something? Maybe I let him down? Is that why he won't come back? Maybe I forgot something? I forget things all the time. Like there's a bear in the area and I forgot to post the warning! It's probably eating someone right now. Because of me!" A tear rolled down Roxanne's haggard cheek.

"There's bears all over Crow Valley," Val said. "I wouldn't worry about it. As for Dale? I don't think you let him down or did anything wrong. He was still talking about you right up until the fire."

Val saw the hint of a smile on Roxanne's face. It was true. Dale always talked about her. He'd mention a new TV show that made her laugh, a song she liked, something she'd done at work.

Dale noticed her.

"For what it's worth—" Val hesitated. Dale had made her promise never to say anything about Benedetto. Not about how he sang in the choir and certainly not how he'd fooled Dale. Val had seen the reports, the language Dale used to describe him: "exceptional," "exemplary." He'd gone as far as to call him a "citizen." She exhaled. "Dale helped an inmate get early parole. In the spring before he died. That inmate got out, went straight to his parents' house and shot 'em. Dale never got over it. The idea that he'd been duped. That he'd made a mistake."

Val bolted, leaving Roxanne behind, speechless and stunned. She hurried past the laundry room and kitchen, where a cook wiped down a prep table, the hood fan rattling and blowing his bayou beard. No sign of a backpack at his feet. Where the hell was it?

By the time she reached the bathroom, she could barely breathe. Navigating her own *forward* was enough. The tiny room gave her goosebumps. She leaned heavily on the sink. Muffled music from the competition drifted in through the ductwork. A green bottle was nestled beside a garbage can overflowing with cheap paper towel. The toilet flushed before she could read the label and take it. Val jumped and stood off to the side, hands folded patiently at her waist.

Caroline Leduc stepped out of the stall. Both women gasped. Val had never seen Caroline this close. Not since the affair. Not since she'd infiltrated her marriage with her pinup hips and rowdy mouth. Not since she'd turned Brett and Val into Brett

and

Val

Val braced herself against the wall. Caroline had crow's feet and a playful dimple. Her cleavage stretched like a long weekend and her eyes were green, not hazel. She'd been crying.

"Excuse me," Caroline stumbled, turning her back on Val. She bent over the sink and dispensed foamy soap onto her hands. A mood ring replaced a wedding band. The stone was the color of ash. Val counted the white threads that dangled from Caroline's frayed denim shorts. *Eins, zwei, drei.* She measured the swath of bare skin between her waistline and her tank top. She memorized the scalloped edges of Caroline's exposed black thong and the fine lines of her tattoo.

Caroline didn't bother to dry her hands. She wiped them on the back of her jean shorts, leaving behind a drag of damp prints. They could've been Brett's. Val rushed inside the stall. It was even harder now to breathe. She kicked the toilet seat down as the bathroom door closed, the faint scent of Caroline, a fresh-cut lawn, lingering in the air.

Val yanked her phone from her pocket and frantically texted her sponsor. *Ichi, ni, san.* Norman didn't reply. She swung open the stall door, pushed the garbage can to the side, and gathered the bottle of Chablis into her arms. The wine shook, a tiny turbulent sea. She wanted to swim inside, pull through the bubbles, float, drown. She brought the cap to her lips. The aluminum was pleasing, the weight of the glass hard against her teeth, taunting.

Her phone buzzed. She set the wine on the back of the toilet.

Her sponsor. "Don't do it Val. You've come so far."

Had she come far? It had been only forty days since her last drink, a full five years since the affair. At their final appointment, the counselor had told Val and Brett that their marriage might come out stronger. That the affair would force them to address the dark parts of their marriage. The fire hazards. And they were everywhere. That much was true. In what they said and in what they didn't. In whether they went to bed with their boots in the hallway, resentment in the sink, or regret in the washing machine. Marriage was flammable.

The scent of Caroline began to dissipate, and the music stopped. Applause reverberated through the hall. Val brought her shirt to her face, taking in Marcel, who had seeped into the fabric. Youth and despair produced a tragic smell.

In her own youth, Val had been a frizz of optimism. She'd laughed at TV shows and sitcoms, at talking dogs in movies. She enjoyed the bad jokes of flight attendants, dads, and teachers. She'd barely drunk. Now she was here. A frizz.

Brett texted: *Last song of the night. Molly.*

Then Norman: *Hang in there, Val. Night's almost over. Just make it to forty-one.*

A back draft of tears surged, spilling onto her phone. She typed: *I can't.*

Brett: *Where r u?*

Norman: *Final performance. Come watch.*

Bathroom, she texted. *Just one sip.* She swapped the phone for the bottle, unscrewed the top, and drove the rim to her lips. The wine sloshed. It slapped her teeth and washed her gums and soaked her throat. One hard sip and then another, the Chablis tiptoeing inside her cheeks like a music box dancer, lovely and enchanting. Lethal.

She remembered a movie she'd once watched with Olivia, about a dog that wanted to be a dressmaker. The dog spoke with a Boston accent and sat behind a sewing machine. Its foot could barely reach the pedal. Val took another haul on the bottle, but the absurdity of the seamstress dog made her laugh. The wine burst from her.

The outside door to the bathroom flung open, followed immediately by the stall door. There was no time to hide the bottle or dry off the wet spot on her front. She continued to laugh.

"What's so funny?" Brett asked.

Norman seized the wine. "Come," he motioned.

"A dog," Val whispered through tight-laughing cheeks. "He wanted . . ."

"He wanted what?" Brett yanked paper towel from the dispenser and pressed it to her chest. He didn't ask about the wine. He knew better.

Norman turned the bottle upside down and poured the wine down the sink.

"Let's go," said Brett. "Molly's about to sing. Final performance of the night and then we'll go home."

Home? Was that even a place?

"Come on, Valerie." Norman's eyes were serious and clear. "Remember, the girls are here."

Brett wiped Val's face, kissed her tears, and pulled her up from the toilet. Norman opened the door and motioned them through. Val's foot scuffed the floor. She was certain a Tic Tac had crunched beneath her shoe.

She saw her reflection in the emergency glass case with the red fire ax. *You never made it to day forty-one.* She slowed, legs heavy, traced the wall with her hand. Wood panel, panel, panel. Tomorrow she'd have to start over. One. Getting sober was about as plausible as a dog sewing a dress. She buried her face in her hands, their alcohol scent palpable, horrifying.

When they reached the main auditorium, the lights had dimmed to a hazy hangover blue. Molly looked radiant and slim. A strange confidence had lifted her shoulders and stiffened her dress. Norman pulled two chairs from an abandoned back table. Val sank heavily into the upholstery, Brett beside her and facing the stage.

Norman placed a hand on her shoulder, and she understood how Marcel must have felt under his watch. The hand lifted and lowered twice more, and then Norman left.

Daphne sidled up to the table, eyes down, playing on Brett's phone. A puzzle game with moving shapes. Daphne's finger moved frantically across the screen. She stomped her foot, rattling the forks on the table. The shapes dissolved. *Do you want to play again?*

Chapter 56

ROXANNE

Roxanne stumbled into her seat, knocking things from the judges' table: pens, songbooks, the karaoke posters. Silas reached a steadying hand, bent to pick up the items.

"You okay?" he asked.

"Dale helped an inmate get early parole, and soon as the inmate got out, he killed his parents."

Silas grimaced. "Add that guy to the *HELL* list."

"Dale never told me. I mean, I remember readin' about it in the paper, but nothing about it being his fault." She planted her hands on the table as if she'd otherwise topple. "He should've told me."

"People don't like to be betrayed. From the way everyone here talks about Dale, a mistake like that would have been devastating. He was probably just too embarrassed to tell you."

"We told each other everything."

"Shame is a twisted thing, Roxanne. It can change a man. It can change everything."

Roxanne was listening, but all she could picture was Dale. The nights she'd discover him out of bed and find him hovering over the fish tank watching the fish swim back and forth, back and forth in a dreadful continuous loop because where else could it go?

She adjusted her headlamp, withdrew a fresh score sheet, and removed the lid from a pen with her teeth.

Chapter 57

VAL

A twinkling of music was released into the air, the coppery synth-pop notes from the 1980s—handwritten, desperate, sincere. *We belong*, Molly sang. The audience was quiet, pensive. *We belong*, Val mouthed. Brett placed a hand on her knee. The words fell on them like theater snow, gentle and unexpected. An anointing. Something in her shifted. Something in her slipped away, like a prisoner into the night. The simple truth about marriage matched the startling truth about life. It was often unfair and sometimes boring. Stale, one-sided, disappointing. Lonely. But it could also be forgiven and celebrated and enjoyed. There was no greater intimacy than the intimacy of effort and nothing more heroic than detecting the fires and putting them out.

Do you want to play again?

She took Brett's hand.

We belong, she whisper-sang, ready to believe it, ready to feel.

To notice.

To play again.

Chapter 58

ROXANNE

A supernatural stillness hovered in the air, giving the hall an illusion of smallness. The ceiling felt low, the walls thick as a fortress. Molly's voice was a spell. All eyes in Crow Valley were fixed on her. Children sucked their thumbs, men wept, women fell silent. Even Silas stooped over his score sheet. He'd only written the letter *M* before his wrist slackened and slit open from the music.

Pat Benatar, a surprise. "We Belong." The problem was the lyrics. They were true. Roxanne belonged with Dale. They belonged together. And yet Dale was missing and she was here, alone and furious. Her hand darted up to the headlamp to turn it up, but the knob had already been cranked to maximum brightness.

Molly lifted her chin. *Don't want to leave you really, I've invested too much time.*

Exactly, Roxanne thought. All that painstaking time caring for the thermos, coddling his ashes, holding her grief. Now was anything but the time to give up, to accept. He had to be out there somewhere. Surely he'd be able to find her. She'd plastered the whole damn town with the posters. There were signs everywhere.

Norman Blanchard stood by one of the exits. Roxanne watched as a baby crawled toward him. He bent to pick up the child, rested him on his hip, and pointed to the stage. Her boys were once that small. Dale would prop them on his shoulders until they leaned sideways, heavy as chef's hats.

They were too big to be carried now. When either of them fell asleep on the couch there was no one to take them to their rooms. She had to nudge them awake and guide them to beds that were becoming too short. Soon their feet would dangle off the end. Avatars would replace action figures. They would ask to use the band saw, drive the car, play *Call of Duty*. Things would change and there would be no father to father them.

One of Molly's boys stood on a chair, watching his mom perform. A sensitive kid the same age as Roxanne's Thomas, he rocked slightly to the music, hands in anticipatory fists, jogging pants twisted at the waist. Amplified by the stage lights, his hair rose in a staticky inferno. Roxanne had seen his brother toddle by earlier, unsupervised, a cast up to his thigh.

A commotion on the balcony—a stampede of footsteps, laughter— drew Roxanne's attention upward. The railing wobbled. Silas looked up too. An empty bag of Fuzzy Peaches sailed to the floor beside him. He nudged it with his foot and added the *o* to Molly's name at the top of his score sheet.

Molly swept her arm from one side of the hall to the other. *Now there's no looking forward, now there's no turning back.*

"Back. If he would just come back," Roxanne blurted.

"Even if he does," Silas replied, "he's still gone."

Kabir stood suddenly, as if he'd just realized he'd forgotten some-thing, cell phone on the toilet paper dispenser, wallet in the car. He wound his way through tables, the light on his reflective pants blinding. The ripples of his abs were visible through his tank top. He moved in a way that was both manly and graceful. Brave. Ready.

Another piece of garbage floated down from the balcony. A soiled fry carton from the canteen. *For fuck's sake.* Roxanne stared up at the railing with her angriest eyes. A boy jumped in the air to catch some-thing and missed. The others laughed at his misfortune and scrambled to retrieve whatever had not been caught. Someone yelled "Fuck."

Molly was in the eye of the song now, her voice taking on more power. Roxanne saw the hairs on the back of Silas's neck stand. Nor-man passed the baby he'd been holding to its mother. The baby was asleep, cheeks puffed and limbs heavy. Norman slipped out of the exit he'd been marking. Roxanne wondered if Norm was going to sneak a drink. Maybe he'd fallen off the wagon, or the "feller-buncher" as they said in Crow Valley. Half the town's loggers were drunks. Same with the prison guards. Kabir was right there on his heels, following Norman into the night.

Chapter 59

MARCEL

Marcel had made it three-quarters of the way across the farmer's field when he slowed to a jog. The piano nearly killed him. So did their youth, his shame. He could still feel the warmth from the boy's home. It was in the carpet, and in the pictures on the fridge, and the bowl of fruit on the counter. He'd spied a growth chart at the end of the hall.

He grabbed at his ribs, willing away a stitch. When he reached the tree line behind the hall, he stopped moving altogether, to catch his breath. Did he hear music? He listened, strained. Marcel had no music. No one had taught him to play the piano. He didn't have any songs.

It was getting dark, and he was on borrowed time. Marcel looked down at his hands, scarred and bloodied. He could go back to the hall parking lot, hot-wire a hatchback, and drive through the night or off a bridge. He could drive into a train. He imagined his foot on the accelerator, he imagined the impact. *Kaboom.*

Or he could go back to prison. Turn himself in. Inmate 113. Finish his sentence in his damp cell, in solitary confinement, in silence. Where he belonged. He took a deep breath and charged onward, branches snapping beneath his feet.

Chapter 60

ROXANNE

Roxanne looked for Val. She and Brett were pressed together at a back table, the curls of their hair mingling, shoulders squeezed as if the room was closing in on them. Val and Brett belonged together too. Dale had been the better husband. The better guard, the better ballplayer, probably the better dad, based on the way Daphne was poking Johnny Mains with a drumstick. But there was something special about Val and Brett. Their love always seemed big somehow, a boreal forest, sprawling and ancient; no matter how many times it caught fire, it always seemed to grow back.

Roxanne's neck tensed. She snapped a pencil in half. Opened her notebook to the *HELL* column. How was it they got to carry on? What about Dale's second chance?

Molly sang, *Whatever we deny or embrace, for worse or for better.*

Roxanne's hands curled into fists. *What about my better?*

Silas elbowed her and produced a wad of plastic.

Roxanne jumped. "What is it?" she asked, fingering the trash.

"A cheese wrapper."

That wasn't what it looked like to Roxanne. Her wrappers were square. The boys left them all over the house, the faint smell of factory pressed into their seams.

Roxanne whispered, "What do you want me to do with it?"

"It's *my* cheese wrapper."

She raised her eyebrows. *What is he going on about?*

"I brought this cheese with me from Vancouver. I left it in the trailer. Why is it here?"

How the fuck would I know? Roxanne shrugged. They both looked toward the balcony. Boys were wrestling. A girl stood beside them stretching a piece of gum like a slide whistle from her lips.

"How did they get my cheese?" Silas asked.

"We've got a deli in town."

Silas unfurled the wrapper. "They sell Benton Brothers Fine Cheeses in Crow Valley?"

"We sell lots of things in Crow Valley. Work gloves, summer camps, maple cream, homemade soaps that don't work, Pokémon cards, fire extinguishers, crushed dreams, and very fine cheeses."

Silas rolled the plastic into a compact ball and pushed it into his pocket. He finished writing Molly's name on the score sheet and slipped back into judge mode like a true professional. Brett kissed Val on the cheek and excused himself from the table. Roxanne turned to Silas. "Do you smell smoke?"

Chapter 61

MARCEL

Marcel dodged thorny bushes and stumps. He wove through trees, hurdled an old mattress someone had dumped. His heart raced. He tripped on a rock, sailed forward in the air, and landed on his face in a depression. His nose bled. He touched the tender spot where the high jump bar had landed. He smelled his body odor. Rancid. He didn't move.

Tangled in the mess of stiff branches above, a nest balanced. No birds. He remembered his bed at Crow Valley Correctional. Roberta Bondar's corn chowder. The tang of Hello Kitty's breath. *Jeopardy!* nights. Norman. He thought of his favorite book. *Hero: Becoming the Strong Father Your Children Need.*

Was it still there? Had someone packed it away?

His escape meant he'd never see his daughter again. He couldn't just go back to Quebec and pick her up from school. Take her to a movie. Braid her hair. Tie her skates. He could never buy her a piano. The Montreal police hated him.

Marcel rolled onto his side. His body sank deeper into the ground. If he didn't serve his time, she'd never learn that he'd liked to paint rocks or collect Hot Wheels, or that mustard pickles and Ritz crackers had been his favorite. She'd never know that he was scared of the dark, or that he'd loved baby animals and the smell of red licorice or that he'd killed his father to save his mother. She would know him only as a convict, a mug shot, numbers on a prison record, letters on a birth certificate. A ghost.

Chapter 62

ROXANNE

"I don't smell anything," Silas replied.

Roxanne faced the balcony and issued a curt "Shh." The straps and cords of a backpack dangled between the rails.

"Two points," a boy argued.

Below, the mayor had fallen asleep. His head was back, mouth open, his legs spread as if in a trance waiting to host a spirit. A dead mother, a demon, Dale.

The mayor's wife sat quietly by his side.

"I'm sure I smell smoke," Roxanne said again.

"Maybe something's burning in the kitchen."

Roxanne remembered getting the call. News that Dale had been seen on the side of the road next to Molly Chivers's car. That it had been Dale's truck parked at the Esso. She'd heard the explosion. The gas pumps and air hoses. The shelves of motor oil, beef jerky, and Skittles, all blasting into orbit. She could see the flames.

Molly's voice lowered to a whisper. It somehow made the song seem louder, the words sharper. It called out to Roxanne. She belonged to no one now. To her boys, sure, and the town, maybe, if she still had a job on Monday. But she was alone in a way Brett and Val were not. Without the thermos to hold, Roxanne's loneliness peaked, flames in the night sky, singeing the treetops, suffocating the clouds, climbing toward the moon, turning out the lights. She clawed at the headlamp, cupping the light, all ten thousand watts, burning her hand.

Chapter 63

MARCEL

Marcel imagined a new life. One in which he kept a job and a schedule. Maybe he'd wear a name tag. Maybe he'd join a fastball league and a volunteer rescue squad. Maybe someone could love him in spite of his wrongness, make treasure from his garbage DNA. Make him a father. Give him a chance.

He hauled himself up off the ground. He had to go. There was no turning back. He picked up his pace. He was running again, long limbs charting the course over moss mounds and roots. The back of the hall soon came into view. His nose twitched. A trigger smell. Fire. Subtle but definite. From where?

He remembered the glugging sound of the gas as it spilled from the red plastic can soaking the lawn, the porch, the empty sandbox, his father's bike. The window boxes. The match had struck on his first try. He remembered the sound. *Hiss.*

Around the corner, a small weathered shed butted up against the hall. Smoke billowed from the ugly slanted roof. Marcel's heart sputtered. He skittered to a stop, inhaled, watched, listened.

At the height of his waist, someone was knocking inside. He raced to the door, wiggled the rusted latch, and yanked on the knob. A soft and tiny fist, a rubbery kick. He remembered pounding on his bedroom wall, begging to get out so he could save his mom. All he could see from the crack below the door was her feet, bare and tumbling across the hardwood as his father dragged her away.

"Get away from the door," Marcel warned. "I'm going to kick it."

There was no answer.

"Fuck." Marcel punched himself in the head. "Stand back."

Chapter 64

ROXANNE

A sudden clanking sound rang from the balcony, causing a metallic echo to reverberate through the back of the auditorium. It reminded Roxanne of Dale's workshop, his hammers and blades and drill bits. The clanking was followed by whispers, shuffling feet.

A boy's voice: "It was your fault."

The lights dimmed. Were they even still on? The music faded. Roxanne stared at the *HELL* column. She added her name to the list because life without Dale was just that. Hell. A living hell. All brimstone and silence. She began to cry.

Onstage, Molly brought the mic closer to her lips. *I hear your voice inside me, I see your face everywhere.* She tipped back her head. Roxanne tipped hers too, heavenward. It started to snow. Ash, gray and dusty, settled in Roxanne's hair, mixing with the tears on her face to form blackened puddles. In the light of the headlamp it resembled a collapsed cloud. Then a bone fragment, no bigger than a Tic Tac, landed on her chest.

Silas scrambled away from the judges' platform, a ghastly expression on his face. Dust was on him too. In the pocket of his fancy shirt, down his neck. A powdery line ran across his shoulder.

Overhead, a boy held a thermos, the lid in one hand, the dented steel cup in the other. He swept the last remnants of Dale over the balcony with his foot, then tossed the thermos to the balcony floor. It rolled to a stop near the backpack.

Chapter 65

MARCEL

Marcel kicked the door at the height of the lock, as the firefighters had when he'd set his house on fire. The shed shook. Flames crept from the roof. The door remained closed. Marcel backed up and tried again, this time throwing his whole body into the frame.

The structure hissed. The scant pounding continued from inside. Marcel heard movement behind him. He did not look. On his third attempt, the lock snapped and the door shivered open. Marcel batted away the smoke, thick as a duffel bag, and felt inside.

"Take my hand," he said waving madly. He bumped against something metal. A garden tool tipped, knocking him in the temple. Flames slithered up the wall toward the ceiling. A doughy hand grabbed onto his ankle. Marcel crouched in the blackness. The first thing he touched was an ear, small and thick. A sloping shoulder, a fleshy rib cage. A boy too big for his age. The kind that ate entire boxes of ice cream sandwiches and couldn't keep up with the others.

Marcel scooped him off the shed floor, laid him across his forearms like a stack of firewood, and staggered outside. He examined the boy in the day's remaining pink light. He had freckles, singed hair, a soft thigh-high cast that had begun to unravel. No shoes. Through the smoke and oil and grass of the shed, Marcel made out the faint scent of hotdogs and socks. Clutched in the boy's hand was a packet of matches. Marcel peeled them away. Crow Valley Billiards.

He tossed them aside. "You can't play with matches," he said. "They set things on fire."

From behind Marcel, a command. "Put him down."

Marcel knew it was coming. He turned, the boy still in his arms. Brett walked cautiously toward him. Beside him was a beautiful firefighter. In behind, a Mountie with feet so turned out they could have belonged to someone else. The Mountie inched closer, face pinched and white as a cue ball. Rounding out the troop was Norman Blanchard. They'd sent the goddamned Village People after him.

Norman stretched out a hand, and Marcel's body slackened. "Pass over the boy," he said. His voice was the Father, Son, and Holy Spirit.

The Mountie drew his gun, though it trembled in his faulty hand. He mumbled, "Malcolm."

"Marcel, pass the boy to Kabir," Norman continued.

The firefighter stretched out his arms. Marcel looked down at the boy. Was this the boy from the yard? The one who'd scaled the fence and enabled his escape? And now his capture? Marcel handed the boy to Kabir.

Brett rushed forward, ripping off his shirt. A button popped and ricocheted off the hall's siding. He draped his shirt over Malcolm's heaving chest. The Mountie was bent over, hands on his knees, sobbing. "What's wrong wit me son?" he whispered.

"He's okay," Kabir replied, checking Malcolm's vitals. He passed the boy to his father.

A man raced from around the front of the building with a fire extinguisher. Out of breath, he handed it to Kabir and then leaned away, coughing.

"Olivia," Brett said. "What are you doing coming from there?"

All of the men turned to face the teenager, who stood nervously at the edge of the woods, her face flushed.

Kabir charged the shed, teeth gritted, spraying wildly at the flames with the fire extinguisher. Norman yanked the hose from the reel and cranked the tap.

Brett went to his daughter. The man who'd fetched the fire extinguisher passed out. Everything slowed.

Marcel staggered forward, took in the scene. All of the men were occupied. This was his last chance.

Chapter 66

ROXANNE

Roxanne should have been horrified. Dale on her upper lip, in her ears, nesting in her clavicle. But she wasn't. He'd come back, in dramatic fashion, to where he belonged. With her. *For worse or for better.* He always knew how to make an entrance, and this, she realized, was his swan song. His final performance. And she knew what that meant: it was hers too.

She watched the sign language interpreter delicately link her fingers together for the word "belong." It was a beautiful sign, a beautiful notion. Roxanne noted sleeping babies, spilled drinks, stepsiblings, and diamond rings. She saw broken hearts and broken glass, carnations and trash. She witnessed lovers and losers. Families and failures. Wounds, scars, smiles, second chances. Acceptance. Roxanne embraced it all.

She shook the fine dust of Dale from her clothes, and transferred the tiny bone into her pocket. She resolved to do better. To put up the bridge signs, to order the chairs, to lock the shed. To not forget. She belonged here, in Crow Valley.

She carefully removed the headlamp. The relief was palpable, nearly euphoric and she understood now what Silas meant when he'd accepted the loss of his mother's ashes. Dale belonged to the light now, to the thunder. She would focus on the memories. She'd record them in her notebook. The pitch of his voice, the shape of his hands, his breath on her skin. The way he whispered good-bye.

Roxanne gave Molly perfect tens, ran her fingers along the strap of the headlamp for one last time, and switched off the light.

Chapter 67

MARCEL

Marcel took a final fleeting glance at the mayhem behind him, and started to run. He cleared the side of the hall, and reached the parking lot. A transport truck trundled past on the highway above Crow Valley. The sky was the color of a Florida hotel. The cooling air brimmed with smoke.

"Marcel."

It was Norman.

Marcel scrambled up the embankment toward the main road, where the girls had crashed their bicycles. He heard footsteps behind him.

"Marcel," Norman called again.

Marcel stopped on the roadside, lungs aching, soot on his hands. Norman clambered up the shallow hill.

"Marcel," he said, heaving. "Boy."

He reached into his pocket and pulled out an angular key attached to a simple plastic keychain. He gestured toward the mountain. "The bus," he said, still out of breath. "Go east. Highway 30."

Marcel wrapped his hand around the key. Norman placed his hand on top. "Do me a favor?" he wheezed. "My daughter's picture. Leave it behind."

Norman released his hand from Marcel's, thumped him gently on the back, and nudged him in the direction of the mountain. "Go, Marcel. Go."

Marcel climbed the hill, and closed in on Norman's brown A-frame, the key to the bus digging into the flesh of his hand. He removed the picture of Norman's daughter from the rearview mirror and hung it on the back door.

The bus started on the first try, like a perfect second chance. He wound down the mountain and turned toward Highway 30, freedom in his foot and something like hope smoldering in his heart. He crossed over a bridge. A scorched wasteland gave way to new growth. Saplings bent in the night breeze. A sign appeared in the headlights. YOU ARE NOW LEAVING CROW VALLEY.

Acknowledgments

Steadfast gratitude to the entire team at Henry Holt, particularly the brilliant Sarah Crichton and the dazzling Natalia Ruiz for their astute and thoughtful editorial insights and unwavering belief in *Crow Valley*. Thank you to my agent, Stacey Kondla, for getting this book on the big stage and to my dear friend and whip-smart editor Sandra McIntyre, who revolutionized my process, craft, and approach to story.

Mad love to my writing family, without whom I could simply not create: paulo da costa, Judith Pond, Leanne Shirtliffe, Bradley Somer, and Elizabeth Withey. And to my extended writing community, who continue to show up, read my work, and support my writing. I see and appreciate you.

Thank you to the Canada Council for the Arts for supporting an earlier draft of this book and to the Edna Staebler Laurier Writer-in-Residence program, in particular Dr. Tanis MacDonald, for supporting the final draft.

Special shout-outs to Eric Volmers and Shelley Youngblut for routinely showcasing my work and to the countless individuals who offered their expertise and professional insights on everything from language and procedure to law and karaoke and everything in between. Amanda Brazil, April Georgekish-Gull, Theresa Kakabat-Georgekish, Bianca Johnny, Wanda Moore Wilcox, and so many others.

To my friends, the old and the new, the next-door and the miles away, those on the soccer pitch and those online, thank you for enriching my life with your friendship.

A heartfelt thank-you to my readers, without whom I wouldn't have the privilege of making art.

And lastly to my family, both immediate and extended, the makeshift and made-up, I love you to pieces and then some.

"Above all, keep loving one another earnestly" (1 Peter 4:80).